No Time
for Ashes

DIANE BROYLES

ISBN: 1540753034

ISBN 13: 9781540753038

Also by Diane Broyles:

Out of Time on Santorini

ACKNOWLEDGEMENTS

My thanks to San Mateo Coroner, the Honorable Adrian "Bud" Moorman; Sergeant Linda Gibbons of the Major Crimes Unit in the San Mateo County Sheriff's Office and Funeral Counselor Bradley E. Sullivan at the Saratoga-Cupertino Funeral Home in Saratoga, California for answering my questions about interrogations, dead bodies, victims' families and murder suspects.

Thanks also to the members of The Novel Idea writing group in San Luis Obispo, California: Barbara Wolcott, Sue McGinty, Carroll McKibbin, Art Dickerson, Ernie Lenz, Valerie Bentz and Ann Dozier. Their input was invaluable.

My appreciation also goes to Susan Lindstrom and Andrea Fine for their keen editing and proofreading skills.

I'm indebted to Sandra Smith of Wheeler-Smith Mortuary and Crematory in San Luis Obispo, California for allowing me to choose and photograph the funeral urn for the front cover.

Special thanks go to Myrt Cordon for her excellent line editing. I don't know what I'd do without her.

In addition, my gratitude goes to the members of the Central Coast Chapter of Sisters in Crime, who brought me into the twenty-first century.

TABLE OF CONTENTS

1

SHOCKING FIND

Christmas Eve 1998

Marissa DeSantos splashed into the icy Pacific, her Gucci pumps in hand, a pale moon above.

This was ridiculous, she thought. All she wanted was a breath of fresh air, a break from the Spindrift Cove Christmas party. And now she was up to her ankles in bone-chilling water.

A strong breeze churned small waves that lapped at the legs of her new wool slacks. It was the sparkle on an object riding the swells that had caught her eye enough to take the plunge. Bobbing in the distance, the shine was almost hypnotic, beckoning her to watch.

She squinted as the object drew closer until she could see a shape that looked like a huge narrow box. Intrigued by the prospect of possible treasure, she shoved her pumps into her pants pockets, sucked in her breath and waded deeper into the freezing water.

The shape was teasing her, appearing and disappearing, when a breaker smashed over it and propelled it toward her.

It's more rounded than a box, she thought. More like a big log. Or maybe a big hunk of driftwood.

Disappointed, she was about to leave, when the breaker carried it within a few feet of her.

Were those ropes around it? Who would tie up a piece of driftwood? This had to be something else. Maybe loot thrown overboard from a passing ship. And the ropes meant someone wanted to keep it intact.

She stepped toward it, splashing her slacks and the sleeves of her jacket. As the form raced past her, she grabbed at the loose end of a rope draped in seaweed and struggled to keep her balance. Repulsed by the feel of slime, she gritted her teeth and hung on.

This was not how she'd intended to spend Christmas Eve.

A calm settled on the water between the oncoming waves and, unwilling to desert the mysterious thing, she tugged on the rope. But with her feet mired in unstable sand, she lacked the strength to pull the object to the beach. Wave after cold wave lapped at her thighs, causing her teeth to chatter. And then the big one came.

She yanked with all her might as the breaker struck the form and knocked her aside, wrenching the rope from her grasp and her cell phone from her jacket pocket. With a struggle to remain erect, she watched the huge wave devour her phone and carry the mysterious object to shore, depositing it on the beach.

Swearing at the loss of her phone, Marissa pulled her feet from the sand and edged her way toward her treasure.

If only she had more than moonlight to help her to see.

As she approached her find, the smell of seaweed filled her nostrils and the details of the object unfolded.

That shine is black plastic, she thought. Thick. The kind used in industrial-strength garbage bags.

She crept forward. Ragged gashes in the plastic revealed several layers wrapped around the object. Three ropes bound it. The one in the middle that she had tugged on and a rope near each end. In all her thirty-five years, she'd never seen anything like it.

Her feet numbed with cold, she stooped for a better view.

Her breath caught in her throat. "Oh, my God. It's got feet!"

And one of the ropes was tied unmistakably around the neck!

She bolted toward the bluff she'd come down, running as if someone were chasing her. The deep sand hardly slowed her as she plunged through the night air, her sopping slacks clinging to her like heavy wet towels.

Why did she ever come to Spindrift Cove? She should have spent Christmas Eve back home in San Francisco with her boyfriend. Her uncle could tend to her sick aunt at the Cove by himself.

She ran up the bluff, wheezing until her lungs could no longer take the punishment. Stumbling, she fell onto the cold sand.

She was right to leave the body, she thought as she surrendered to the mounds of beach grass. This was a police matter. The corpse could be a murder victim, washed twenty miles down from San Francisco. Gruesome scenes played in her head. She wanted no part of this.

But as she regained her breath, she wondered if the corpse could be a hefty teenager, the size of a linebacker. Maybe his parents were wondering why he didn't show for Christmas Eve dinner. Or maybe he'd been missing for days.

A shiver ran through her. No family should endure the agony of wondering if one of its own were dead or alive. She had to do something.

She surveyed the deserted beach and looked farther up the bluff. Everyone in Spindrift Cove was still at the town Christmas party. If she left to get help, the tide could pull the body back out and no one would find him. She could at least ensure he'd stay put. She stopped. Why had he suddenly become a "he" instead of an "it?"

Slowly, she turned and retraced her steps, still trembling from the cold.

Maybe the waves had already reclaimed her find.

The walk back down the bluff seemed much longer than the walk up. When the glisten on the plastic shown once more, she knew the corpse was still on the beach and she'd made the right decision.

Her heart pounded as she crept closer and prepared herself for the slippery seaweed-covered rope. She grabbed the loose end secured at the corpse's middle. Steeling herself, she kept wrapping the rope around her hand until she stood a couple feet from the form.

Could she touch the body to dislodge it from the sand?

She pushed on it with her foot and reeled back at the feel of the corpse's belt on her toes. No question. This was a real person.

Her stomach lurched and she gulped the sea air. She'd come too far to quit now. If she could just pull him a few feet, he'd be safe from the waves.

Determined, she yanked the rope taut and tugged. She shook her head, thinking she should have more sense than to expect her small frame to pull something so many pounds heavier.

Shaking with cold, she was contemplating her next move when a giant breaker crashed toward her. Quickly, she planted her feet and watched as the wave grew and finally broke at the shore, almost submerging the corpse.

She yanked as hard as she could.

With a jolt, the body dislodged and the swish of the plastic bags brought her an almost pleasurable sigh. Using the momentum, she dragged the corpse through the sand until the pain in her cold hands could take the torture no longer.

She stopped and looked back at the shoreline. She'd come far enough.

Slowly she unwound the slimy rope and rubbed her hands together, feeling the blood return. The body would be safe until the tide changed. What she needed now was a phone.

Marissa trudged up the bluff again, cursing herself for losing her cell phone. The deep sand slowed her steps. A rehash of the events on the beach brought clarity to her thoughts. What if someone else should find the corpse? Would it be obvious that she pulled it to shore? The police would question her motives. She should have thought this through.

She walked faster. She had to tell someone before someone else discovered the body. Soon she was racing up the bluff. Her short puffs became heaving gasps and she stopped for air, brushing strands of dark hair from her eyes.

Where was that coffee shop she passed on the way down from town? Wasn't it at the top of the bluff and the bottom of the hill to her uncle's place? She scanned the top of the bluff for the shop's sign. Only sparse weeds and a patch of pampas grass waved in the breeze. Cold and clammy, she continued on. She thought she could go no farther when a dark roof emerged at the top of the bluff. A spotlight shone on the words, *Spindrift Cove Perk and Turf.*

Please let this place be open on Christmas Eve.

2

STUMBLING BLOCK

The bell jingled over the warped wooden door and Marissa stumbled into the dimly lit restaurant. The heat of a blazing fire in a huge stone fireplace instantly warmed her cheeks. Red Christmas candles in glass chimneys threw dancing shadows on paneled walls. Tinsel-draped garlands hung on the doorway to the kitchen where the sweet scent of apple pie drifted toward her.

"Is anyone here?"

"Howdy!" A stocky woman, somewhere in her sixties, emerged from the kitchen. Marissa remembered seeing her at the Christmas party. Petticoats rustled under a long red skirt that matched the woman's brightly dyed-red hair. Wire-rimmed glasses added authenticity to her costume from Dickens' Christmas Carol. "Name's Tizzie," she said. "Lordie, girl. How d'you get so wet?"

"Quick!" Marissa shouted. "I need the police."

The woman eyed her. "You must be new in town. Spindrift Cove's got no police. What's your—"

"A dead body's washed ashore."

"Oh, my Lord!" The woman's eyes widened. "The deputy sheriff's at the Christmas party."

"Phone him there."

Tizzie headed toward a wall phone covered in red streamers. She stopped. "No sense calling. Party's about over." She hustled to the window and looked out. "He and the town folk are on their way down here now."

Marissa yanked open the door. The cold air hit her face. "What's he look like?" She rushed out the door.

"Blond bruiser about fifty," Tizzie called after her. "He's also the funeral director . . . and the town mayor. Name's J.J. Haggersby."

Marissa sped up the hill toward the town.

"Say," Tizzie shouted, "Where on the shore is that body?"

Marissa ignored her and rushed toward the partygoers. When she was close enough for them to hear, she shouted, "Is J.J. here?"

"J.J.," a man called. "The new lady from the Christmas party's looking for you."

A tall husky blond man in a cowboy shirt emerged with a woman half his age on each arm. He swaggered toward Marissa, favoring his left hip, where a holstered pistol hung. After giving the women each a squeeze, he released them to extend his hand. "J.J. Haggersby," he said with a firm handshake. "Looks like you took a dip in the ocean, little lady. What can I do for you?"

She bristled at his condescension. "I'd like to speak to you alone."

With a frown, he broke from the crowd. "You're Walter Schmidkin's niece. I saw you at the party." He stepped closer. "Noticed your shiny black hair. Pretty little thing that you are, you—"

"I just found a dead body in the ocean."

He seemed to stifle a chuckle. She was about to lose her cool when he placed a firm hand on her back and guided her away from the crowd.

"Are you sure it's not a piece of driftwood? Sometimes city folk mistake it for all kinds of things."

She faced him, eluding his touch. "Not unless the driftwood around here has a head and two feet."

He frowned again. "Take me to it."

It was bad enough she had to deal with a corpse on Christmas Eve. Now she had to tiptoe around the ego of a chauvinistic deputy sheriff.

She led him down the bluff toward the ocean.

Halfway down, J.J. turned to the chattering crowd that followed them. "Bill, Jake, corral these people into Tizzie's place."

The men called to the throng and herded them back toward the Perk and Turf.

Thank God J.J. had some clout, Marissa thought. "The body's out this way." She indicated the shoreline.

She half hoped the corpse had disappeared, but there it was, just as she'd left it.

J.J. walked to the body, grunted and knelt to inspect the wrapping. He seemed to be taking his time.

"This is a murder," Marissa said. "Shouldn't we be calling someone?"

J.J. continued inspecting the black plastic. After a moment, he looked up at her. The moonlight on his leathered face revealed a small scar over his left eye. "Did you touch anything?"

She hesitated, thinking about the rope. Fingerprints didn't stick to slime, did they? "No."

"Tell me what happened."

"I left the party at the school auditorium to get a breath of—"

"How long ago?"

"I don't know. Maybe forty-five minutes."

"Were you alone?"

"Yes. If you'll let me talk, I'll tell you everything."

He looked around as if to ensure they were alone. "Go on."

"I was on the shore."

"On the shore where?"

This was getting exasperating. She spoke more quickly, hoping he'd let her say more than a few words at a time. She indicated a spot on the beach.

"I was standing there when I saw the body. As the waves washed it in, I noticed the shine of the water on the black plastic. I was curious, so I waded in and pulled it to shore. I didn't know what it was until it was beached. Then I dragged it here so it wouldn't wash out."

"I thought you said you didn't touch it."

"I pushed it with my foot. Then I tugged on the ropes. No way I was going to touch it with my hands."

His brow knit and he remained silent, seemingly contemplating her story. Even though her teeth were chattering, he appeared not to care.

"Why'd a pretty little thing like you want to drag a dead body to shore?"

She felt the blood rising to her cheeks.

"It's huge," he added. "And you're only a mite of a lady."

Her fists tightened and her voice rose. "Rescuing corpses on Christmas Eve is not my favorite thing to do, but that body probably has a family. I wasn't about to let it wash back into the ocean."

"Okay, okay!" J.J. circled the corpse as if deep in thought. "Any idea who it is?"

"Of course not. Do you?"

He raised an eyebrow and studied her face. "Let me have your name and address." He slipped a notebook from his pocket. "There'll be others who have questions."

A wave of concern enveloped her for having touched the rope. Would the authorities think she was involved?

She waited until J.J. found a pen. "I'm Marissa DeSantos. In Spindrift Cove for the holiday. I live in San Francisco." She gave him her home address.

"You staying here with your uncle?"

"Yes."

"What's your phone number in the city?"

He scrawled the information into his notebook as if he could see what he'd written in the dark.

She asked, "What happens now?"

"You go back to your uncle's place and wait. I'll call the Ocean Bluffs coroner. You'll hear from someone tonight."

"I'll wait with you," she said. "I'd like to know what happens."

J.J. stuffed his notebook into his pocket. "No sense you freezing out here. It may take them a while to get here."

Strange, she thought. In the movies, they keep all the witnesses around until the coroner arrives.

"I'd rather wait," she said. "Ocean Bluffs can't be more than twenty minutes away."

He shifted his weight to his good hip and frowned. "Look. I know what I'm doing here. You're gonna catch cold in those wet duds. You high-tail it up to Walter's place and get into some dry clothes."

His take-charge attitude reminded her of why she divorced her second husband. She would have stood her ground, but she hadn't stopped shivering since she first waded into the ocean. So she allowed him his macho attitude. If the police and coroner wanted to chase after her while she changed clothes, that was fine with her.

"It's your show." She pulled her wet jacket around her. "Is my uncle in the coffee shop?"

"Uh-uh. Walter left the party before it was over. Said he had to tend to your Aunt Candi."

She turned and continued plodding uphill toward town, concerned her old uncle's young wife Candi might be more sick than she thought.

Almost to Main Street, she stopped when a flash of bright light temporarily blinded her.

She squinted. "What the . . . ?"

When her eyes adjusted to the dark, she saw Tizzie slinging a camera back over her shoulder.

"Sorry," she said. She made some notes in her notebook and looked up. "You're Walter's niece, aren't you? Tell me, is it a man or a woman down there?"

"Are you some kind of reporter?" Marissa asked. She certainly didn't look like one in her hoop skirt.

"Owner of the *Spindrift Sun*," she said without hesitation.

"You better ask J.J. your questions."

One of J.J.'s men joined them and took Tizzie by the arm. "Oh, no, you don't," he said to her. "Back to the coffee shop. Orders from J.J."

Tizzie did a reluctant about face, mumbled to herself and allowed the man to escort her down the hill. Marissa crossed the deserted road called Main Street and headed toward her uncle's place.

Wait till Uncle Walter hears about this, she thought.

3

MAJOR DISCLOSURE

The moon and twinkling Christmas lights guided Marissa up deserted Ferndale Road, where giant redwoods towered above her like spirits hovering in the light wind. She was alone with the soft sound of her footsteps.

Had she spent Christmas Eve with her boyfriend Gregory or her brother Tony, none of this would have happened. On the other hand, her Uncle Walter needed her and, God knows, she owed him more than this visit.

She prayed Candi's illness was no more than the flu. Her aunt was too much of a spitfire to wallow in bed for more than a few days.

The corpse crept back into her mind. She thought of her hands on the rope and she shuddered. The last hand that had touched it was probably the killer's.

The wind stopped. Were those footsteps she heard behind her? She stopped and looked over her shoulder.

No one.

She quickened her steps and replaced thoughts of the corpse with those of a soothing hot shower and the comfort of a visit with her uncle on Christmas Eve.

She turned right at the stone pillars with gas-lit lamps on each side of a walk that led to a circular driveway. Steps led to the huge Victorian house at the top of the hill.

Another uphill trudge made her realize how exhausted she was. She plodded up the driveway and finally up the steps.

The Christmas wreath and a light over the porch made her feel as if she'd finally arrived home. What surprised her were the dark windows. She tried the door and found it unlocked. According to her uncle, no one used keys in Spindrift Cove.

She pushed open the huge front door and stepped into the high-ceilinged foyer, expecting to feel warmth. Instead, the cold inside matched the chill on the front porch. And Walter's usual cheery greeting was missing.

She flicked on a light showing the way to the dark parlor on the left. Walter sat in an overstuffed chair gazing out the window, seemingly unaware of her presence, an unlit Christmas tree at his side.

"Uncle Walter?"

"Huh?" He looked up. "Oh, Marissa. I didn't hear you come in." He frowned. "What happened to you? I looked for you after the party and you were gone. Jeepers, you're soaked. Come in and turn on a better light."

Marissa hung her jacket on a coat tree in the foyer and set her wet pumps below. She switched on the light in a wall sconce above her uncle's head. The orange bulb shed an eerie glow on the wrinkles in his face. When she'd arrived that afternoon, she'd noticed how thin his brown hair had become since her last visit. Now his shoulders were hunched forward and he looked as if he'd aged since she saw him earlier.

Marissa's concern about the corpse temporarily faded. "Are you all right?" she asked. "You look worse than I do."

"Yes, it is," he said. "It's been this cold since yesterday."

Uncle Walter's hearing was getting worse, she thought. She noticed before, if she wasn't standing nearby or speaking loudly, he only pretended to hear what she said.

She stepped close enough for him to hear. "Can I get you something?"

"No, no. You look upset. Tell me what happened to you. How'd you get so sopping wet?"

Marissa took a breath and fought back unexpected tears. The memory of the corpse became real. She swallowed hard and said, "I left the party to get some air and I . . . I found a dead body floating in the ocean."

Walter sat up, his eyes wide. "What?"

Tears welled in her eyes. "It was wrapped in black plastic." Sniffling, she explained what had happened, ending with her encounter with J.J. and her unexpected dismissal.

Walter offered his handkerchief. "You've had quite an evening. One ripe for nightmares. Don't worry. I'll look into this. You try to relax. Can I get you something? Maybe a cup of hot cocoa?"

Marissa blew her nose and wiped her eyes. "I think I'll be all right. I was fine until I walked in the door."

"You've had a nasty shock. Better get yourself out of those wet clothes. And don't worry about J.J. He has his ways but he's a good man."

Ashamed of her breakdown, she changed the subject. "What about you? Why were you sitting in the dark?"

Walter shrugged. "Guess I'm tired, too. It's been a long day."

Marissa didn't buy that, but she knew him well enough not to prod him. She thought about the woman at the restaurant. Walking toward the fireplace, she asked, "Do you know someone called Tizzie?"

"Maybe a little light-headed," he said, lifting a bottle from the table. "Comes from the beer." When Marissa looked back with a raised brow, he said. "Oh, you must have asked me about Tizzie. I . . . I wasn't sure."

At least her uncle realized he had a hearing problem. "She sure was curious about the body," Marissa said.

Walter smiled. "Tizzie writes the local newspaper. Gives her reason to nose around in everybody's business." He sipped from the bottle. "The woman can't spell worth a hoot."

Marissa chuckled. She was about to go upstairs to change when her thoughts went to Candi, Uncle Walter's much younger wife. Yes, she was ill, but since Marissa's afternoon arrival, Candi hadn't even acknowledged her appearance. And Walter's haggard look made Marissa even more suspicious. Something was going on that he was keeping from her.

"Is Candi feeling better?" she asked.

"Not much. She's sleeping in the guest room. She gets more rest when I'm not traipsing in and out."

Sleeping all day since I arrived? Marissa thought. "She must be quite ill."

Walter failed to reply and Marissa was too exhausted to pursue the issue. She climbed the winding staircase to the upstairs hallway and stopped at the closed door of the guest room. She tried the knob. The door was locked.

Not at all like Candi.

"Candi?" she called.

No reply. "Candi, are you all right?"

Nothing.

Perplexed, she proceeded to the other guest room to undress and then to the bathroom for a hot shower. Afterwards, she descended the stairs in her robe and nightgown.

She stepped close enough for Uncle Walter to hear. "Do you think Candi might have something more serious than the flu? Maybe we should call a doctor."

"What?" Walter shot from his chair. His lackluster blue eyes became fire. "No!" he shouted, sending her a step back.

He'd never raised his voice to her before.

"I . . . I'm sorry," he said. "I'm upset. I . . . I don't know what to do."

Marissa put an arm around his shoulders. "Is her condition serious?"

He hesitated. "You might say so."

She braced herself for the worst as Walter retrieved a sheet of paper from the mantle and handed it to her. It looked as if it had been read, crumpled and smoothed.

"Candi's not sick," he said.

"But at the party you told everyone she had the flu." Confused, Marissa took the paper to the light to decipher the flamboyant penmanship.

> *Dearest Walter,*
>
> *I've gone to see Gunther in Munich. Please don't try to contact me. There's so much I've wanted to tell you. I just couldn't find the words.*
>
> *You've been a good husband. I hope you'll find it in your heart to forgive me.*
>
> *Love,*
> *Candi*

My God! Marissa thought. Who wrote this? It's Candi's writing but it didn't sound like Candi. She and her aunt were good friends. Why hadn't Candi told her?

Marissa thought back to two years before, when her uncle announced to the family that he was marrying a woman he'd only known for a few months. Marissa's brother Tony kidded that Candi was closer to Marissa's thirty-five years than to Uncle Walter's sixty-five. Shapely and vivacious Candi seemed a strange match for her quiet uncle.

Marissa placed the note back on the mantel. "This is unbelievable." Retracing her steps, she said. "I'm so sorry. Everyone at the party thought she was sick." She embraced her uncle. "Why haven't you told them?"

Walter gave her a gentle squeeze and broke from her hug. He returned to his chair and sat down, his jowls sagging. "People said she'd leave me and she did. She took off for that Gunther guy."

"Who's Gunther? She never mentioned him to me."

"Last name's Friedlich. Ever since she came back from a conference in San Francisco, she's been talking about Gunther Friedlich." He spat the name out in a mocking tone.

Marissa had never seen this side of Walter.

He continued, "She said he offered to help her. You know how excited she gets about her mail order business. I figured it was all work. How could I be so dumb?"

Marissa knelt beside him. "When did you get this?"

"A week ago."

"A week! Why didn't you tell me?"

"Don't get excited. I didn't want you rushing down here when there was nothing you could do."

"How long were you planning to keep this from me?"

"You offered to come for Christmas, so I decided to tell you when you got here."

"My Lord. What you must have gone through this last week." She took his hand. "You shouldn't be going through this alone. What can I do for you?"

He caressed her cheek. "Your being here for Christmas is enough."

"No, no, I owe you much more. I still haven't repaid you for my schooling after Mom and Dad died and for being there when I was short of cash." Her words tumbled out. "Tony couldn't have raised me if it weren't for your help."

When she finished spouting, a smile crossed Walter's face. "Your brother's a fine man. He's the one you should be thanking."

Frustrated at his refusal of her help, she stood silent. Then she thought of all the questions she'd answered about Candi at the party.

"I told everyone Candi was sick. Why didn't you tell me the truth *before* the party?"

"It wouldn't have been fair," Walter said. "That's what you believed. I didn't want you to have to lie."

"But you can't tell them she's sick forever."

Walter rubbed his forehead. "I was hoping you would help me with that."

Marissa looked to the ceiling. Had her dear uncle become crazy as well as deaf? "Think about what you're doing. You need to tell everyone the truth before this lie gets out of hand. And the sooner, the better."

Walter shook his head. "We can keep things as they are for now. You'll be going back to San Francisco tomorrow. After that, the problem's all mine."

"No," Marissa said. "No problem is all yours. I'm here for you, no matter what. But you can't expect me to continue this lie."

Walter shifted in his chair. "You may be right," he said. "But it's Christmas Eve. How about we talk about this in the morning?"

Marissa knew there was no sense in pushing her uncle any further. She was headed up to bed when Walter called to her. "That dead body you saw . . ."

"Yes?"

"Was it a man or a woman?"

4

COVERT AFFAIR

Marissa woke early Christmas morning to thoughts of the dead body and the fact that neither the coroner, nor the Ocean Bluffs police nor J.J. had contacted her yet. And why was her uncle so interested in the sex of the corpse? That really puzzled her. Life in Spindrift Cove was like life on another planet.

The silence of the house hung over her like a cold shroud. If Candi had been home, Marissa thought, she would have been singing carols as she scrambled eggs for breakfast. And they would have been cracking jokes together. Would Candi have really left without so much as a phone call?

Although she felt less than festive, Marissa donned the green sweater and pants she'd brought for the holiday. She looked into Walter's room and was surprised to find him gone and his bed unmade. As a professional who helps others to manage their clutter, seeing an unmade bed drove her crazy. She tried to ignore the mess, gave in, plumped the pillows and pulled the sheets and bedspread over them.

Downstairs was as quiet. She checked the kitchen for her uncle and instead found a worn stuffed teddy bear sitting on the table. It was her favorite from her childhood. Uncle Walter must have saved it all these years. She allowed herself a few moments of nostalgia and then hugged it to her and gingerly set it back on the table.

Coming back into the present, she searched for the Spindrift Cove phone directory and, upon finding the flimsy book, looked up J.J.'s number. When she punched it into the keypad, the line was silent.

Drat. Walter had mentioned the town had been having trouble with the phones. You'd think by now Uncle Walter and all of Spindrift Cove would have joined the rest of the world of cell phones. No wonder neither the coroner nor the police hadn't called. On the other hand, why didn't the officials just show up on her uncle's doorstep?

Her brother Tony and the kids probably couldn't get through either. She wished he'd chosen to spend the holidays with her and Uncle Walter again this year, instead of in Lake Tahoe.

She revisited her conversation the previous night with J.J. Phone lines up or not, she had to find out why he was so eager to send her away. She grabbed her jacket and marched out the door.

Outside, the air had the nip of a northern California winter. From her vantage point on the front porch, Marissa could see misty outlines of small houses with curling chimney smoke that reminded her of Currier and Ives prints. Beside the house sat Candi's baby blue Cadillac convertible. Had she seen the car there last night? She couldn't remember.

Someone must have driven her to the airport—someone who knows the truth about her. How would Uncle Walter explain the car?

Marissa set off down the hill. The redwoods seemed friendlier in the daylight with the sun peeking from behind gray clouds. When the ocean appeared at the end of the road, the memory of the corpse crept into her thoughts again. Maybe if she found out who it was, she'd stop thinking about it.

She turned on Main Street, one of only a few streets in Spindrift Cove. Passing the old Pajama Factory, she promised herself someday she'd explore it. Walter told her the old factory had been converted into artists' galleries and apartments.

She continued on to her uncle's hardware store, a small one-story building covered with weather-beaten cedar shingles. The dark inside and the unlit Christmas lights verified the CLOSED sign that hung on the door.

Farther down the street, a light shone in the window above the holly-draped sign for the Spindrift Cove Funeral Home. A black hearse was parked in front.

If J.J. is the funeral director, she thought, there's a good chance he lives in the apartment above.

She walked along the grove of cypress trees in the side yard, passing a white Ford Crown Victoria in the driveway. As she approached the backyard, she saw a black Lincoln and a motorboat. She was rounding the back corner of the home when she heard voices. Looking up to the landing at the top of the open wooden staircase, she saw J.J. kissing a voluptuous blond, his hands wandering from her neck to her curvaceous back side.

Intrigued, Marissa slipped behind a clump of oleanders. When the two came up for air, J.J. gave the woman a pat on the behind and helped her into a leather jacket. The woman descended the steps and strode to the Crown Victoria. As she passed within several feet, Marissa could see she was much younger than J.J. Even with smeared lipstick the woman could win beauty contests. A silver badge was clipped to her belt as was a cell phone. At least someone in the Cove believed in cells, Marissa thought. More importantly, a gold wedding band on the woman's left hand was hard to miss.

If Tizzie knew about these two, Marissa thought, she'd have a field day with the front page of the Spindrift Sun.

The woman started the car, J.J. disappeared into his apartment and Marissa climbed the stairs.

She waited until J.J. answered her knock, his hair combed and his face free of telltale lipstick. "Marissa, what brings you here?"

"Merry Christmas," she said.

"Yeah," he said. "Almost forgot."

"I haven't heard from the police yet. I thought I'd stop by to find out what the coroner said about the body."

Although she saw goosebumps from the cold rising on J.J.'s bare arms, he refrained from inviting her in—an obvious indication he didn't want her to see the interior of his apartment. She could imagine the unmade bed and the scattered clothing.

"A deputy coroner came about a half hour after you left," he said. "In fact she came back this morning. You might have seen her drive out as you came in."

A smart man covers his ass, Marissa thought.

"I won't have any information until at least tomorrow," he said.

"They must know something about the body by now. Was it a man or a woman?"

"No word yet. You might want to give me a call from San Francisco."

How can they not know? She thought. "It sure looked like a man. Wouldn't you say? They must have at least unwrapped the body by now. What did they find?"

"No sense hanging around here," he said. "If I was you, I'd have my Christmas with your uncle and then head north."

Besides ignoring her question, he was a bit too insistent she leave town. Two reasons that convinced her to stay.

"I'll do that," she said.

5

STRANGE CURIOSITY

Marissa returned to the house and found Walter at the kitchen table, nibbling on a piece of toast. He looked debonair in a red flannel shirt, except for the creases still in it from the way it had been folded in the box he probably bought it in.

She stopped in the doorway. "Merry Christmas!"

"You like it?" he asked, holding up his wristwatch. "It was a gift. Candi left it for me."

Marissa wondered how he could mistake a Christmas greeting for a compliment on his watch—an impressive Rollex. She stepped within Walter's hearing range.

"Quite a beauty," she said. What a heartbreaker, she thought, that Candi left him an expensive gift and then disappeared.

She hugged herself. "Brr. It's cold in here. Mind if I start a fire?" She headed for the fireplace.

"Flue's jammed. Been meaning to get Bubba up here to fix it."

She looked back. "Bubba?" The name had been mentioned several times at the party.

"The local handyman," Walter said. "He left town for the holidays. You can turn up the thermostat."

Marissa adjusted the heat and sat down across from her uncle.

"Went for my walk this morning," Walter said. Didn't see you when I got back. Thought you might have gone home."

"You know I wouldn't have left without saying goodbye. I plan on spending at least another day. You shouldn't be alone."

He sat up. "No need to do that. Your brother and the kids will be waiting to see you."

"Not this year. When I told Tony you and Candi couldn't make it to San Francisco, he gave in to spending Christmas at his in-laws' place in Tahoe. It'll be strange not all being together for the holiday."

Walter pondered a moment. "You have a boyfriend to spend Christmas with. Gregory, isn't it? Right fine young man. Good job, too. You ought to hang on to him. Candi was already making wedding plans for you two."

Marissa would miss sharing her love life with her aunt. "I think Candi was jumping the gun. Gregory and I haven't even discussed marriage." How she wished he would. "We'll see each other tomorrow night—after I find out about that dead body."

"Not much you can do here. I'm sure the police are taking care of it."

"I just can't imagine Candi leaving so abruptly."

"Yes, it's pretty darn strange. Then again, even though you two were close, she probably wasn't about to tell you she was up and leaving your uncle for another man."

He's probably right, she thought. "I noticed Candi's car by the house this morning. Whoever drove her to the airport knows something. Who do you think that was?"

"I wondered about that. Could've been anybody in town."

Yes, that was strange, she thought. Her driver was probably at the party and could have caught Walter in the lie.

"Are you doing all right?" she asked.

His hand visibly tightened on the knife he was using to butter his toast. "Isn't much I can do. I'm going to have to face the truth."

Marissa softened her tone. "Do you plan to look for her?"

Walter heaved a giant sigh and shrugged. "No sense doing that. She doesn't love me anymore. Now I wonder if she ever did."

Her heart went out to him. "Is there anything I can do?"

The blood rose to his face and he seemed either angry or about to cry. "There's not a damn thing anyone can do." He dropped the knife onto his plate with a clatter. "Let's talk about something else."

Marissa put a comforting hand on his shoulder. She dropped a slice of bread into the toaster and waited until the red left his cheeks. "I went to see J.J. while you were out," she said. "I saw him with a pretty blond wearing a badge," she added, testing the waters.

"At this hour? Must be Daphne, the deputy coroner. What's she doing in Spindrift Cove this early? Didn't she haul that corpse you saw last night to Ocean Bluffs?"

"Even more strange, her lipstick was smeared when she left J.J.'s apartment." She dropped her hand from his shoulder and watched for his expression.

Walter straightened. "You've got to be pulling my leg. Daphne has a good looking husband up in Ocean Bluffs and J.J.'s got a flock of single women right here in town that would do-si-do with him if he asked them."

Marissa winked.

"Why that old coot," he said, a warm smile crossing his face. "No wonder he dragged me off to Ocean Bluffs to see that stupid play she was in last month. He told me he was supporting the Ocean Bluffs Drama Group."

"You two are pretty good friends, aren't you?"

"For five years. We been buddies since the day he moved into the apartment above his funeral home. He's the mayor, you know. And I'm his vice mayor."

"Congratulations. So you've become a politician," she said with a sly smile.

Walter's eyes cast down. "Not a real one. Haven't had to perform any official duties since I was elected."

"How about J.J.? He must be pretty busy, being both deputy sheriff and mayor. And also the town mortician. Has he any family?"

"None in town. Been divorced forever. His daughter Stephanie drops in from Phoenix once in a while." He plucked the toast from the toaster and offered it to Marissa. "I might head over to J.J.'s and give him a little nonsense about Daphne," he said, taking his empty coffee cup to the sink.

"Before you go, let's talk about how we'll tell the folks in town today about Candi."

"Yes, fine and dandy," he said with his back to her.

Was he feigning deafness or using it as an excuse?

"Uncle Walter!"

"It's a holiday, honey. We'll worry about it later."

Marissa swallowed hard. "How much later?"

"Can't hear you, sweetie."

"When? When? When?" she asked progressively louder.

"How long you staying?" He kept his back to her.

"As long as you need me, damn it."

He turned around and leaned toward her, both hands on the table. "I appreciate your concern, sweetheart, but I'll be all right."

A crease formed in his brow. "You go on back home and spend the day with that Gregory fellow."

The blood rose to her temples at his patronizing attitude. Even worse, he promptly strode out of the kitchen, leaving her no chance for further conversation. This wasn't at all like her uncle.

Marissa was about to clear the table when she noticed a single sheet of paper tucked under the salt shaker.

"A special issue of the Spindrift Sun," she read. She chuckled at the headline: *Dead body washes assure.* Below it, slightly askew, a photo of Marissa's wide-eyed face spread across the page. Her wet bangs hung in her eyes and she looked infuriated. The story of her find on the beach filled the remainder of the typewritten page.

The article didn't mention the body had been wrapped. J.J. must have done a good job keeping Tizzie from seeing the corpse, she thought.

She struggled through the misspellings and ink-filled lowercase *e*'s that looked as if they'd been pounded out on an old typewriter.

Marissa looked up to see her uncle had come back to the kitchen. He looked over her shoulder. "Quite a reporter, that Tizzie," he said as if their previous words were never spoken. He made a few feeble attempts at conversation and then asked, "When you saw J.J. this morning, did he say whether the corpse was a man or a woman?"

"He said he hadn't heard. Don't you think that's strange?"

Walter stood silently as if pondering her reply. "Probably find out later." He turned and left the kitchen once more. She would have followed him this time, questioning his curiosity about the body, if the ring of the phone hadn't surprised her. Pleased the lines were up, she answered it.

"Gregory!" she said at the familiar sound of her boyfriend. "Merry Christmas!"

His deep voice warmed her and she settled in a kitchen chair as he told her the details about Christmas Eve with his parents. Then she related her discovery of the body.

"You must be pretty shaken," he said. "I've been rattling on about my spectacular evening and yours must have been awful. Are you all right?"

She liked the fact he was concerned. She pictured his soft maroon cashmere robe covering his muscular chest. "I'm managing. The hard part is getting the corpse off my mind."

"I can imagine. Tell me more . . . or would you rather give me the details when you get back to San Francisco?"

Marissa hesitated. "I'll wait."

"I'll stop by your place tomorrow. I'm aiming for 6:35."

Timing to the minute. It's the price she paid for dating an efficiency expert.

"I may have to delay our Christmas celebration a day or so. My uncle needs me here. I can't go into details now. I'll call you."

"When?"

"As soon as I can. Probably tomorrow."

"I'm disappointed but I understand. We'll have a quiet celebration this year. Wear that red angora sweater I gave you."

"I love you," she said.

"Me, too."

They were his same old words. Never "I love you." And the two words would only come after she'd expressed her feelings for him.

Wistfully, she made a pact with herself to confront him regarding his lack of commitment.

Walter joined her in the hallway. "Were you talking to the police?"

Funny, she thought, that he could hear her when he was in the other room.

"Do they know who the body is?" he asked.

"No, I was talking to Gregory."

"Fine man," he said, absent-mindedly. "I'm going out for a while."

Why was her uncle so curious about that corpse?

6

SECRET BARGAIN

J.J.'s phone rang and he put down his ham sandwich to answer it. "Stephanie!"

A familiar wave of guilt washed over him whenever his daughter called. He'd all but forgotten her until she tracked him down a couple years ago.

"What's happening, Steph?"

"Something's come up. Can we make our dinner plans earlier this month?"

"Uh . . . sure. What's the problem?"

"My boyfriend's been on my friggin' back about some money I borrowed. I want to pay him off and dump him. How's next Wednesday sound?"

J.J. had thought of asking Daphne out on Wednesday. "Uh . . . sure, but I won't be able to come through with as much on our little business deal."

"Didn't you go to that gem show last week?"

"Yeah, but I only wangled a few bargains. Worth a couple thou at most."

"Awesome. That should cover what I need."

"I'll have a couple cold Molsen's ready for you."

"Don't bother. I'll be flying in and out of San Francisco on the same day. How 'bout I meet you at the Top of the Mark?"

J.J. thought a moment. He hadn't planned a trip to the city. "I . . . guess that'll be all right."

"Thanks, Poppy."

He hated that name. He was sure she was getting back at him for fooling around with a barmaid while his wife was pregnant with Stephanie. It was bad enough Steph's mother kicked him out on the street. He never thought the kid would find out why.

A knock on the windowpane interrupted another attempt at his sandwich. He smoothed his hair, looked through the window and opened the door. "Oh, it's you."

Walter strode past him and into the apartment. "I know who you're expecting. And Merry Christmas to you." He handed him a red and green box tied with a red string.

J.J. accepted it and followed Walter into the kitchen. "You don't know nothing, old man," he said loud enough for Walter to hear. He'd been noticing the old man was going deaf. "Who'd you think I was waiting for? Santa Claus?" He offered Walter a gift the same size.

A smug smile crossed Walter's face as he took the box. "I've heard from a reliable source you been shackin' up with Daphne."

J.J. stiffened. "Not true." He thought fast. "And where'd you hear a cockamamie story like that?"

"Can't reveal my source." Fingering a towel on the table, he added. "Sure looks like this has got lipstick on it." J.J. snatched it and hid it behind his back. Walter said, "And I know she came out of your driveway this morning."

How could Walter have seen her? He'd never been up before 7AM.

"She was here on business. Your niece must have told you we found a body on the beach last night. Daphne came to give me an update."

"On Christmas morning? And that doesn't explain the lipstick."

J.J.'s thoughts raced. "You got me there, old man. What the hell. You know how it is when you haven't been laid for a while. She's one hell of a woman, don't you think?"

"Not if her husband catches on. As a cop he can make life pretty tough for you."

It was something J.J. thought about constantly. "Come on, Walter. We've been friends a long time. You're the only one who knows about Daphne and you're not about to tell."

Walter looked at his feet. "I could if I wanted to."

What kind of game was this? "What the hell do you mean? I can't believe you'd rat on me."

"Why don't we say I might? Unless . . . "

"Unless what?"

"How about we make a deal?"

"You're acting crazy, old man. Why are you doing this?"

"Let's suppose I need a favor from you."

Maybe all the old man needed was a few flowers from a funeral arrangement, J.J. thought. Maybe for his niece.

J.J. offered Walter a chair and sat with him at the kitchen table, J.J. with the damning towel tucked under him. "Shoot me with it," he said.

Walter took a deep breath and looked at the ceiling. "Remember at the bowling alley when I told you Candi was sick?" Now he looked directly at J.J.

"Yeah. How's she doing? She must be over that flu thing by now." The old man fidgeted and J.J. could tell he was hiding something. "It's nothing serious, is it?"

"She's . . . " Walter shook his head.

"She's what? Have you called Doc Masterson?"

Walter sighed. "She's gone."

"Gone where? You mean she's out and out left you?"

Walter nodded.

"Where'd she go?"

"She ran off with some damn German guy she met at a conference." His face became red.

"Gees, old man. I'm sorry. Are you sure she's gone for good and not on a vac—"

"She left me a note."

"So she's really not sick like you been telling everybody?"

Walter looked down. "I can't face anyone. Everybody told me she'd leave me if I married her. They were right."

"So you want me to tell them?"

Walter looked at J.J. "Yup."

J.J. thought for a moment. It would be an easy favor. Now he had the advantage. "Let me get this straight. You want me to spread the word she's run off?"

"No. I want you to tell everyone the body that washed up on the beach was Candi's."

A wave of nausea hit J.J. "Dammit old man, you gotta be out of your mind. Nobody's gonna believe that . . . and I could lose my job."

"Only tell them for a few days. Until everybody forgets about her."

Had the old man gone bonkers? "Listen here. People don't forget about somebody who's lived in the Cove. Her name and what happened to her are bound to keep coming up. Ocean Bluffs may be a ways away but someone from there's bound to bring the news here."

"Well, I guess I could tell a few people in town what Marissa saw this morning from below your steps."

J.J. leaned forward. "She saw Daphne?"

"I know all the details and I maybe could let a few of them slip."

"Why you son of a—" He stopped. He needed Walter on his side. And this cover-up might not be so hard. Besides Daphne, Marissa was the only one who knew the corpse had been wrapped. Unless she told Walter.

His mind whirled. He had to test the waters. "Your niece is going to know the body's not Candi's."

"How's she going to know? She said it was wrapped in black plastic."

This was what he wanted to hear. No need for Walter to know the corpse weighed a hundred pounds more than Candi. He leaned forward. "Tell you what, ol' pal."

Walter's eyes widened.

"I'll pretend that body is Candi's if you get Marissa out of town. And I mean quick. You planning a service for your supposedly dead wife?"

"Haven't thought that far ahead. I guess I better."

"We better do it soon. We keep it small and out of the papers. We'll say she's cremated. I'll bring the urn to the service. No one outside of the Cove is invited. Once Pastor John says the final 'amen,' I give the urn to you and Marissa is out of town, pronto. Understand?"

"Guess I can arrange that. We got a deal?"

J.J. offered his hand. "Deal."

"What? I can't hear you?"

The S.O.B. was pulling his chain. "I said, 'Deal,'" he shouted.

Walter took the wrapped gift J.J. had given him and headed toward the door. "Thanks for the Christmas present."

J.J. shut his apartment door and pulled back the curtain to watch Walter descend the steps to the backyard.

All these years of fooling around and not getting caught, he thought . . . except for the blond whose husband took a potshot at him. Now this happens. Never thought Walter had the brains to catch him or the balls to call him on it.

He tried on the fishing hat Walter had given him for Christmas and glanced at the bathroom mirror.

"Damn good cap," he said. Exactly like all the others he'd bought him. This was the first one that fit.

He rehashed the bargain he'd made. Walter's niece wouldn't be a problem. She'd be gone. The only hitch was Daphne. A knot twisted in his stomach. She could lose her job if she went along with Walter's loony idea. He had to convince her to help. All they had to do was keep the body out of the news until Walter devised a better plan.

He reached for the phone to call her and then changed his mind. He better think about this first. He'd really taken a chance this time, fooling around with a cop's wife. He ran his hand over his balding head.

How did he get himself into this mess?

Marissa woke the next morning to an empty house. Confused the authorities still hadn't questioned her about the body, she called J.J.'s home number. When the phone rang unanswered, she called the funeral home, only to reach his answering machine. She grabbed her jacket and headed out to find him.

The sun hid behind a cloud as she walked down the driveway. A gray mist hung in the air. She was almost to Main Street when she saw a lone figure coming up the hill. A fishing pole balanced on one shoulder and a tackle box swung from one hand. As the person drew near, she recognized Tizzie in faded jeans, a brown shirt and a baseball cap with the visor to the back.

Tizzie waved, dropped her pole and box and rushed toward Marissa at surprising speed for a woman her age. From her troubled eyes, Marissa could tell something was wrong.

"I'm so sorry," Tizzie said, hardly huffing. She wrapped her arms around Marissa. "And on Christmas Day."

Marissa felt as if she'd entered the middle of a conversation.

"Walter's pretty upset," Tizzie said. "Candi was his life."

It was about time Uncle Walter came clean about Candi, Marissa thought.

"She was so young," Tizzie said. "Flu must have made her delirious. It's hard to believe she walked all the way to the beach."

Walked to the beach? Marissa hid her confusion.

"J.J. stopped by the coffee shop after Walter called him. Said Walter wanted to talk to him today about the arrangements."

Arrangements?

"Walter was wise to request cremation."

Marissa gulped. Good god.

"Candi must have looked awful after being tossed about in the ocean. The waves are down today, but they can be treacherous this time of year. An open coffin would have been a bad idea."

Marissa's head spun. Was Tizzie talking about the corpse she'd rescued? That body was much too large to be Candi's. J.J. knew that and he knew it had been wrapped.

Heat rose in her cheeks.

"There, there, child," Tizzie said. "You need women folk to talk to." She took Marissa's arm and strolled with her. "Don't you worry about a thing. J.J. will do a good job. You and Walter won't have to lift a finger."

What a pack of lies! Marissa thought. "Do you know where my uncle is?"

"He didn't tell you where he was going? He's probably at J.J.'s arranging the memorial service. I'm surprised he didn't ask you to come along."

Memorial service? He must think I'm an idiot, Marissa thought. He pretends Candi's the corpse, plans a memorial service and I'm supposed to go along with it?

"I think I'd better go find him," she said. She pulled her arm from Tizzie's and headed toward the funeral home.

7

ANOTHER LIE

Marissa's shoes crunched on J.J.'s gravel driveway, almost drowning out the strains of "Pink Cadillac" that wafted from the apartment window above. She followed the music to the back of the building and climbed to the top of the steps. She knocked and the music stopped.

"J.J., I know you're in there!"

She waited.

"Damn it! Come out here and tell me what's going on!" This time she pounded with both fists. A shadow moved behind the drawn window shade.

"J.J., come out!"

She sat on the top step. She'd wait him out.

Minutes became an hour. When the apartment remained quiet and leg cramps set in, she stood and stretched.

Okay, he won this one, she thought. But she wasn't giving up.

She tiptoed down the stairs like a crook leaving the scene. J.J. deserved to spend the day waiting for her to leave.

When she reached Main Street, she resumed her normal gait and looked back.

The rat was probably watching her from the window, she thought. She waved in case he was.

As Marissa climbed up Ferndale Road, she planned her approach to Walter about the lie. Somehow she'd convince him to come clean. And doing so now would be easier than later.

She walked up the circular driveway and was surprised to see a tall, muscular man in his mid-thirties on the front porch. He tossed his shoulder-length hair from his eyes and set down a toolbox and shovel before knocking on the door.

Marissa bounded up the steps as he opened the door and was about to step in. "Hold it."

The man turned with no sign of embarrassment. "I'm here to fix the flue." His clean T-shirt and fingernails belied his explanation.

"So you just walk in?" She joined him on the landing.

She couldn't help her attraction to his handsome Greek profile and shiny brown hair. But his good looks wouldn't sway her. "I don't see any truck in the driveway. Who are you?" she asked.

"I'm Nick Devereaux. I'm sorry I didn't bring my calling card," he said with a hint of sarcasm. "We don't have much use for them around here."

"You're a pretty clean looking fellow for a chimney sweep."

"Look, Marissa—"

She stepped back.

"Now don't freak out because I know your name. I was told at the Christmas party you're Walter's niece."

"But that doesn't give you the right to walk into his house un-announced. He'd probably come to the door if you rang the bell."

She steamed when he chuckled under his breath.

"I knocked. I didn't ring the bell because I know your aunt's sick in bed with the flu."

He's one lie behind, Marissa thought.

"I'm not being fair," he said with a smile, revealing straight white teeth under his mustache. "I'm filling in for Bubba, the local handyman, while he's in L.A. Your uncle left a message on Bubba's machine asking him to fix his flue. Said to go in if he wasn't home."

"What do you know about fixing flues?" Marissa asked.

"I'm only a lowly photographer," he said, "but I'm pretty sure I can handle the job. Your aunt and uncle shouldn't have to spend the holidays without a fire in the fireplace."

"Uh . . . thank you . . . for taking time to help my uncle." Marissa pushed the door open, hoping he wouldn't notice the blush on her cheeks. "Come on in."

She led him to the parlor and switched on the stereo to fill the void while she recovered from her strong reaction. Strains of "Take the A Train" filled the room.

Nick removed the screen from the hearth. He threw down a ragged towel and lay on his back to check the chimney with a poker he found on the hearth. His T-shirt stretched over the muscles in his chest.

"Jammed tight as a cork in a wine bottle." He grunted and made clanging noises with the poker. He banged on the inside of the chimney. "There it goes. The damper was stuck." He slid out. Soot spotted his face and lingered on his dark mustache. "Let's give it a try."

He wadded up a newspaper on the hearth and threw a log in with some kindling. Within minutes a roaring fire threw shadows on the wall. He stood and she approached the fire to absorb its warmth.

"I'll check the fireplace in Walter's room," he said, "to make sure the flue's working up there, too."

Thinking quickly, Marissa blocked his way.

"Your uncle said his room shares the chimney." He walked around her.

Wait!" Marissa shouted. "You'll disturb Candi."

"She has to be awake," he said, stopping on the first step. "No one could sleep through all my banging. Give her a warning I'm coming."

"Uh, that won't be necessary. I'm sure the fireplace upstairs is all right."

"I can't come back. And I won't be around later tonight."

"No problem."

He stepped down. "Suit yourself. Call me tomorrow if you see smoke. My number's in the book."

Duke Ellington finished playing on the stereo.

"You like the old jazz?" Nick asked, folding the dirty towel and tucking it under his arm.

"Guess it's a family thing."

"Do you play?"

She stretched her imagination for a way to impress him. "I had a two-bar singing solo in a community theater production last year."

He laughed and the warmth of embarrassment flooded her cheeks.

"They have a great combo at the Do Drop Inn in Ocean Bluffs," he said. "Have you had a chance to catch it?"

"I've only been here a couple days."

"Sure. I thought you might want to stop by."

As he gathered his tools, she found herself wishing he'd invite her to go with him.

This was ridiculous, she thought. She didn't know anything about him. And she already had a boyfriend she was looking forward to seeing.

She turned at the sound of the front door opening and the sight of Walter. Bags hung under his eyes and his sparse hair stood on end.

"Uncle Walter, what's happened?"

He closed his eyes and then opened them. "I think we better sit down."

Nick headed for the door but Marissa offered him a chair in the parlor, hoping Walter would act more sanely in front of company. Instead, her uncle ignored Nick. He sat beside Marissa on the couch, and she readied herself for whatever tale he would tell.

Walter took her hand. "I . . . I don't know how else to tell you this. I . . . Candi's dead."

"What?"

"Oh, man," Nick said. "I thought she was upstairs."

"What are you doing here, Nick?" Walter asked.

Nick stood. "I'm standing in for Bubba. You left a message on his machine, so I came over and fixed your damper. I'm so sorry about Candi."

Walter's brows drew together. "My hamper? Marissa, did the lid come off again?"

Marissa exchanged glances with Nick. He seemed to understand. Walter leaned to the side to take his wallet from his pants. "Glad you fixed it. Damn thing kept slipping off. How much do I owe you?"

"Not a thing." Nick wiped his sooty hands on the towel and shook hands with Marissa, the warmth of his hand lingering in hers. "I'm really sorry," he said. "I'll show myself out. If I can help, call me at the Pajama Factory." He went out the door.

Marissa looked at Walter. "I thought you said Candi had run off. How can this be?"

"She did and I was so upset about it. Now I find out she's not only gone, but she's dead."

He appeared so distraught. Could he be telling the truth?

She thought of Tizzie's story that Candi walked into the ocean. "What happened to her?"

He stood. "Come with me." he said.

Marissa followed him through the kitchen to a woodpile in the backyard.

"She was way too gullible," he said. "She should have stayed with me."

Chilled without a coat, Marissa hugged her body to ward off the cold. Walter grabbed a hatchet from the shed and set a hunk of wood on end. Lines of fury crossed his forehead as he brought the hatchet down and smashed the wood into two pieces.

Marissa stood back, afraid of his next move. She moved to leave when, with a shrug, he flung the hatchet down and collapsed on a huge log near the woodpile. Making room for her beside him, he looked about to cry.

Marissa sat down. She put her arm around him and waited, hoping he'd continue his story.

After a moment, he wiped his nose on his handkerchief. "J.J. called me this morning. You were still asleep."

She'd heard no phone ring that morning.

Walter continued, "He asked me to come down to the funeral home. Said he had something to tell me real important." He took a Hershey's kiss from his pocket and offered it to her.

Marissa refused.

"The body you found Christmas Eve. It was Candi's. She was shot."

"Shot?"

"I know it was that German boyfriend of hers."

Marissa dropped her hand from his shoulder. "Wait a minute. That body couldn't have been Candi's. It was the size of a football player."

Walter looked at her. "I know you want to believe Candi's still alive. It's only natural. I wish she was, too. It was dark when you found her. She was bloated with water. You had a few drinks at the party. It probably affected your judgment."

No, No, Marissa thought. She wasn't drunk. Yes, the body could have been bloated. Still, it was much taller and bigger than Candi.

"Tell me this. Why has no one except J.J. questioned me about that body?"

Walter's brows drew together. "That I don't know. J.J. probably had all the answers the coroner needed."

"How do you know she was shot?"

"Police in Ocean Bluffs told me. They showed me her body." His eyes filled with tears. "I don't know what I'm going to do without her."

Marissa wavered. Could she be wrong about the size of the corpse? Surely she hadn't been drunk on only one glass of wine. How awful to have to look at a loved one who's been shot. Still, how could this be?

"I don't believe it," she said, drawing away. "Why did Tizzie tell me she drowned?"

He looked up as if in a dream. "I couldn't tell the people in town the truth. They'd say they were right all along—that Candi would leave me."

Still the same old story, Marissa thought. At least this part was consistent.

"But you can't make this tale stick. There'll be police reports. Ocean Bluffs isn't so far away that the news won't eventually travel down here. The longer you keep this up, the bigger fool you'll make of yourself."

Walter looked into the distance.

Marissa asked, "How did J.J. get involved in this lie?"

"I asked him to. Only you two knew the body was wrapped. I told him to tell everyone she drowned."

Marissa shook her head. "This is too much. Think about it. If she's actually dead, you could be a suspect in her murder. Especially if she were cheating on you, as you say. You can't go around telling people different stories. The lies are going to come back to bite you." When Walter didn't reply, she rose. "I think you better give this some thought. I'm going inside," she said, stepping away.

"Get fried? Drinking's not going to make her come back."

She was too upset to laugh. She opened the kitchen door and then looked back. "Why in the world would J.J. agree to go along with this? If the truth came out, he could lose his job."

Walter stayed seated. "J.J.'s my good friend. He'd do anything for me. All he has to do is tell the town folk she drowned."

Marissa leaned close enough for him to hear. "Didn't you say Candi's boyfriend was in Germany? If so, how could he have killed her here? And what motive would he have?"

"I don't know. Maybe he was some whacko. They didn't know each other very long."

Marissa thought. Maybe they knew each other longer than her uncle suspected. Had her uncle ever considered all those out-of-town conferences Candi attended might have been bogus? She might have been seeing Gunther for a year or more. This could be, but even Marissa found it difficult to believe.

Walter looked so grief-stricken that this was not a good time to present the possibility.

"Look," he said. "J.J. is here to take care of everything. You don't need to hang around to babysit me." He rose and walked to the kitchen door.

"There's no way I'm going home. I don't care if J.J. goes down the tubes, but I can't let you go with him."

Walter's sad expression became one of concern. "That's real nice of you," he said, taking her hand. "You have to understand I helped you out years ago because I love you. I don't expect anything in return." Rising, he accompanied her into the kitchen. When she softened with a smile, he added, "You know, there might be something you can do for me."

She squeezed his hand. "Name it."

"I could use some help at Candi's office. I got a call from her landlord. Her mail's been piling up."

8

UNEXPECTED REQUEST

On the drive to Ocean Bluffs, Marissa reflected on Uncle Walter and how he'd been a positive influence in her life when she was down. Now, a defeated man, he sat hunched in the passenger seat beside her. How in the world could she get him through this if he insisted on acting crazy?

She stopped at a light and then proceeded. "Who's running Candi's business?" she asked.

"To tell you the truth, I'm stymied. I figured she shut the company down."

Marissa thought of what she would do if she were in Candi's place. If she left to live in Germany, wouldn't she have stopped the mail and closed down the business? Or if she were in love with Gunther, wouldn't she move her business to Germany?

She wished her brother Tony were there. He'd have some suggestions.

"Make a right at the end of this street," Walter said. "Pull into the lot."

Marissa obeyed and parked beside a newly painted two-story white stucco building with a forest green canopy that stretched from the door to the sidewalk. The words *Fifty-One Park Avenue* shone in the sunlight.

"Candi Enterprises must have been doing pretty well," she said. She thought of the hand-carved mahogany desk Candi had given her when Marissa first started her business.

"Yup. She did it up big. Never asked a penny from me."

They crossed the marble floor to the elevator and Walter pressed the button for the second floor.

The elevator deposited them on a thickly carpeted hallway that led to an office door with *CANDI ENTERPRISES* lettered in gold. A hand-lettered sheet of paper was taped below: *MOVED TO 321 MISSION STREET.*

Walter removed the paper. "What's this? Candi never told me she moved."

Unbelievable, Marissa thought. Another shock was all her uncle needed.

After jostling over a street filled with potholes, Marissa parked on Mission Street in front of a small wooden building that needed paint. Stains from the rusted metal frames on the windows ran down the walls.

Inside, she and Walter walked the dingy wooden hallway on a faded runner that had seen better days. The floor groaned with each step and Marissa could hear conversations through the paper-thin walls of each office they passed.

Walter shook his head. "This place is a dump."

What could have caused Candi to move from an upscale building to one like this? Marissa wondered. Lack of funds? Her pride? So much pride that she couldn't ask her husband for help?

Soon they came to a door with a yellow Post-It sticker announcing *CANDI ENTERPRISES* in ballpoint pen.

A man in a Fedora and a loud green tie was about to unlock the office next door. "You must be Candi's business partners." He leered at Marissa. "Quite a looker that Candi, if you know what I mean."

Walter stepped toward him. He appeared about to take a swing. Marissa pulled him back.

"Bill Richards," the man said, offering his hand to Marissa. "You folks from around here?"

"No thanks," Walter said. "Too early for beer this morning."

"We live not far from here." Marissa replied.

"From Spindrift Cove, like Candi?" the man asked.

Marissa nodded. "Have you a key?" she asked Walter.

Frowning, Walter fumbled in his pocket. "She gave me this a couple months ago when she said the locks got changed. She never told me she moved."

"My wife's sister lives in Spindrift Cove," Bill Richards said. "Maybe you know her. Name's Margaret Potter."

"Yup," Walter said. He opened the door and Marissa nodded to Bill.

"Nice meeting you."

She followed Walter into Candi's office, tripping over a mountain of mail that had accumulated beneath the mail slot. She picked up the top layer and carried it to a mahogany desk that covered half the floor space in the tiny office. A giant philodendron plant behind the desk begged for water and a dead coleus drooped over the edges of a filing cabinet. On one of four windowless walls hung a framed poster proclaiming, *The difficult I can do today. The impossible may take a little while.*

Marissa sat on a cushioned chair behind the desk and inspected the carved drawer handles. "This desk is exactly like the one she gave me for my new office at home. And the chairs she gave me match the desks. I'll bet she bought all the furniture at the same time."

"Her other office was twice this size," Walter said. "She probably gave you the extra stuff when she moved."

"It's all so expensive. She had me believing she got it for a bargain price at a garage sale. She wouldn't let me pay her a cent."

"Sounds like Candi. She took a real shine to you. That money I gave you for your office was mostly hers."

Marissa blinked hard. "Why didn't you tell me?"

"She told me not to. Was afraid you'd try to pay her back. Why didn't she tell me she was losing money?"

The phone rang in Bill Richard's office and Marissa tried to ignore the conversation coming through the wall. She could even hear the squeak of the springs when he shifted in his chair. The guy sounded like some kind of private eye, like the sleazy ones in old TV movies.

Walter joined her at Candi's computer and scanned the top page of a large notepad propped against the monitor. His knuckles whitened on the desktop as he read.

"Why that son of a—"

Marissa read the note that was scrawled in the same handwriting as the Dear John letter Candi had left Walter:

> *Dear Bubba,*
> *You'll find all the computer folders just as I explained. If you process the hard-copy orders as I indicated and download and send out the online orders, you should have no trouble.*
> *You're a dear and I love ya. Good luck!*
> *Candi*

So Bubba, the handyman, knew she was leaving. Marissa checked for a date on the note but Candi hadn't bothered. Bubba was probably the one who drove her to the airport. He could have brought back her car while Walter was at work.

The note says she loves him!" Walter shouted. "Bubba's been screwing my wife!" His eyes bulged as he tore the note into shreds. "I'll kill him!"

"Don't be ridiculous," Marissa said. "Candi says that to everyone. I heard her use those same words with Pastor John."

Walter dropped into a chair. "Maybe Pastor John's been screwing her, too." He rubbed his face. "I can't trust anybody in the Cove anymore, excepting J.J."

Marissa shuddered at the thought. She sorted the mail into orders and bills. "So you think she had an affair with Bubba and then ran off with Gunther? It doesn't make sense."

He watched her sort the mail and then drew his hands over his face. "I don't know what makes sense anymore." He blinked a few times. "If Bubba is only a friend, how come he hasn't taken care of all this mail like he must have promised?"

"He went to L.A. for Christmas, remember?"

"Oh, yeah."

She couldn't help but feel sorry for Walter. "Seems the trip was unexpected," she said. "He didn't think to have someone water the plants, either." She filled a large coffee cup with water from a water cooler in the corner and doused the two plants. "I'm curious why she would ask Bubba to help her out. Didn't you say she had a son? Wouldn't her son be a more logical choice?"

"Her son lives in Omaha. Bubba was probably more convenient, especially if he was screwin' her."

Marissa let him rant. She penned a note to Bubba, in case he stopped by before she had a chance to meet him. When she replaced the pen into a pencil cup, a small painted swan next to it caught her eye. She flipped it over. Made in Japan. She checked a few other knickknacks. None made in Germany. And no framed photos of Gunther.

As a professional organizer, Marissa knew the signs of someone who was having an affair. She checked the drawers for snapshots. After a few keystrokes on the computer, she checked Candi's electronic address book.

Aha, an address for Gunther Friedlich. And a phone number.

While Walter paced, still insisting the whole town was sleeping with his wife, Marissa copied Gunther's phone number and slipped it into her bag. Then she checked for e-mail from him. Candi's password was easy to guess: Walter.

No e-mail from Gunther. She looked at the list of e-mails Candi had sent. Only one to Gunther. She clicked the mouse and opened it: *Arriving in Munich at 2:45 Dec 21. You have all the info. See you then.* No signature. No loving phrases. Not even a "can't wait to see you."

"What're you looking at?" Walter squeezed behind her and leaned over her shoulder to read the screen. "Who's Gesund?"

"It's Gunther's e-mail address."

"See! I told you. He's probably written her a slew of love letters."

Marissa twisted in her chair. "You're jumping to conclusions. This e-mail is not *from* Gunther. It's *to* him. It has no indication of any love relationship."

Walter read the e-mail, left the desk and sank into a chair. "When was it sent?"

"December 19th."

"Maybe he showed up here before she had a chance to leave."

"I doubt that." She rounded the desk. "Is there anything about Candi's behavior you haven't told me? Did you and she have a fight before she disappeared?"

The corners of his mouth drooped. "I've been wracking my brain. I wish there was something more I could remember. We went to bed at the same time and everything seemed fine. When I woke up the next morning, she was gone. All I found was the note." He wiped his mouth with a handkerchief.

She took his hand and looked into his eyes. "If this is really what happened, I'll believe you and I'll help you. But I need more to go on. Think about any clues she might have dropped before she left."

Walter thought for a moment. "I know something you can help me with."

Finally! she thought.

"Nobody in Spindrift Cove knew Candi very well. I'd like it if you'd give a nice little speech about her at the memorial service."

9

UNSPOKEN WORD

Marissa dropped several coins into the pay phone in the booth on Main Street and pressed the buttons for Gregory's number. The walk from the house was worth keeping Walter from eavesdropping. Gregory answered with the hint of a growl. "I miss you. I thought you'd never call."

"I couldn't tell you before," Marissa said. "Candi isn't ill. She's disappeared. Uncle Walter says she's dead."

"What? My God. I'm so sorry. She's so young."

"Don't be sorry yet. I don't know if I even believe him, but he's holding a memorial service day after tomorrow. Can you come down?"

"Of course. What happened?"

"I'm not sure. My uncle's telling everyone in town she drowned. I'll tell you the details when you get here."

"I can come tonight if you need me. Are you all right?"

"Tomorrow is fine." Talking to Gregory brought her comfort. "I love you," she ventured.

If he said, "me too," she'd scream.

"Can't wait to see you," he said and the connection broke.

Unbelievable. No putting off the talk she planned about commitment. She'd do it when he arrived in Spindrift Cove.

She dropped more coins into the box and pressed the buttons again. A young woman answered. "Ocean Bluffs Coroner's Office."

"My name is Marissa DeSantos. My aunt's been missing for at least two days. I . . . I think she may be dead. Do you have a body in the morgue with the name Candi Schmidkin?" She heard the tap of keys.

"Would you spell the last name for me, please?"

Marissa complied.

"I'm sorry, we have no one by that name. Could she perhaps go by some other name?"

Maybe she kept her maiden name when she married Uncle Walter. It would make sense, seeing as she was in business. She'd never mentioned her maiden name.

"I don't know of another one."

"Have you filed a missing persons report with the police?"

"Uh. I'm not sure if anyone has yet. I'll check. Do you have the number?"

Why hadn't she thought of that? She took the number and dropped more coins into the box.

You'd think they'd have a phone in this town that accepts phone cards, she thought.

When an officer answered, she introduced herself. "Has anyone filed a missing persons report for Candi Schmidkin?"

She waited.

"I'm sorry, Miss. I have no one listed by that name. How long has she been missing?"

She could have been missing long before Christmas, Marissa thought.

"I'm not sure. Would you check back a week or two?"

"I've checked way beyond two. I'm sorry."

She thanked him. What had she found out? That she may not know her own aunt's last name and she had no idea how long she'd been gone? And, worst of all, she forgot to ask if they'd identified the body that washed into the cove.

She took Gunther's phone number from her bag, deposited more coins and punched in the number. When the operator asked for a dollar more, she emptied her change purse. Only three pennies and a nickel. "Rats."

Marissa slouched at the roll-top desk in Walter's guestroom and gazed out the window at the lighted front lawn. The grandfather clock downstairs struck 2 AM, reminding her she had made no progress on Candi's eulogy.

How do you write a eulogy for someone you don't believe is dead? But maybe she is. Could her uncle be creating this lie to cover a worse deception?

She tossed one more ball of wadded notebook paper into the wastebasket. She thought of her brother Tony. Something was wrong for him to neglect calling her at Christmas. If only she had his number on the slopes. It was strange that Uncle Walter didn't seem to be concerned.

She stretched her arms before resuming the task at hand. If she wanted to spend the day with Gregory, she had only tonight to complete her speech.

She wrote, "Candi Schmidkin, or whatever she went by, was a woman we knew and loved." Damn. She wadded the page and slam-dunked it into the basket with the rest. She closed the roll-top, took her robe and nightgown from the closet and prepared for bed.

Marissa tossed, waking twice, only to stare at the ceiling. She lay still, thinking first of Walter's delusion, then of J.J. refusing to answer the door, then of Bubba's friend Nick, who fixed the flue.

Why was she thinking of Nick? she wondered. He may even be married. He sure knew how to get to her.

Okay, she'd think of Gregory instead. The alarm clock showed 7:45 AM. He'd soon be here. She would have enough time to work on the eulogy before he arrived.

After a shower and a quick breakfast, she opened the roll-top and prepared herself for another bout of writer's block. The grandfather clock bonged 8:30 and she heard Walter stir. Several minutes later, he appeared at the door. "Working on the eulogy?"

"Trying," she said, staring at the blank sheet of paper. She flipped it over and invited him in.

"No need to be lying. You had some good times with Candi." He settled into the chair beside her.

She ignored his misunderstanding. "I'm confused and concerned. I checked the coroner's office. They have no Candi Schmidkin listed. You have to level with me. What's going on?"

Walter looked her in the eye. "I'm really trying to. So much has happened in the past few days. I can explain no listing at the coroner's office. When Candi and I got married, she kept the name Pomeroy. It was her previous husband's name."

Marissa thought back to when she'd first met Candi. Yes, she had mentioned an ex-husband—someone she'd married young and divorced soon after. "And it was all right with you that she kept her ex's name?"

"No. It bothered me at first. Then she told me she hadn't seen the guy in twenty years. Said she'd already changed her name once. We had quite a talk about it. She was afraid it would be bad for her business to change it again. I guessed it would be all right. I was marrying her, not her name."

This was the uncle Marissa remembered years ago, making concessions, sharing his feelings and making her feel as if she could share hers.

He patted her hand and got up to leave. "There's no reason to be checking into the coroner's records. You've done all you can. And I already identified Candi's body."

"Yes, I'd like to believe that . . . unfortunately, I can't."

Walter sat back with a start.

"The corpse in the cove was way too big."

How could he explain that? she thought.

He hesitated and was about to speak when a horn tooted in the driveway. Only Gregory would arrive a half hour early.

"You better tend to your boyfriend."

"We need to finish talking about this," she said on her way to the door. She ran a hand through her mussed hair and muttered, "Does every man become evasive as he ages?" Still feeling the heat of exasperation, she opened the door.

Gregory's spotless black Camry sat in the driveway with the trunk open. His head was lost under the trunk lid as he unloaded an Armani suitcase and a Nordstrom's shopping bag filled with wrapped gifts. His blue Austrian ski sweater topped navy blue pressed jeans, flaunting his perfect physique. All coordinated. Sometimes she wished he'd leave a shirttail hanging. Even his brown hair matched his brown eyes—eyes that had a way of making her feel all warm inside. He looked younger than his thirty-four years, probably because of his shiny, scrubbed cheeks. He lifted the suitcase in one hand and the gifts in the other.

"Come on up," she said. "Have you had breakfast?"

When he looked up, he dropped the suitcase and the gifts and raced up the stairs. "Merry Christmas!" he said, twirling her around in his arms. "I couldn't wait another minute." He planted a kiss on her lips and then pulled away and looked at her. "It's sooo good to see you."

Marissa caught her breath, remembering why she was so attracted to him. He ran back to retrieve the suitcase and gifts.

When they entered the foyer, Walter greeted Gregory warmly with a pat on the back and a handshake. "Merry Christmas, son." His eyes were filled with warmth and sparkle. "Marissa, show Gregory to his room while I get us some eggnog."

Wouldn't you know? Separate rooms, Marissa thought. But there was no use arguing with old Uncle Walter.

"First I shower you with gifts," Gregory said, carrying the bag into the parlor.

Walter came back with the eggnog and Marissa sat back and listened to the two men talk about the football playoffs. Marissa remained silent but kind enough to "oo" and "ah" the gifts each had to exchange.

She lavished praise on the calfskin computer case Gregory gave her for her laptop even though she'd hoped for a red silk nightgown or a weekend at a resort she liked—something more personal. Gregory seemed delighted with the camelhair blazer she presented to him.

On Walter's turn to offer gifts, he crossed to the mantel where a small box sat, wrapped in gold paper and a silver ribbon. His eyes filled with the anticipation of a child. "Marissa, this is for you. I saved it for today."

Marissa removed the ribbon and opened the box. Tears immediately clouded her eyes. A gold ring with a small diamond and two diamond chips on each side nestled in a bed of blue velvet. "It's the engagement ring you gave Candi. This was Grandma's wedding ring."

It was final closure on the fact that Candi was gone.

"Are you sure you want me to have this?"

"No sense letting it sit in a drawer."

She wrapped her arms around Walter's neck and kissed him on the cheek. She placed the ring on her finger.

"Look how it sparkles." She extended her hand toward Gregory, wishing the ring were from him.

After an awkward silence, Gregory said, "Uh, nice. Guess I better unpack."

Marissa led Gregory to the guestroom, upholding Walter's rules of propriety. If she knew Gregory, he'd later sneak into her room. And if she knew Uncle Walter, he'd look the other way. But did she really know her uncle anymore?

Gregory set his suitcase on the stand at the foot of the bed. Marissa hugged the computer case he had given her. She was about to kiss him, when he took the case from her and opened it. "See inside? It has three pockets for notepads, two for pens and pencils, one transparent place for ID and two large sections for papers."

"And a partridge in a pear tree?"

He looked to the ceiling. "I'm doing that counting thing again, aren't I?"

She nodded. "It doesn't matter. It's a handsome case."

"I guess I shouldn't tell you about the altimeter I stuck in the pocket."

"You didn't." She felt inside the case. "You did."

"I thought you might want to know how many feet above sea level you were on your hikes."

She kissed him a long and lingering kiss that warmed her from head to toe. Yes, he had his ways, but he also had some pretty powerful assets.

When she came up for air, Gregory broke the silence. "I missed you," he whispered. "Do we have to go back downstairs?"

"Mmm. It would be nice if we could stay here. Unfortunately, my uncle's expecting us."

Another kiss almost changed her mind. "I missed you, too. A lot's happened since I arrived here."

He sat down on the bed and patted the place next to him. "Tell me about it. Maybe I can help."

Marissa shut the door and related everything she knew about Candi's disappearance and all the various stories she'd been told. Gregory listened silently, with eyes riveted, until she was finished. "An unbelievable series of events. What can we do?"

"I'm not really sure. My immediate problem is getting my aunt's eulogy written before the service. I really don't believe she's dead."

Gregory rubbed his chin. "That's a tough one. Give me a few minutes to unpack and maybe I can help."

She left the room, silently scolding herself for delaying the confrontation with Gregory about those three important words she longed to hear.

Nick stepped into the crowded Chapel of the Roses, thinking the newly stained oak pews made quite a contrast against the white paint he'd applied on the interior walls. He thought of Bubba brushing on the final coat of varnish last week. Now, even in the low light, the old wood shone like brand new.

He made his way down the center aisle. It seemed the whole town had shown up for Candi's memorial service. Too bad Bubba couldn't be here, he thought, to see how the whole town came to remember Candi.

Spindly Margaret Potter passed by with her organ music in hand. Nick had seen her earlier in the day replacing the bright Christmas decorations with funeral wreaths.

Candi's going to be missed, he thought.

Having heard several of Bubba's compliments about Candi, Nick wished he'd taken the time to get to know her. Bubba thought she was sharp as well as shapely. He's going to be devastated when he hears, Nick thought.

He looked toward the front of the chapel where Marissa was already seated next to her uncle. He damned the lost black sock that made him arrive too late to claim a seat nearby.

A real spunky woman Marissa was. He would have invited her to the jazz concert if she hadn't been struck with the news of her aunt. Then again, maybe she'd have refused him. Word had it she had a serious boyfriend.

He sat midway in the chapel on the aisle. Settling in, he scanned the crowd, grateful for his life among caring people after years in L.A. The city was fine, if you liked parties and conversations about movies and who was doing who. Spindrift Cove, on the other hand, was a place where someone was always eager to offer a helping hand. This place was more to his liking.

He stretched his neck to ease the itch from the collar and tie he hadn't worn since the last memorial service he attended. The solemn faces around him reminded him of the drug-abuse death of a co-worker. Had it not been for that wakeup call he might still be living in L.A.

Nick's reverie was interrupted when J.J. Haggersby, in finely tailored funeral attire, strolled past and stopped to speak with Walter. Lines of concern etched J.J.'s face, as he placed his hand on Walter's shoulder and bent toward him.

Nick cringed when Margaret Potter hit a sour note on the organ while playing "Nearer My God to Thee." He moved to the right so he could see the shine of Marissa's black hair. Damn, she was gorgeous.

He scanned the townspeople who lined the walls and those in pews who were making room for more. The only person missing was Bubba. Nick wondered why he hadn't answered the voicemails Nick had left at Bubba's parents' house.

A young boy placed a Bible next to a bronze urn on the altar. Nick moved to the side to see Marissa lean closer to Walter and whisper into his ear. He imagined what it would be like for him to be on the receiving end of that whisper. Other women seemed attracted to him. Yet Marissa held her distance. Maybe because of the boyfriend?

A tall stranger in an expensive-looking suit marched down the aisle and Nick's gaze followed him. One by one, the women's heads turned.

Was that a handbag he had under his arm?

The man stopped at Marissa's pew and handed her the purse.

She must have forgotten it, Nick thought. The guy must be the boyfriend Tizzie talked about. Looks like a rich boy.

The man put his arm around the back of the pew so his hand fell on Marissa's shoulder.

Also, looks like the guy's pawing her.

Suppressing a tinge of jealousy, Nick watched them, wishing he could see the expressions on their faces. Without these clues, he could tell little about their relationship.

Get your lousy manicured hands off her, he thought. Nick would know how to treat her if he had the chance. A guy carrying a handbag couldn't be a hell of a lot of competition.

When the organ music ended, Pastor John waddled to the altar and stood beside the urn. His girth extended on each side of the lectern and his bald head and small eyes peeked only a foot above the top. Nick had planned to provide him a box to stand on. He'd probably hear about it later from the pastor.

Although he tried to concentrate on Pastor John's short eulogy that could apply to anyone, his mind kept wandering. He was glad he wasn't the pastor, having to make up niceties about a woman he hardly knew.

Pastor John concluded with, "Walter, would you like to say something now?"

Walter rose slowly, stood behind the dais and lowered his eyes to the three-by-five cards he held. "Candi was the best wife a man could ask for. I was blessed to have such a beautiful and kind woman as my wife. We were so happy together. I don't understand . . . I don't know how . . . I . . ."

Nick felt sorry for him as he choked on his words.

Marissa immediately rose to Walter's aid. After she helped him to his seat, she faced the group, Walter's notes in hand. "Would you like me to continue with these?" she asked him. He nodded.

Poor man, losing a wife. Nick imagined the magnitude of his grief. The devastation he'd felt during his own divorce was the closest he could come.

Marissa cleared her throat. She looked sharp in a tasteful black dress that came just below her knees. What a knockout photo she'd make. He thought of how he'd pose her in his photography studio. Then guilt crept in when his mind wandered past how she might look with her hair mussed.

Quietly, she began, "Candi held a special place in my heart." Her voice cracked and Nick could feel her pain.

"Speak up," J.J. said loud enough for the whole congregation to hear.

J.J., leave her alone, you idiot, Nick thought.

Marissa set aside Walter's notes and spoke her own words. "Candi . . . she . . . my aunt . . ."

Nick leaned forward. She'd looked so composed a few minutes before.

Her eyes darted around the room.

That look is apprehension, he thought, not grief.

"I'm sorry," Marissa said. "This is difficult for me."

"Tell us what happened to her," Tizzie whispered from the second row.

"My Aunt Candi . . . Candi . . ."

Tizzie stepped to the lectern and placed her hand on Marissa's arm.

Nick shifted in his seat. Why didn't that numbskull of a boyfriend help her out?

Tizzie looked at the crowd. "Candi met an untimely death," she said with authority. "As you may have read in the Spindrift Sun." She paused to check for nods of recognition for her newspaper. "She had been ill with a severe case of the flu and, in her delirium, walked into the ocean here at Spindrift Cove and drowned."

The drama Tizzie seemed intent on invoking was successful. The only sound Nick could hear was Marcus Frobush's wheezy breathing.

Tizzie resumed. "Were it not for her niece Marissa, we might never have known what happened to her. It was Marissa's heroic efforts that brought Candi to shore on Christmas Eve."

Marissa made eye contact only with her shoes.

That poor woman, Nick thought. Seeing her aunt like that. Nick's respect for her grew and he knew he had to see her alone.

He watched her shift from one foot to the other. Not in an embarrassed way. More as if she couldn't wait for Tizzie to finish. Finally Tizzie asked her for final words.

"She was a good woman," Marissa said. Her eyes were on Walter, who was checking his watch.

Checking his watch? Nick looked again. What was that about?

Then Marissa's gaze shifted. Nick could swear she was looking directly at him. "She didn't dr . . ." She cleared her throat. "We all loved her." She bowed her head. "Thank you."

What was she about to say? Why didn't she finish?

Marissa sat back down and Pastor John closed the ceremony. Margaret played the first chord on the organ so loudly that everyone jumped and Lulu May's baby let out a cry. Nick cringed at another assault on "Nearer My God to Thee" and the young man beside him stifled a chuckle.

Nick waited in his seat until almost everyone had left the chapel. He was sure Marissa had intended to tell the townspeople something and he was determined to find out what.

10

MISSING ASHES

As Marissa received condolences with Walter and Gregory at the door of the church, she thought of the fool she'd made of herself. Her brother Tony would have helped her if he'd attended. The fact that he still hadn't called worried her.

Margaret Potter clutched her organ music in one arm and approached Walter in the receiving line. As Walter accepted her handshake, he looked almost animated. Marissa could swear she detected a bit of a smile.

Margaret moved toward Marissa. "What a brave woman you were to pull Candi's body ashore."

"It wasn't Candi's," she wanted to shout. She half-heartedly accepted a hug with the organ music pressed between them.

Only a few mourners remained near the altar. The lights had been dimmed and Marissa couldn't make out their faces. But she recognized J.J.'s profile as he fussed in the front row. Then he marched down the aisle toward her.

Marissa swallowed hard. J.J. had been playing hide-and-seek with her since she found the body on the beach. He approached the receiving line, murmured something to Walter, handed him the bronze urn and then offered Marissa his hand. Her reflexes took over and she shook it.

"I'm so sorry for your loss," he said.

She sputtered, wanting to grab him and tell him what she thought of his false sympathy, but he quickly moved on to Gregory. "And you must be the boyfriend."

Gregory nodded. The two shook hands.

"Guess you'll be taking your girlfriend back to San Francisco," J.J. said to Gregory, his eyes trained on Marissa.

Marissa steamed. No one, especially J.J., was going to tell her when she was to leave the Cove.

J.J. walked away without looking back.

Not so fast, Marissa thought. She was about to chase after him when she saw Nick coming toward her. His grim expression couldn't overshadow his good looks. Shaking Walter's hand, he said, "I'm so sorry." Walter acknowledged him with a nod.

Marissa's eyes met Nick's. "So nice to see you," she said at the same time as he expressed his condolences. Unexpected warmth filled her as she offered her hand. But instead of accepting a handshake, for a brief moment he wrapped her in his arms, his mustache tickling her ear. "You're one special person," he whispered.

As quickly as he'd grabbed her, he let her go. Briskly, he caught up with the departing crowd.

Later that day, when the last mourner had left the gathering at Walter's house, Marissa kicked off her shoes and collapsed on the sofa.

No more lies, she thought, at least not for now. How genuinely thoughtful the townspeople had been. Not like those in the city where she swore most people show up only to be seen.

The hug from Nick had lingered throughout the afternoon. She was disappointed he hadn't come to the reception. J.J., supposedly Walter's best friend, had also failed to attend, a fact that convinced her he was avoiding her.

She watched Gregory gather the paper plates and napkins, wishing he had come to her aid during her eulogy. Thank God Tizzie took over. Sometimes she wondered why she kept hoping for a future with Gregory. Yes, he had helped her get promoted and then start her own business. Yes, Uncle Walter thought Gregory could provide her a good life. Yes, Gregory was handsome and, when he looked at her, she'd melt like butter. That seemed to be the main reason. Hormones!

She got up and pushed the vacuum cleaner across the parlor and then paused to watch Walter bustling about, humming and cleaning up the last of Tizzie's canapés.

What a weird attitude, she thought. This was not the uncle she once knew. Surely he must realize the hole he was digging for himself. And what would she say when everyone found out she'd covered the truth for him?

Walter took the trash into the kitchen and then poked his head into the parlor. "I'll leave you two some time alone," he said, retiring upstairs.

Marissa shut off the vacuum cleaner. "Pretty strange behavior, wouldn't you say?"

Gregory sat down on the sofa. "He sure seems happy for someone who's lost his wife." Marissa sat down beside him. He added, "By the way, you did fine at the service."

She could have used his words a little earlier. "I've heard better eulogies," she said.

"No one cared. It all went well."

He whispered, "Were you about to tell the congregation the truth?"

"What truth? Uncle Walter's told me so many lies, I don't know what's the truth." She tucked her legs under her.

"You could have told as much as you know."

A knot tightened in her stomach. Maybe she should have. She'd done what she thought was best. To Gregory, all in life could be measured and categorized. Everything was either black or white.

"You know what was strange?" he said. "All of Spindrift Cove seemed to show up today, but I didn't meet anyone who claimed to be Candi's relative."

Marissa pictured the mourners. "You're right. Everyone I saw was from the Cove."

"I'd say that's weird. Where's Candi from?"

"Originally from L.A. I would think she'd have friends and family there. She only moved up here to marry Uncle Walter."

"Weren't you expecting Tony and others from your side of the family?"

"Tony's all we have. Any chance to spend time in Tahoe with his kids and he's off."

"Wouldn't he have cared enough to come back for Candi's service?"

"I'm sure he would have if he'd known. His in-laws pride themselves on having no phone in the cabin and Tony told me his cell phone doesn't work up there. So there was no way to contact him. And Uncle Walter is an only child, so there's no one else."

Gregory was quiet for a moment and then said, "This may not be what you'd like to hear, but even if the body in the cove wasn't Candi's she might still be . . ."

"Be dead?" Marissa had to admit Gregory was right. "Then what in the world could have happened to her?"

She thought of the possibilities.

Gregory leaned back and crossed his legs, revealing a black sock and a square gadget on his ankle.

"Are you wearing a pedometer?"

"I always do when I go out of town. It tells me how much ground I've covered. We're exactly three-tenths of a mile from the church."

Marissa burst into uncontrollable laughter. She'd been holding back her feelings about Walter, J.J. and Gregory for too long. The pedometer summed up Gregory's whole measured existence. Tears filled her eyes and she held her stomach.

He snickered. "It's not all that funny," he said, dabbing at her eyes with a handkerchief.

When she stopped laughing he pulled her to him. A familiar warmth crept through her when he gazed into her eyes.

"You look especially pretty today," he said.

"And?"

"There's no 'and.'"

"Come on. You're usually after something when you butter me up."

"Well, you *are* a pretty woman. But since you asked, I'm a bit curious about that long-hair who hugged you after the service."

The spell was broken. She pretended to think.

"Tall," he said. "With a mustache. He sure seemed interested in you."

She rubbed her ankle. "Darn. A run in my stocking."

"Don't change the subject. Who was he?"

"You mean Nick Devereaux? He's the town photographer."

"He's one of those hippies who lives down on Main Street, isn't he?"

Marissa cringed. "What makes you say that?"

"He didn't look too comfortable in a suit. That was quite a bear hug he gave you."

Marissa placed both feet back on the floor. "Gregory, how do you feel about me?"

His eyes widened. I . . . I like you. You know that."

She stood and padded to the other side of the room. "We've known each other for two years. We've dated exclusively for a year and that's all you feel?"

He looked away and then back at her. "You're . . . special."

Marissa fought a lump in her throat. From Nick, those words had made her tingle. From Gregory, they were a laugh.

"Damn it!" She grabbed a cushion from the arm of the couch and flung it at him. It missed his head and soared toward the urn of Candi's ashes.

Both gasped when it made contact.

The urn fell from the mantle and clattered to the floor, sending the top rolling into the dining room. Marissa's heart leapt as she bent to inspect the damage.

The urn was empty.

11

UNFORESEEN COMPLICATION

J.J. Haggersby drove his black Lincoln from the driveway and onto Main Street, humming "Everything's Coming Up Roses." The memorial service had gone better than expected and he was eager as hell to tell Daphne. He hadn't felt so good since before Walter put the screws to him.

Main Street became Highway 1 and he stepped on the gas. No need to keep Daphne waiting.

Soon the Do Drop Inn appeared in the distance and his heartbeat quickened. As he drew near, he saw Daphne seated in her gray Ford Taurus, her personal car, waiting in the side parking lot. He drove into the lot, stopped beside her car and waved, watching her slide from her seat and lock the door. She smiled and his gaze traveled from her face to jeans that accentuated every curve. Even the loose-fitting T-shirt looked sexy, hinting at the full shape of her breasts. She slid into the passenger seat of his car.

God, she was beautiful.

"Hi there," she said. Her husky voice was sultry, like Lauren Bacall's.

"I could ravage you right here," he said, inhaling the sweet essence of gardenia perfume. He grabbed her to plant a kiss but she recoiled.

"Let's go someplace less obvious. Pull onto a side street somewhere."

J.J. obeyed, eager to feel her warm body against his. He drove north on Main Street and swerved right at a dirt road lined with redwood trees. After making another right to ensure no one from the highway could see them, he pulled into a side street and parked on the shoulder under a camphor tree.

He kissed her deeply and she responded. Nibbling at her ear, he whispered, "I did it. The service went better than expected."

"Really?" She pulled back. "Tell me about it."

"Tizzie not only grabbed the bait," he said stroking her arm. "She also passed it around to all the other little fishes. She couldn't have put on a better show if I'd told her the truth."

Daphne squeezed his hand. "Do you think everyone believed her?"

J.J. had expected Daphne to be more excited about the news. All through the service he'd been planning how he'd tell her. "You bet they did. Every word. I talked to quite a few of them."

Her smile faded and her blue eyes became serious. "You kept your promise. Can you trust Walter to keep his?"

He'd been through this before with Daphne. "Of course. Walter's reputation's at stake. That's all he cares about."

Daphne wrung her hands. "If he tells my husband about us, I hate to think what would happen."

"Don't you worry. Chet won't find out." Running his finger along her cheek, he asked. "Any news on who the corpse is?"

"Not a thing." She took his hand from her cheek and held it. "And they're having a devil of a time locating the woman who found the body. There's no record of her living in San Francisco or anywhere between here and there. Is there a chance you might have misspelled her name when you gave it to me?"

He tried not to smirk. Damn, he was good. "No way. I'm crazy when I'm with you, Daph, but I keep my head when it comes to my job. It's all in my report, including her disappearance. I couldn't believe it. I looked away for two seconds and she'd vanished."

"Which way did she head?"

J.J. thought fast. "I didn't see. It was dark as hell. And I had to keep an eye on the corpse until you got there." He took her hands in his. "When I think of what these hands could do to me." He wrapped his arms around her and cursed the steering wheel.

She returned his embrace until he caressed her breast. "I've gotta run."

Damn! "Only one more kiss."

She pecked him on the cheek. "We take too many chances. I need to get home before Chet comes back. He thinks I'm at play rehearsal."

Chet and her damn plays always came first. She was sure calling all the shots.

He slid his hand from her body, took a breath and started the car. "Don't worry so much about Chet. Walter will keep his word. We're doing him a big favor."

He made a U-turn and drove toward the highway, damning the way she could set him on fire and then ice him.

When they arrived at the Do Drop Inn parking lot, he pulled up to the Taurus. "When will I see you again?"

"Soon," she said. He grabbed her and kissed her long and deep. She responded with less fervor than he hoped. After sliding out, she closed the door, her fragrance lingering.

He waited several minutes until she and her car left the lot and disappeared down the highway.

Thank God, she lived in Ocean Bluffs. Not as much chance of those in the Cove knowing her. And he was lucky only Walter and his niece knew about them. Why hadn't his niece left town like Walter promised?

Then a thought crossed his mind. Damn. His niece's boyfriend probably knows, too. He was a complication J.J. hadn't foreseen.

12

BEWILDERING ASHES

Marissa quickly reassembled Candi's empty urn and headed upstairs to confront Walter.

Gregory grabbed her arm. "Whoa, there."

"This has gone too far," she said, escaping from his grasp. "I need to confront my uncle."

Gregory reached for her again. "Not so fast," he said. "I think we should act like nothing's happened."

"What?" Heat filled her cheeks. "You're as crazy as Uncle Walter."

"Let's not back him into a corner until we find out what he's up to. If we keep quiet, he may give a few more clues."

She stood on the third step with him. This was far from what she would have planned alone. "How long do you think that'll take?"

"Is there a problem?" Walter asked, looming over them at the top of the stairs. Tying the belt to his robe, he ambled down to the parlor. "How about a backyard barbecue for dinner tonight? I have some T-bones in the fridge."

Marissa heaved a silent sigh of relief that he hadn't heard them—unless he was faking.

"I have a better idea," Gregory said. "You've had a rough day. I'm taking you to the inn for T-bones you can enjoy without cooking."

"Aw, thanks," Walter said, "How about we do that some other time? I just got comfortable."

"I'm beat, too," Marissa said. "I'm not ready to face any more people." Or tell any more lies, she thought.

"Then let me do the honors," Gregory said. "You two put your feet up. I'll pour the wine and toss on the steaks."

Marissa rubbed her sore feet. "You're on." Whenever she was ready to declare Gregory a lost cause, he had a way of coming through.

Walter chose his favorite chair by the window and settled in. "Nice fellow," he said. "I hope you keep him around for a long time. I forgot how you said you met him."

All inane chatter, Marissa thought. Why was he talking like all was well? Candi was gone from his life. He couldn't be suppressing his grief that much. Why wouldn't he come clean? "I met him at work when I was a programmer—before I started the Clutter Clinic."

Walter leaned back in his chair. "He told me they're considering him for a director's job."

Marissa had had enough. "Uncle Walter, Candi's gone. Shouldn't we talk about this? Don't you have some feelings? What are we going to do?"

Walter flinched. Then his tight lips relaxed. "I wish I knew," he said. "I've gone over and over this and I keep coming up empty."

A tear formed in his eye. It was the first sign of grief he'd shown Marissa since the memorial service.

She stepped towards him. "Why weren't any of Candi's relatives at the service? Surely she has someone besides us who cares. What about her parents?"

"Both gone," he said quickly. He added, "Her other relatives are spread around different states I can't remember. I couldn't find her address book. She must have taken it with her. Her son is the only one I could trace."

"Why didn't he show up?"

"I left a couple messages. He never called back."

"This is unbelievable."

He shifted in his chair. "Probably gone for the holidays. I'll call him again tonight."

"Couldn't we have held the service a few days later? Maybe you could have found him."

"I doubt it. I wanted the whole thing over."

His answers were too pat for Marissa. "Let me have his number. I'll get in touch with him."

"No need," he said and quickly added, "By the way. I forgot to tell you. Tony called."

Marissa came to attention. "He's all right, isn't he?"

"He's fine. They got snowed in. There's no phone in the cabin and his cell phone doesn't work up there."

Marissa sunk into a chair across the room from him. At least her brother was all right.

"Said he trudged a mile in the snow to let us know he's okay. Said they were having so much fun, he wasn't coming back with the kids until after New Year's."

If Tony knew about their aunt, he wouldn't have stayed in Tahoe, Marissa thought. "How did he take the news about Candi?"

"Pretty bad. Was going to come down with the kids right away. I told him there was nothing he could do now. The service is over."

This was not at all like Tony. Her frustration was mounting and she was glad when Gregory ducked his head into the parlor. "Where do you keep the Worcestershire, Walter?"

"I know where it is," Marissa said, leaving her uncle in his chair.

Marissa tossed in the creaking bed in Walter's guestroom. The empty urn confirmed Candi wasn't dead . . . or did it? None of her relatives showing up at the memorial service would support the fact that she might not be dead or that Walter might have purposely not told them.

Marissa couldn't go on without knowing. She had to find proof one way or another. And what a chicken she'd been in her confrontation about Gregory's feelings for her. She still had no concrete answer. Maybe she should take the clue that he doesn't care. Maybe all he wants is her between the sheets. And maybe she should investigate Candi's disappearance by herself. And why did Nick keep sneaking into her thoughts?

She was about to doze when she heard the floorboards creak downstairs.

She listened.

Leaving the doors unlocked at night gave her the creeps. She searched for a likely weapon and found only the black shoes she'd worn to the memorial service. Shoe in hand, she set out in the dark.

"Uncle Walter," she whispered outside his room.

No answer.

"Gregory?" She opened his door. "There's someone downstairs."

"What? I thought I heard a noise, too." He grabbed his robe. "Stay here."

Marissa waited at the top of the stairs as Gregory pulled on his robe and tiptoed down. "Walter, is that you?"

"Of course it is," Walter replied. "I came down to get some milk."

Marissa joined them in the parlor. "You scared us to death."

"I'll be up in a minute," he said. "After I switch the light off in the kitchen."

Gregory climbed the stairs but Marissa waited for Walter. When she heard him still fussing in the kitchen, she yawned and went up alone.

Back in her room, she waited for the sound of Walter walking the upstairs hall. Even after he went back to his room, she lay awake for hours. Her intuition nagged her. Before they'd discovered him downstairs, she'd heard the outside kitchen door open and shut. And when he told them he was getting milk, she noticed specks of ash on his robe.

She rose and padded down the stairs, feeling her way on the railing. Once through the foyer, she made her way to the fireplace. She ran her hand along the cold hearth in search of matches.

Stopping, she listened. No one stirred.

Quietly, she lit a candle on the mantle and lifted the lid on the urn to check inside.

The urn was filled with ashes.

13

NEW CLUES

Pastor John removed the last funeral wreath from the altar, thinking about how he'd tell the church board in San Francisco how nicely the service went. Surely the members would see he'd taken positive action toward improvement.

He thought of the last meeting he had with them before they banished him to Spindrift Cove. "It's for the betterment of the church," they'd said. But he knew the real reason. They'd spoken to him several times about not knowing his congregation and their needs. And they said he moved too slowly when taking action on important matters.

It was a setup, he thought. There was nothing in the Bible that said you had to make quick decisions.

He was sweeping the floor when Margaret Potter burst through the door, holding her feathered hat on her head. Still dressed in the dark wool suit she'd worn to the memorial service, she hurried toward him. For a woman in her seventies, she moved remarkably fast.

"I'm so glad I caught you, Pastor, before you went home to bed." Even in the low light, he could see the flush on her face and she was wringing her hands. Gray hair stood out from under her hat and her large swollen eyes made her look like a raccoon.

"I don't know what to do," she said. "I've been thinking all day since the service and then when I went home I kept thinking about it and I still don't know what's best."

Pastor John cleared his throat. "Now calm down." He used his most comforting tone—the one he'd cultivated since he'd moved to the Cove. He led her to the nearest pew, where she sat down and he squeezed in beside her.

"And then," she said. "I thought maybe I should keep my mouth shut. Then again, somebody should know. So I—"

"Now take a deep breath and start from the beginning."

She removed a lace hanky from her suit pocket and blew her nose with surprising force. "I don't know where to start." Her hands trembled. "Yes I do. It was a week ago when I was at work at the post office. You know, I give out the applications for passports. And who should come in but Candi and she wanted an application. I said, 'Two?' and she said, 'No, one.' Oh, dear, I didn't know what to think."

She stopped for a breath and Pastor John dove in. "What's upsetting you so?"

"*One*, Pastor John. She only wanted *one!*"

"Are you concerned because she didn't want a passport for Walter?"

Her eyes widened. "Of course I am. She hasn't been married more than a couple years. I'd think wherever she was going, she'd go with her husband."

"Couldn't the passport be for a business trip?"

Margaret stiffened. "No." She hesitated. "Well, maybe. Except Candi looked so distraught. I asked her about Walter and she ignored my question like I didn't ask it. She left in a flurry and next thing I heard, she was dead." She shook her head. "You know what a floozy she was. She dressed and flaunted her figure like a teenager. I think she was running off with somebody and Walter caught her and killed her."

Pastor John stifled a smile at her wild accusation. "Couldn't you be jumping to conclusions? There are so many other explanations."

"Like what?"

"Like I said, the trip could be for business. Or maybe she has family out of the country. You know Walter is rooted here. There would be no reason for him to join her."

"But I haven't told you everything." She folded and unfolded her hands. "The day after Candi asked for the application, I ran into Walter in Ocean Bluffs at Walgreens and he was buying rat poison."

Pastor John squeezed her hand. "And you think—"

"He gave Candi an overdose and dumped her into the ocean. If he thought she was leaving him, he was going to kill her. I was so upset when I heard she was dead. I was in such a turmoil at the service, I could hardly play my music."

Same god awful playing as before, Pastor John thought.

"I had to tell somebody," she said. "I don't want to be an accessory for keeping my mouth shut."

The pastor gently touched her arm. "I assure you, you have nothing to worry about."

"I would have told the deputy sheriff, excepting he's such a good friend of Walter's and all."

Pastor John led her to the door. "You did the right thing."

She wiped her eyes. "I tell you Pastor, she had other things on her mind beside her new hubby."

"Now you get a good night's sleep. Poisonings are for soap operas. They don't happen in Spindrift Cove. You'll feel better in the morning."

She looked at him. "If I don't, I'll be back."

"That's fine, Margaret."

He watched her go down the path and then closed the door.

This congregation was a piece of cake, he thought, compared to the one he had in San Francisco.

The sun was high when Marissa and Gregory stopped their uphill hike for a breather.

"Nobody braves a December morning to hike to the sun," Gregory said, panting between words.

"We've only come a few hundred feet. And look at the view." She surveyed the fields of tall grass on the sides of the trail. A panorama of Spindrift Cove spread below them. They were only a few minutes from Walter's place and they were already in the country.

"Check the altimeter I gave you," Gregory said. "You can see how high up we are."

Marissa searched her backpack.

"You forgot it, didn't you?" He gently cuffed her on the cheek. "What am I going to do with you?"

She headed toward a large flat rock and sat down.

"A bit uncomfortable if you had sex in mind," he said. "I should have brought a blanket."

"Not now," she said. "I have something serious to discuss."

Gregory brushed off the rock and sat beside her. Taking her hand, he asked, "Are you going to tell me why we had to hike all the way up here?"

"I wanted to talk to you away from Uncle Walter. I wasn't sure if he'd be staying home from his hardware store for another day. Besides, you and I can both use the exercise."

She looked over the rolling meadow and out to the serene ocean. She'd discovered the view the last time she visited and it had become a favorite. Why couldn't Gregory appreciate it as much as she?

"What's the big secret?" he asked.

She opened the wrapper of a granola bar and offered him half the bar. "Last night, I was curious about Uncle Walter's bathrobe. It had ashes on it."

"So?"

"After you were both asleep, I sneaked down to the parlor and checked Candi's urn."

"What in the world for?"

"It was full of ashes."

"Oh, God, do you think that's why he wanted me to barbecue? He needed ashes for the urn?"

"Bingo. They would substantiate his story. What he didn't count on was anyone looking into the urn before he was able to fill it."

"So what have we proved?"

"Only that there are so many possibilities."

"You're right," Gregory said, taking a piece of paper from his shirt pocket. "But never fear, my dear." He opened the paper into a large blank computer-generated matrix. "We can use a decision table to solve this problem."

This was the ultimate, Marissa thought. "You carry blank matrices in your pocket?"

"Yes. I use them to—"

"When you go hiking?"

His cheeks became pink. "I'm being a bit compulsive again, aren't I?"

More than a bit, she thought. Sometimes she wondered how much she could endure. "Only a bit," she said, spreading the paper on the ground. "Show me how these things work."

"Now on this axis," he said, pointing with a pen, "we list all the things that could have happened to Candi. Up here we write down who might have been involved. And in the boxes, we put our comments."

She took the pen from him. "Let's make a list."

"I suppose we could cut corners." He bit his lower lip. "We can do it chronologically. What was the first story your uncle told you?"

"He said Candi was sick."

"If she were sick, where would she be now?" he asked, taking a bite from his half of their snack.

"In a hospital, maybe, but not dead."

"Okay. That's one possibility. What's another?"

"She walked deliriously into the ocean and drowned."

"Possible but not likely. What else could have happened to her?"

"She ran off with a German guy she met at a conference."

"Where would she be now?" Gregory asked

"Maybe in Munich. Maybe anywhere. Not dead." She added, "And I forgot to call Gunther."

Gregory's eyes grew wide. "You have his number?"

"I found it in Candi's office. Uncle Walter and I went to clean up her mail. I tried calling him from a pay phone and didn't have enough coins. I didn't want to call him from my uncle's house."

Gregory took a cell phone from his pocket.

"Does this work overseas?" she asked.

"Oh, right," he said. He pulled a larger phone from his backpack and handed it to her.

"You carry a special phone for overseas calls when you hike?"

He smiled sheepishly. "It's for business. I forgot I put it in here."

Marissa didn't venture to ask why he'd bring a backpack to work. Instead she mulled over the trade-off of marrying someone so prepared for anything compared to having fun with someone more impulsive . . . like maybe Nick.

Abandoning her short reverie, she found Gunther's phone number in her purse and punched it in. She waited. "It's ringing." After more than ten rings, she was about to hang up when the call was answered. She listened. "It's his answering machine. It's in German."

"I'm afraid my one semester of college German won't help. You better hang up."

Disappointed, she asked, "Did we cover all the possibilities for Candi?"

Gregory tilted his head. "I hesitate to say this but she could have run off with the German guy and something serious could have happened to her."

"I guess I have to face the fact that she may not be alive." Marissa looked out to the ocean. "So what do we have? She could be dead, alive and almost anywhere."

Gregory finished off the last bite of the granola bar. "If she's dead, who would have killed her?"

"Her boyfriend."

"Why?"

"I don't know. Maybe for money. She was quite flamboyant. She might have flashed around whatever she had."

Gregory shook his head. "Who else had reason to kill her?"

"No one I know. The people in town thought she was a bit loud and flashy for Spindrift Cove, but I think most accepted her."

"What about Walter?"

"You mean if he couldn't have Candi, maybe he didn't want anyone else to have her?" Marissa shuddered.

She thought of the times Walter had held her and comforted her. How he'd called every day after her parents died. How compassionate he'd been.

"If Uncle Walter killed her, then where's her body? She's too small to be the corpse that washed into the cove. I'm sure of that."

"Then where would she be? In Walter's backyard?" His eyes lit up. "Maybe those ashes are not from last night's barbecue. Maybe he buried her in the backyard. Maybe he's cremating her body, piece by piece."

This was too gruesome. Marissa thought of the fireplace and how sparkling clean it was. And of Nick's comment that Walter had built so many fires that the damper got stuck with soot. "Oh God, could he have burned the body parts in the fireplace? Is that why he'd cleaned it so well?"

"I doubt it. The stench would have been unbearable, not to mention the smell that would alert the neighbors."

Marissa stood up. Walter's stories flooded back—his not being able to contact Candi's relatives and Tony deciding to stay in Tahoe. She repeated Walter's stories to Gregory. "He doesn't want anyone except the townspeople to know about Candi."

"About her leaving him," he asked, "or about him killing her?"

"It could be either. But if he killed her, he wouldn't have invited me to spend Christmas with him. He knows I'd be curious about her disappearance."

"Did he invite you?"

"Of course. Why do you think I came? I could have spent Christmas with you as planned."

Gregory rose from the rock. "Think back. When you told me you were going to visit your uncle, you said you wanted to help him with Candi. You thought she was ill. Did he ask or did you offer?"

Marissa thought about their telephone conversation. "He said Candi was sick and . . . and I guess I offered to help."

"So it wasn't his idea?"

"No, but that doesn't mean he killed her."

Gregory brushed off his pants. "Maybe not, but it's something to think about."

"But tell me this. If Uncle Walter killed Candi—and I'm not saying he ever could—do you think J.J. had anything to do with it?"

"I suppose it's possible. What's J.J.'s relationship to Walter?"

"They've been friends since J.J. moved here five years ago."

"Is he a good enough friend to help in a murder?"

The word gave Marissa goosebumps. "That's a pretty weak motive." She started down the hill. "Let's go back to the Cove. I'm more confused now than ever."

"I've got a better idea," Gregory said. "Let's stop somewhere for breakfast."

"And then we should go to Ocean Bluffs and find out who that corpse is."

14

MOUNTING SUSPICIONS

Nick Devereaux sat on his bed, tapping a pencil on his nightstand. Maybe he should have gone to the wake. He would have if Marissa's boyfriend weren't in town. This wasn't a time to cause more problems for her. Under any other circumstances, he'd have given the boyfriend a run for his money.

What did she say at the service? Candi didn't dr—? Didn't dream? Dress? Drown? She didn't actually drown? If she didn't, then what happened to her?

He grabbed the phone and called Information. "Give me the number of the coroner's office."

"Ocean Bluffs Coroner's Office." A young woman's voice came over the line.

"My name is Nick Devereaux and I'd like to inquire about a body found by Marissa . . ." He realized he hadn't asked Marissa her last name. On a chance, he used Walter's. "Schmidkin."

He heard the click of keys "I'm sorry Mr. Devereaux. We have no record of anyone by that name."

Marissa searched for the coroner's office as she and Gregory drove slowly down Veteran's Boulevard. "There it is," she said. "Go into that lot."

Gregory pulled the car into a parking lot in front of a three-story white brick office building and parked in an empty space next to four white Ford Crown Victorias, like the one Daphne drove for business, Marissa thought. And sometimes for pleasure.

She followed Gregory to the door of an office with a poster in the window that read, "You Drink, You Drive, You're Ours."

They stepped into a room filled with several desks with nameplates for deputy coroners. Three of the five deputies sat at their desks, tapping on computer keyboards.

"Where do we inquire about a body," Marissa asked a shapely brunette receptionist.

"Who are you inquiring about?"

"I'm not quite sure. I'm the woman who dragged the body from the ocean on Christmas Eve in Spindrift Cove. I reported it to Deputy Sheriff Haggersby and no one has questioned me since. I'd like to know who the corpse is."

"Please have a seat," the woman said without hesitation. "May I have your name?"

"Marissa DeSantos."

"And Gregory Townsend," Gregory added.

"That's strange," the woman said. "I received a call about a Marissa today—only her last name was Schmidkin."

"That's my uncle's name. Who was it that called?"

"Hmmm. I'm afraid I don't remember who he said he was. I'm sorry."

Marissa turned to Gregory. "Who would call the coroner's office about me? And why would they think my name was Schmidkin?"

"Beats me."

The receptionist tapped at her keyboard and peered at the screen. "Don't go away," she said, her voice riddled with urgency. "Coroner Williams will want to see you." She jumped from her seat and rushed toward an office down the hall.

Marissa sat down opposite an imposing wall plaque. In gold letters, it read, "Honorable Jacob Alan Williams."

"We're being sent right to the top," she said.

Soon a tall, dark man strode out to see them. Although he appeared to be in his late fifties, he had a full head of brown wavy hair. Clean-shaven, posture erect and clad in a neatly pressed shirt and pants, he presented an almost military image.

"I'm Coroner Jake Williams. Please come with me." A waft of Irish Spring pursued him.

Marissa and Gregory followed the coroner into a large office lined with bookcases. A huge oak desk at the back of the room faced them and a long table extended out from it and halfway to the door. The coroner took a seat behind the desk and offered them chairs at the table.

"Our receptionist tells me you're the woman who found the body in Spindrift Cove," he said to Marissa.

She cleared her throat. "Actually I pulled it from the water. I was afraid it would drift away."

He listened with a sober face. "Our records say a Mary Ann DeSardo found the body. That's not your name?"

"No," she said, thinking back to her conversation at the beach with J.J. He'd taken her name and address in the dark. Maybe when he passed the information to the deputy coroner, "Marissa DeSantos" looked like "Mary Ann DeSardo." Or maybe J.J. gave Daphne a phony name on purpose so she couldn't contact her.

"Do you live on Clipper Street in San Francisco?"

"I live in San Francisco but on Douglass Street."

He shook his head. "This body weighed about two-hundred-fifty pounds. How did you manage to haul it to shore?"

Marissa explained the best she could.

He smiled. "Stay right where you are. Officer Hendrick has been trying to locate you since Christmas Eve." He punched some numbers into the telephone pad. "Hendrick? I've got a woman here who says she recovered the body from Spindrift Cove. You want to come down here?"

Marissa looked up when a handsome man with curly blond hair and rosy cheeks knocked on the doorframe of the coroner's office and strode in. He was followed by a squat dark-haired man with piercing black eyes and the jowls of a bulldog. Both wore dark business suits and ties.

"Hendrick," the coroner greeted the blond man. "And Sanchez." He introduced everyone and then ushered Gregory to the reception area, leaving Marissa alone behind a closed door with the two detectives.

"Am I glad to see you," Hendrick said. His trim, solid form towered over her.

"You are?"

He slid into a chair on the other side of the table. Sanchez pulled one up beside him. "Off course, I am," Hendrick said. His blue eyes shone from a square face with a strong jaw. "Why did you flee the scene?"

Marissa sat up. "Flee what scene?"

Sanchez kept his mouth shut, his dark eyes trained on her like those of an attack dog ready to spring.

"My report says you pulled the John Doe out of the water and took off," Hendrick said.

John Doe, she thought. Does that mean for sure it was a man?

Marissa pushed her chair back from the table. "I wanted to stay until the coroner arrived. J.J. was the one who insisted I go back to my uncle's."

Sanchez let out a barely perceptible snort of disbelief. Marissa ignored his attempt to rile her.

"You never got in touch with Haggersby after that?" Hendrick asked.

"Of course I did. I kept asking him for an update. I got nowhere."

Sanchez rolled his eyes and Marissa swallowed her anger. She would not lose her temper at this man.

Hendrick asked, "Why didn't you call the police?"

"I did—" She thought a moment. Her call to the police was to check on a missing persons report for Candi. She'd forgotten to ask about the body. "I tried but the lines were down in Spindrift Cove."

Sanchez squinted as if he weren't convinced. Marissa could feel the blood rise to her face.

Hendrick asked, "Why did you give a false name?"

"Wait a minute," she said. "I came in here on my own because no one contacted me and I was concerned. I gave my correct name and address. I don't know how this DeSardo name and phony address got into your report. I'm here to help in any way I can. But if your friend here keeps looking at me like I'm some kind of an idiot, you're not going to get a lot of assistance from me."

A mischievous smile crossed Sanchez's face. "Sorry," he said. "No offense. You have to admit, your story's tough to believe."

What is this? Marissa thought. Good cop, bad cop? Only now she couldn't tell which was which.

Hendrick rubbed the side of his face and sat back in his chair. "Maybe we got off to a bad start. Let's do this again from the beginning."

Marissa took a breath, unsure which man to address, so she related her story to both. After she explained how a female so small could drag a mighty corpse out of the ocean, she inquired whether they had any leads as to the identity of the corpse.

Sanchez opened a briefcase and handed her a sketch of a man with deep-set eyes, a strong nose and full cheeks. Beside the face was the description:

SEX:	MALE
RACE:	CAUCASION
HEIGHT:	6'2"
WEIGHT:	ABOUT 250 lbs.
AGE:	21 TO 23 yrs.
HAIR:	SHAVEN, BLACK
DENTAL:	YES
FINGERPRINTS:	NO

"Does this mean no fingerprints were taken?" Marissa asked.

"It means there were none. Somebody burned them off with a propane torch."

Marissa shuddered. She read the circumstances printed beneath the description:

ON DECEMBER 24, 1998, THE BODY
OF A WHITE MALE ADULT WAS FOUND
ON THE BEACH IN SPINDRIFT COVE,
CALIFORNIA. SUBJECT WAS WRAPPED IN
FOUR SHEETS OF HEAVY BLACK PLASTIC.
A .38 CALIBER BULLET WAS LODGED
IN HIS CHEST. EXCEPT FOR JEANS AND
UNDERSHORTS, HE WAS DRESSED IN ILL-
FITTING CLOTHING AT LEAST A SIZE
TOO SMALL.

"Strange only some of his clothes didn't fit," she said.

The report listed the clothing the corpse wore, including a light blue Oscar de la Renta tuxedo jacket, size 46R and sizes for a long-sleeved ruffled Van Heusen cotton shirt, blue Levi jeans, Florsheim shoes and Fruit of the Loom underwear.

"Levis with a tuxedo jacket and dress shirt? Isn't that a bit unusual?"

Sanchez stretched and yawned. "You might say, but I've seen stranger."

She read further. "He wore a Princeton University ring? That must tell you something about him."

"You would think so. We've checked with the university. So far, no luck."

Marissa studied the sketch again. When she finished, Hendrick asked, "Any chance you might know who he is?"

"I'm afraid not." She sat back in her chair. "What's next? Do I have to view the body?"

Chuckling, he said, "That only happens in the movies. We provide photos or sketches to identify. We don't allow any viewing in this jurisdiction."

So Uncle Walter was lying about viewing Candi, Marissa thought. A big, bold-faced lie.

She asked, "What do you think happened to him?"

"The bullet was a .38 caliber. That's all we've been able to determine," Sanchez said.

"May I have a copy of this report?"

Sanchez handed her a page from a stack of papers. He and Hendrick rose, signifying the interrogation was over. They handed Marissa their business cards. "Call us if you think of anything that might help solve this case," Hendrick said. "Any time. We work late."

Marissa took their cards. "It's kind of sad," she said. "A man can struggle through life trying to make something of himself and when he dies, no one knows who he is or that he's even gone."

"Yeah," Sanchez said. "Thanks for coming in."

On the way out of the coroner's office, Marissa stopped at the reception desk. "Would you please check your computer and tell me if someone by the name of Candi Pomeroy has passed away?"

The woman put down her coffee cup and tapped on her keyboard. "I don't find anything. Is she related to the case you were discussing with Detective Hendrick?"

"Uh. No. I know this sounds strange. I usually don't have so many dead bodies in my life at one time."

The woman raised an eyebrow.

Gregory joined Marissa at the desk. "She means it's a coincidence that her aunt is missing and she found a dead body at about the same time."

Marissa ignored Gregory's comment and wished he'd let her speak for herself.

The woman looked at Marissa. "You poor dear. I guess it's good news your aunt isn't on record here. If she's been gone more than twenty-four hours, you might want to go to the sheriff's office and file a missing persons report."

"We're on our way," Gregory said. "Thanks."

Marissa stayed put. "Can you tell me anything about the man who called about Marissa Schmidkin?"

"Not too much. He had a kind voice. I remember he introduced himself. I wish I could remember his name."

"What did he want?"

"He wanted to know if we knew of someone called Marissa, who found a body."

This was too weird, Marissa thought. She thanked her and joined Gregory at the door.

"It must be J.J.," he said.

"Why would J.J. be checking on me here? And why would he say my name is Schmidkin?"

"Can't answer that one," Gregory said.

Once they were outside, he said, "So what did those guys ask you?"

"They thought I'd flown the scene. Something screwy is going on. When I gave J.J. information that night, I was very clear about my name and address. I don't trust him one bit."

She walked with Gregory down the sidewalk and to the car.

"Do you think they suspect you of killing the guy?" Gregory asked.

Marissa had wondered the same thing. "Neither detective mentioned me as a suspect but, as I left, Hendrick asked me to be available for more questions."

"Does he know yet who the corpse is?"

"That's the funny thing. They still haven't received any missing persons report on him. Sanchez gave me a copy of the sketch they made." She handed it to him. "Here's what he looks like."

Gregory studied the face. "Maybe he's homeless and hasn't any relatives." He opened the car door for her. "Did Candi's name come up in the conversation?"

"Neither detective mentioned her, but I told Hendrick about her. Our next stop should be the sheriff's office to file a missing persons report."

"J.J.'s office?"

"No, J.J. has no office. He's only a sheriff's deputy . . . and the mayor. The police and Missing Persons are at the sheriff's office here in Ocean Bluffs. Hendrick told me filing a report was the only way I'll find out what happened to her." She buckled her seat belt. "And here's an interesting tidbit: They don't allow anyone to view dead bodies. That means Uncle Walter was lying when he said he viewed Candi's corpse. I can't believe he'd lie to me."

"I guess you never really know anyone," Gregory said, starting the car.

His words hurt. The trust she had for the uncle she loved for so many years was slowly eroding.

She bit her lip to fight back a tear. "I made a copy of the note Candi wrote. When we file the missing persons report, I'm giving it to whoever's in charge."

15

FRAGILE SECRETS

J.J. slipped a ten to the Mark Hopkins maitre d' and followed him to a window table overlooking San Francisco's Nob Hill. He set down his briefcase and gazed out the window at the red and white car lights inching through the narrow streets.

The traffic was probably keeping his daughter, he thought.

"Hello, Poppy!" came from behind.

J.J. cringed at the name and looked up in time to receive a half-hearted embrace from Stephanie, a petite mini-skirted blond, who looked younger than her twenty-three years. Maybe it was the hair-do, fluffy and full around her face. Truth was she was attractive in her little red jacket, skirt and heels.

"Good to see you, Steph."

"Yeah, me, too," she said with little conviction.

He stood and pulled out a chair for her. She could at least show some manners, he thought. After all, he was her father. "How was your trip from Phoenix?"

"Not bad," she said, sitting down.

He was always at a loss for conversation with his daughter. The only thing they seemed to have in common was an interest in expensive gem stones.

"So you're kicking out your boyfriend?" he asked.

A startled look crossed her face and he quickly said, "You told me over the phone."

"Oh, yeah. You could say that." She glanced at her watch. "I'll stay if you want to chat but I'm on a tight schedule."

"Uh—"

"What have you got for me tonight?" she asked before he had time to respond.

Relieved he wouldn't have to play the father bit, he lifted his briefcase from the floor. "Not as much as usual. Gem show was almost a bust. Got a few more rubies. Same instructions."

"Good enough." She rose and extended her hand for the briefcase. After accepting it, she handed him her empty one. "I already have some buyers." She hiked up her shoulder bag. "Next time I'll stay for those beers you promised."

"Sure."

She patted his shoulder and bent toward his ear. "Bye, Poppykins."

The heat rose in his face and he clenched his fists. "Steph!"

She looked back.

"Don't call me that."

She winked at him and trotted in her heels to the elevator. "Whatever," she called over her shoulder.

Damned if she didn't always find a way to show she was in control.

On the other hand, Steph was a lot like him, he thought, and the best business partner he ever had.

He called to the waiter. "I'll have the T-bone."

Back home, J.J. was buttering a slice of bread when someone who sounded like Daphne called at the door. He looked out the window to ensure that Marissa woman wasn't trying to fool him.

"J.J., let me in," Daphne said.

"What's all the commotion?" He opened the door to see Daphne's pink, perspiring face. She was panting. When he bent to kiss her, she pulled away.

"You haven't been straight with me," she said.

"Sit down. Let me take your jacket."

She remained standing with her jacket on, lines of fury crossing her face. "I was willing to go along with Walter's lie but why didn't you tell me the woman who found the corpse was Walter's niece?"

J.J. stopped short. Daphne had found out sooner than expected. He should have planned ahead. "I . . . I didn't see as it would make any difference."

"Are you crazy? I could have lost my job!"

"Now, now. That's not going to happen."

"Don't patronize me. You gave me the wrong name when I came to get the corpse."

"Let me help you with your jacket," he said, reaching for her. "No need to be upset."

"Me? upset?" she said, brushing his arm away. "What about my boss and everyone in the police department? I passed them all a bogus name."

He offered her a kitchen chair, which she refused. "So I got the spelling wrong. Sit down and tell me what happened."

The pout remained on her lips. "Marissa and her boyfriend came to see Coroner Williams this morning."

J.J.'s ulcer gave a twinge. All he needed was that little snoop putting her nose where it didn't belong. "How do you know that?"

"I saw this woman come into the reception area. About five foot three, shiny black hair. Came with a tall, lanky guy. She told our receptionist she was the one who found the body in Spindrift Cove and she wanted to know who it was."

J.J.'s knees trembled and he sat down. "So what happened?"

"Of course, the receptionist immediately ushered her in to see Williams."

"How'd you find out she was Walter's niece?"

Her eyes were blue daggers. "Coroner Williams told me afterwards . . . before he chewed me out for getting the name wrong. Said the guy with her was her boyfriend. Somebody by the name of Townsend. Let me tell you, I was sweating bullets."

J.J.'s ulcer gave another twinge. Why hadn't Walter gotten those two out of town yet? "I would have told you but you'd only worry. Besides, Marissa's on her way back to San Francisco. No harm done." He hoped Walter's promise was good.

"You lied to me. She knows the body isn't Candi's. She knows Walter lied to her and she's out to learn the truth. She probably has strong allegiance to her uncle. She could tell the whole town about Candi. Then what's to stop Walter from spilling the beans about us? And now her boyfriend probably knows, too."

Damn him, J.J. thought. "Don't you worry about the boyfriend," he said.

"And what if Candi comes back?"

J.J. shook his head. "Not a chance in hell. Walter says she's run off to Germany with some guy. Neither of them has any reason to show up in Spindrift Cove again. And Candi sure won't come back to see old man Walter. Not with a new sugar daddy on her arm."

Daphne leaned on the table, face to face with him. "Damn it, J.J. It's the lie you told me that makes me so mad. How can I ever trust you?"

He looked up at her. "I made a mistake. I should have told you. What can I do to make it up to you?" Taking her hand, he said, "I saw a great ruby ring that would look perfect on your finger. If I bought it for you, could we call a truce?"

Fire was in her eyes. "You can't buy me off."

"Could you keep your husband from seeing the ring?"

Her anger seemed to melt and a smile crept to her lips. "Of course I could."

"How would you do that?"

"I'd put it in my panty drawer. Chet hasn't been interested in my lingerie in years. I think he's having an affair." A frown crossed her face.

J.J. caressed her hand. "He's a damn fool. You deserve much better."

"Thanks, J.J.," she said. "You can be sweet sometimes."

"Then it's a deal?" he asked.

"No more lies?"

"I'll have it for you the next time we're together. Leave everything to J.J. You don't have to worry about a thing."

"I don't know why I keep coming back to you," she said with a coy smile. She raised the zipper on her jacket and was about to leave. "I won't be comfortable until we know for sure where Candi is." J.J. was about to rise when she said, "I forgot to tell you the rest of my story."

This time she took the chair he offered and he waited for the inevitable shoe to drop.

"Someone called the coroner's office about the corpse. I heard the receptionist on the phone."

J.J. felt the sweat forming on his upper lip.

"I wrote his name down," she said, taking a yellow Post-It from her pocket. "It's Devereaux. I didn't get the first name. You know him?"

Damn, he thought. He managed to maintain his cool. "Uh huh. He's the photographer. Lives in an apartment in the Pajama Factory. He was at the memorial service."

"Why would he be interested in the corpse?"

His temples throbbed so hard, he was sure she could see. "Beats me. Has the body been identified yet?" He sat on the edge of his chair.

Daphne shook her head and a thousand-pound weight lifted from J.J.'s shoulders.

"He had no I.D," she said. "We couldn't get any prints. The fingertips had been seared with a propane torch. Whoever killed him knew what he was doing." She rose to leave. "Who is this Devereaux guy and why would he be nosing around the coroner's office?"

"He's just a long-hair with nothing else to do. Name's Nick. I wouldn't worry about him."

J.J.'s stomach churned at the thought of Nick getting involved in addition to Marissa and her boyfriend. Even more, he was worried about himself. If Daphne ever found out he knew who the body was, he was doomed.

16

STERN WARNINGS

J.J. saw the light inside Walter's hardware store, ignored the *CLOSED* sign and, finding the door unlocked, he entered. He strode past kitchen faucets and plumbing supplies to the back, where Walter, in a leather apron and green eyeshade, was sorting finishing nails.

Same time, same place, J.J thought, every day after five. The most predictable man in Spindrift Cove.

J.J. approached Walter without a greeting. "Memorial service went damn well."

Walter poured a box of galvanized nails into a bin before glancing up. "You're looking pretty good yourself."

Gees, the old man is losing it, J.J. thought. "I said we had a good memorial service."

"I already thanked you. It went real good."

J.J. watched him pick an errant screw from the nails. "Music was fine?"

"As good as Margaret can play," Walter said, tossing the empty nail box into the trash.

"And everybody bought the story?"

"As far as I can tell. What are you getting at, J.J.?"

"I want to be sure I upheld my part of our bargain."

"You did fine."

J.J. put his hand into a bin full of washers and let them run through his fingers, scattering some on the floor. "'Cause you don't seem to be holding up your end at all." He waited for Walter's reaction.

Walter looked him in the eye. "I haven't said a word to anybody about you and Daphne."

J.J. circled a table of fluorescent light bulbs and then faced Walter. "Your niece is still in town."

Without a word, Walter took the broom from the end of the nail bins and swept the washers from the floor. J.J. knew him well enough to tell he was thinking. He added, "And you didn't tell me anything about a boyfriend coming to town."

Walter stopped sweeping. "I didn't know he was coming. I couldn't tell him he had to leave."

"Women talk," J.J. said, stepping closer. "If she tells him, that's one more person who knows."

"Not Marissa. She wouldn't tell anyone."

"And how come she hasn't gone back to San Francisco like you promised?"

Walter set the broom aside. "She said she was leaving and then she didn't." His voice rose to a shout. "What do you want me to do? Kick out my own niece?"

J.J. remained calm. "I heard she and her boyfriend were at the coroner's office today. If they blow the whistle on what you and I did, I'll be in a heap of trouble."

"I promise she won't tell." Walter backed away and J.J. moved forward, within inches of him.

"If the two of them aren't out of town by tonight, something bad could happen to Marissa."

"They . . . they'll be gone. I'll make sure they're gone today."

"I knew you'd understand." He patted Walter on the back and headed out the door, thinking how easy it was to rile the old man with a few carefully chosen words.

After an hour at the sheriff's office, Marissa was trying to make sense of all she'd learned.

"I can't believe my uncle never reported Candi missing," she said, as she and Gregory left the building. "Do you think he actually knows for sure she's in Germany? Or maybe he really thinks she's dead."

"Could be either," Gregory said. "I'm glad you filed the report and I think Candi's Dear John note you gave the police will give you more credibility with them."

On the drive back to the Cove, Marissa thought of the possibilities. On the one hand, Candi could be living the high life with a man in Germany. On the other hand, she could be six feet under. If the first case were true, she could understand why Candi might not have shared her secret with her. She probably wouldn't want to tell her she was cheating on her uncle. The fact that Candi's disappearance was unannounced was beginning to make sense.

Gregory drove into Walter's circular driveway and parked. Marissa walked with him up the front steps to the sound of a ringing telephone. When she opened the door, Walter called to her, "It's for you."

"Go ahead in," Gregory said. "I want to get the dust off my shoes."

An all-day task for Gregory, she thought. She did a quick shuffle across the doormat, leaving him outside.

Walter closed the door. "It's Nick Devereaux," he said. His look was of disapproval.

Marissa ignored his scowl and hurried to the phone. "Hi, Nick. It's good to hear from you." She took the phone into the pantry and closed the door.

"I'm calling to see if you'd like to join me for wine at the Do Drop Inn tonight. That jazz group I told you about is playing."

"I'd love to." She peeked out the pantry door at Gregory, who stood in the foyer with his shoes in his hand. "But could we make it another time?" She took the phone into the hallway.

"Tonight's the only night they'll be playing."

Gregory strode past her and sat down at the kitchen table with Walter, who was sipping a cup of coffee.

"I'll have to call you back on that," Marissa said loudly enough for Gregory to hear. She hung up the phone and joined the men at the table.

"Was that a client you need to see in San Francisco?" Gregory asked.

Walter's eyes met Marissa's, as if he were challenging her to tell the truth.

"Uh, no . . ."

"I think I'd better call in," Gregory said. "I'm supposed to complete a failure analysis before the New Year. I'll call from upstairs."

Marissa stifled a smirk and helped herself to the last of the coffee in the pot. She and Walter sat in silence. She was sure he was about to ask her about Nick when Gregory came back.

"I'm afraid I have to head back to the city. Will you be coming with me?" he asked Marissa.

"Sure she will," Walter said. "No need to babysit me anymore."

"If it's all right with you, Uncle Walter, I'd like to stay a while."

Strange, she thought, that Uncle Walter's hands quivered as he carried his empty cup to the sink.

"I have some things I'd like to do in town before leaving," she said.

Gregory winked at her, as if to say he knew she'd be sleuthing after Candi. Marissa hoped Walter wouldn't press her.

"You'll be back to San Francisco in time for the New Year's Eve party," Gregory said more as a statement than a question.

"I'll talk to you before then," Marissa said. "Uncle Walter, are you all right? You look a little pale."

Marissa sat on the bed while Gregory folded his soiled clothes and meticulously placed them in his suitcase. She had all she could do to keep from wadding them into a ball and shoving them in.

He took his dark suit from the closet and was about to slide a garment bag over it when Marissa noticed something sticking out of the jacket pocket.

"Did you know you have something in your pocket?"

With a curious scowl, he pulled out a folded piece of paper. "I don't remember putting anything into my jacket." He unfolded the paper and his scowl deepened as he read.

"Don't keep me in suspense. What does it say?"

"I don't understand." He read it to her:

Gregory:
Curiosity killed the cat and it will kill you too. Get out
of Spindrift Cove or you'll find out I'm serious.

"What? You're pulling my leg. Who wrote it?"

"It's not signed."

"Let me see."

Gregory passed the note to her and she immediately recognized the ink-filled e's. "This was written on Tizzie's typewriter."

"Tizzie? I hardly know the woman. Why would she want me to leave town? And how did she get this into my jacket?"

"When's the last time you wore it? Candi's memorial service, wasn't it?"

"Yes, but I was sitting with you the whole time."

"Could she have slipped it to you when you were with me in the receiving line?"

"I suppose so."

"I can't believe Tizzie would have written such a threat. She has no reason to. And her spelling's so bad, I doubt she'd spell 'curiosity' right. Anyone at the service could have slipped it to you as they went through the line. There were a few people who stopped by our seats to give condolences. Or it could have been anyone who came over here afterwards."

Gregory slid the garment bag over the jacket and sat down next to her. "Seeing as I'm leaving town, I think we can forget about it. Whoever wants me gone will get his wish."

"I suppose so," Marissa said, too curious to dismiss it so easily.

"This has been a frustrating couple of days," Gregory said.

"I know," she said, feeling he couldn't be as frustrated as she. "Aunt Candi's disappearance has me going in circles."

"That's not what I meant." He brushed her cheek and fingered her hair. "We've been together for two days and you haven't let me touch you."

He was right. There were times when she wished she were alone. Why was she cooling toward him? He was a promise of a bright future for her.

She gave him a peck on the cheek. "You know how Uncle Walter feels about us sleeping together in his house."

"Walter is downstairs and we're here." He gently pushed her backward on the bed.

His warm breath on her neck made her remember how she missed being close to him. "At least shut the door."

He closed it with his foot. "Now, where were we?" he said, unbuttoning her blouse.

A gentle knock came at the door. "Marissa, are you in there? I need to talk to you." Marissa thought quickly. Before she could reply, Walter poked his head into the room. "I think you'd better go back to San Francisco with—" His eyes grew wide at the sight of her open blouse. He slammed the door and his loud footsteps echoed down the hall.

Marissa sprang from the bed to follow him but Gregory pulled her back. "God, Marissa, you're a grown woman. You can't let him make you feel guilty. He burst into this room with no warning."

"He knocked," she said. She fumbled with the buttons on her blouse. "I can't alienate him now. He's been like a father to me. And he's my only source of information about Candi." She stopped, thinking of how much he'd changed. How he'd completely closed down. "I'm so sick of our tiptoeing around, nobody saying what's on our minds."

"What are you going to do? Accuse him of murder?"

She sat back down on the bed, fighting a mixture of emotions. "I don't know."

"He really has you upset," he said, caressing her hair.

Gregory didn't understand at all.

"See what you can find out tonight" he said, "while you're in town. Maybe stop at the Perk and Turf. If you learn anything new, maybe you can talk it out with him. And try to call that Gunther guy again."

There's so much more to it than that, she thought. "You're probably right," she said.

What she wanted was to escape from her worries, at least for a short while. She was certain her plans for the night would not include digging up clues about Candi.

Marissa kissed Gregory goodbye at his car and confirmed their plans for New Year's Eve in San Francisco. Her kiss was perfunctory and when he seemed all right with that, she thought again how the relationship was cooling. Did she really want a rock-solid one—one in which everything was carefully measured? She missed the excitement of the uncharted, the unexplored.

Back at the house, she found Walter sitting in an armchair by the window. Tension filled the room and she thought she'd suffocate if she had to continue playing his charade.

"We need to talk," she said.

"I took one this morning," he said. "You go on by yourself."

She approached him and firmly placed her hand on his shoulder. When he looked up with surprise, she sat on the arm of his chair. "Gregory and I went to the coroner's to find out who the body is and to the sheriff's office to file a missing persons report for Candi."

"I know. They called here. You could have given me some warning. Why did you file a report when I told you she was dead?"

"The body I dragged from the ocean is still in the morgue and it's a man. The coroner never heard of Candi and no one from her family showed up at the memorial service." Hiding her nervousness, she crossed her arms. "Also, you couldn't have identified Candi's body because they don't allow people to view bodies at the morgue. Now I want to know the truth about Candi."

Walter folded his hands. He opened his mouth and then closed it. Finally he said, "Candi's not here."

"I know she's not here. Where is she?"

"She was killed in Germany. I received the death notice in the mail." His eyes avoided hers.

"You told me she'd been shot in Spindrift Cove. Now, which is the truth?" She took a breath and knelt beside his chair. "You have to level with me. Both of us could be accused of murder."

His back straightened and a tic twitched over his eye. "I'm telling you the truth. She's dead."

"Then tell me who killed her and who sent the death notice?"

"I told you before, I don't know. Probably her German boyfriend killed her. He's the one who sent me the notice."

"That's ridiculous. What man would kill a woman and then announce it by sending her husband her death notice? Let me see it and I'll believe it."

Walter scratched his head, sighed and rose from the chair. "Wait here." He climbed the stairs to the second floor.

Marissa knew he was lying. If she could only break through the hard shell he'd built around himself.

She heard a door open upstairs followed by the sound of drawers being opened and shut. His footsteps resounded as he scurried on the hardwood floors. Maybe she should offer to help. No, she'd already backed him into a corner. She'd let him find his own way out.

Finally he came down the stairs empty handed. "I don't know what I did with it. I must have thrown it out."

Marissa's temples burned and she laughed out loud. "What a fairy tale!" She stood at the foot of the stairs and waited for a better explanation.

Walter blew his nose and jammed his handkerchief into his pocket. "As long as we're clearing the air, you better figure out what you're doing with them two men courting you. You're sleeping with the one who can provide you a future, but you're going out with the long-hair when the other one's not looking."

Marissa clenched her fists to control her temper. This was none of his damn business.

He approached her and wagged his finger in her face. "I could tell from the minute you got the phone call, you were planning on spending time with that long-hair. I can't put up with this kind of behavior. What am I going to tell that Gregory fellow if he calls? You better pack your bags and go home."

Whoa, pretty rash edict for Uncle Walter, she thought. What's gotten into him? Someone wants Gregory out of town and now Walter wants her to go, too.

She was about to reason with him but her anger got the best of her. "I know you filled Candi's urn with ashes!"

She grabbed her jacket from the coat tree and stormed into the cold, slamming the door behind her.

17

ADDITIONAL CLUE

Marissa walked for a couple of hours, calming her temper. She finally stopped at the beach.

She'd really blown it with her uncle.

Even the ocean breeze failed to cool her. The sun was sinking beneath the horizon when she trudged up the bluff, past the Perk and Turf. Gregory would know how to calm her. She stopped at the phone booth outside the Pajama Factory and gave him a call. Waiting for an answer, she watched someone in a battered Ford trying to park between the only two cars on Main Street.

"Nut," she muttered, watching the driver back up until he nudged the car behind him. Then he straightened the wheel and drove forward until he rammed the bumper of the Honda Civic in front. "Klutz," Marissa mumbled. "Is it so important to be smack dab in front of the Perk and Turf?"

The door of the truck swung open and she was surprised to see the man was actually Tizzie in a pair of jeans and a baseball cap with the visor to the rear. Tizzie waved to her and proceeded to unload a vintage typewriter and stacks of paper, which she carried into the restaurant.

Maybe that's the typewriter that was used to write the threat to get out of town, Marissa thought.

She waved back and her attention went to the sound of Gregory's answering machine asking her to leave her number. Rats.

Nick Devereaux grabbed a blue wool sweater from his dresser and tugged it over his head. He looked in the mirror at a day's stubble on his chin.

Not worth shaving, he thought, smoothing his mustache. No women to impress tonight.

He was about to draw the shades but stopped to watch the sun leave a trace of pink on the horizon. It would have made a nice photo. He looked down.

That looks like Marissa in the phone booth in the parking lot, he thought.

His phone let out a shrill ring. "Nick? It's Marissa DeSantos, Walter's niece. Is there any chance you still want to go to the Do Drop Inn?"

DeSantos. That's her last name.

He carried the phone to the window and watched her curling the telephone cord around her finger. Maybe she was as nervous about him as he was about her.

"You bet," he said. "I can pick you up in half an hour."

"How about if I stop by the photo shop instead?"

Nick placed the receiver on the bed, raced out the door, down the steps and around the corner to the phone booth. When he knocked on the glass, Marissa looked up with surprise. "You've been watching me from upstairs!"

Marissa sat beside Nick in his old Chevy on their way to the Do Drop Inn, a few miles up the coast from Spindrift Cove. He pulled into the lot and she was surprised to see an attractive natural wood restaurant and inn surrounded by flowering bushes—a step up in class from what she'd imagined.

Nick parked and they climbed the wide wooden plank steps to the reception area, where mellifluous canned strains of "I'll Be Seeing You" provided a romantic ambiance. A woman, who called Nick by name, told them to take any seats, so Nick led Marissa to a booth midway to the stage.

Marissa slipped into the cushioned booth and surveyed the room, half-filled with a dozen casually dressed patrons. The dark beamed ceiling hung low and dim lights from wall sconces and candles on tables provided a cozy atmosphere. Green Christmas wreaths hung on the corners of a stage only large enough for the guitarist, bass player and flautist who were setting up.

Marissa put her cares behind her and, for the first time since Walter told her of Candi's disappearance, allowed the spirit of the holidays to engulf her. She felt attractive, even in the blouse and jeans she'd worn all day.

"You look especially nice tonight," Nick said, slipping in beside her.

Beside her, she thought. So they'd both have a good view of the stage? She liked being close to him. A warm feeling stirred a tinge of guilt about Gregory.

"I guess I should tell you up front, I have a boyfriend in San Francisco."

Nick looked less than surprised.

"Would you consider platonic?" she asked.

"He's the one who would have been happy to shoot me in the heart at your aunt's memorial service?"

She was intrigued he'd noticed. "Gregory tends to be jealous, but he's a good boyfriend."

She'd done her duty, she thought. Now she could relax and enjoy the evening.

"Did he give you the antique ring you're wearing?"

She displayed her fingers. "This was my grandmother's."

A hint of a smile crossed his face and she relished the feeling he might be pleased with her answer.

She leaned back, engrossed in the live music that replaced the recorded tunes. The musicians played "Stompin' at the Savoy" and when the piece ended, she clapped vigorously.

"We have a celebrity among us," the guitarist announced through the mike. "Nick Devereaux, come on up and join us for the next set."

The crowd clapped with enthusiasm and several cheered.

A celebrity? Marissa was impressed.

Nick lowered his eyes. "I swear I didn't know this was going to happen."

"Go ahead. I'd like to hear you perform." She watched the musicians chat while Nick slung on a guitar from a chair in the back of the stage. The leader struck a chord and the others followed, jamming to "The Lady Is a Tramp."

Marissa tapped her foot to the music as Nick's fingers flew over the frets, proving he was no amateur. And when his deep, mellow voice filled the room, the crowd grew noticeably still. The piece ended and the customers begged for more.

Nick stepped to the microphone. "We have a famous singer from a San Francisco show in our audience tonight."

Marissa looked around to see if she might recognize the entertainer.

"Marissa DeSantos. Stand up and show us where you are."

Marissa slid down in the booth. How could he make fun of the two bars she'd told him she'd sung in community theater?

Nick held his hand in the direction of their booth and she threw him a disgruntled look and waved, cringing at the perplexed expressions in the crowd.

A man in a cowboy hat called out to Nick, "Play 'Mexicali Rose.'" Instead, the other guitarist announced the group would be taking a break. He and Nick crossed the dance floor and joined Marissa at the table.

"This is Paco," Nick said, giving her no chance to chastise him for embarrassing her. "And this is my friend Marissa," he said to Paco.

"You both play very well," she said. She would have liked to pop him one.

"Our pleasure," Paco said, offering his hand and tossing a lock of long dark hair back from the side of his face. His smile matched the mischief in his eyes and he seemed to exude warmth to those around him. "Would you like to join us in a number after the break?"

She aimed a perturbed look at Nick. "No thanks. Nick was pulling everyone's leg. I'm not really a singer."

"I must have misunderstood," Nick said. He called over a young waiter and ordered everyone drinks. "What have you been up to?" he asked Paco.

The man grinned. "I'm coaching my nephew's peewee football team."

"Hey, great. You always wanted to do something with kids."

"Yeah, and he even likes my music. I might teach him guitar if he shows any interest. Of course I'd have to teach him something different from what the folks here like."

"Looks like mostly an Ocean Bluffs crowd," Nick said, glancing around.

"Mostly," Paco said. "You from Ocean Bluffs," he asked Marissa, "or really from San Francisco?"

"From the city. I'm visiting."

"Marissa is Walter Schmidkin's niece," Nick said. "She's here for Candi's memorial service."

Paco lowered his eyes. "I'm sorry for you and for Walter. He's a fine man. Comes in here with J.J. on the nights we play fifties and sixties tunes. They'd stay all night if we let them keep requesting songs." He asked Nick, "Seen much of Bubba lately? Last I heard he and J.J. were going fishing."

"He's in L.A.," Nick offered. "Said he was surprising his parents for Christmas. I thought he'd be back by now, seeing tomorrow's New Year's Eve. He planned to go to the party at the school."

"Have you met Bubba yet?" Paco asked Marissa.

"I'm afraid not. I've heard a lot about him."

"Big kid," Paco said. "With a heart as big as himself. Isn't anything he wouldn't do for any one of us in Spindrift Cove."

Nick said to Marissa, "He came to the Cove without a job and the people in town made one for him."

"I'm not surprised," Paco said. "You've got to like the guy."

Marissa thought about Candi leaving Bubba in charge of her company. "Is Bubba an accountant?"

"He's planning eventually to go into some kind of business. For now, he works as a 'filler.'" A light twinkled in Paco's eye.

"I'm not sure what that is."

Nick said, "Whenever anyone in the Cove gets sick or needs help, they call Bubba and he fills in. He knows a lot about everybody and their business."

"You mean he's a gossip?"

Nick chuckled. "Not on your life."

Paco said, "The only time I ever heard him slip is when he's had a few drinks. Only harmless stuff. Like the time he told the guys about J.J. running low on embalming fluid and diluting it with vodka. I'm surprised J.J. let Bubba leave for the holidays, what with the service for Candi."

"He was already gone when Candi drowned," Nick said.

Paco's eyes widened. "Man, doesn't he know?"

"I left several messages," Nick said. "He never called back."

"Bummer. He's gonna be pretty upset. He really dug Can—" He looked at Marissa. "I mean, he liked doing odd jobs for her. Said she was always fair." When Marissa didn't respond, he added. "You gotta admit. She was quite a looker."

"You don't have to backpedal," she said. "I know what you mean."

Paco's eyes met hers.

"You seem to know a lot about Bubba," she said. "Are you and J.J. friends, too?"

Paco looked down at the table for a moment and then broke the silence. "I've known J.J. for quite a few years."

He seemed relieved when the flute and bass players climbed back on stage. He quickly excused himself to join them.

A soon as Paco was outside earshot, Marissa asked, "Why did you embarrass me like that? I'm not a singer."

Nick leaned back in the booth with a snicker. "I left L.A. because I got tired of dealing with phonies. Pretenses drive me nuts. I knew when you told me you'd sung in a musical, you were trying to impress me. So I thought I'd let you impress the folks here."

He knew her too well. "Wouldn't you have been surprised if I'd gotten up and belted out 'God Bless America?'"

He laughed and tiny wrinkles formed in the corners of his eyes. She liked a man she could laugh with.

"Paco seemed disturbed when I asked him about J.J. Did I say something wrong?"

The trio struck up a lively rendition of "Take the 'A' Train" and Nick moved closer so he could be heard. "Paco used to help J.J. at the funeral home," he said. "Until he caught J.J. doing something illegal."

She leaned toward him. "I've had my suspicions about him from the day I met him. What happened?"

Nick took a drink of his tonic. "I can't really say more. It's never been proved."

"It's important for me. I think it may help me to understand a lot of strange things that have been going on around here."

Nick tossed several bills on the table and took Marissa's hand. "Let's go somewhere quiet where we can talk."

18

SLEUTHING PARTNERS

Unsure where the quiet place to talk might be, Marissa was surprised when their drive ended back in Spindrift Cove at the entrance to the Pajama Factory. Except for having embarrassed her by introducing her to strangers as a celebrity, Nick had been a gentleman all evening. Now he was bringing her to the place where he'd told her he lived. It was late, the evening had been fun, but what did he have in mind?

He opened the car door for her and she followed him into the center of the *U*-shaped redwood structure where several shops and galleries lined the downstairs walls. Moonlight shone through a giant skylight in the ceiling two stories above. Beams from small track lights illuminated the atrium and the wooden staircases at each end of the U. Their footsteps on the concrete broke the silence.

"This is impressive. How long have you lived here?" Marissa asked.

"Ever since it was converted. It's even nicer during the day. Parts of the skylight are stained glass and the sun shines through."

Her eyes followed a staircase that climbed to a second-floor balcony, which served as a means to enter the apartments above. It formed a continuous catwalk around the edge of the atrium, ending in another staircase at the other end of the *U*, with steps down to the main floor.

"From pajama factory to architectural gem," she said. "How did this place come about?" She looked into the window of a yarn shop nearby and Nick joined her.

"Bubba found it. He'd left me and his other L.A. friends. Said he wanted to chill out and earn enough money to go back to school. This was a real pajama factory back then, but sales were down and the factory finally closed. Bubba knew I was looking for a place for a photo studio. When he told me about it, I flew up, took one look at it and spent my life savings refurbishing it. It needed a lot of work."

"You bought the whole factory?"

He nodded. "Much of the renovation was done by volunteers, except for the design. I hired an architect to do that."

Marissa circled the galleries, peering into the storefronts that displayed hand-painted T-shirts, Indian jewelry, oil paintings and other arts and crafts. She walked back to Nick, who was standing outside the photo shop at the other end. The sign above the door read, *Smile for Me*.

"Was construction your business at the time?"

"Hell, no." He chuckled. "I was VP of manufacturing for an electronics firm. I got tired of the phony business culture, or maybe it was L.A. I've always loved photography so gritted my pearly whites and went for it."

He unlocked the door to the photo shop. "Excuse the paint smell. I spent the last couple of days sprucing the place up."

Flicking on the overhead lights, he said, "Thought you might be more comfortable here than in my apartment . . . seeing as we're being platonic." His wink caught her off guard. Now she was almost sorry she'd told him about Gregory.

Her gaze traveled the stark white walls filled with framed color portraits.

Nick picked up a letter that had been slipped under the door and flung it into a basket of mail on a counter. Then he stopped and retrieved it from the basket.

"Something of interest?" Marissa asked, following him inside.

Nick studied the envelope. He tore it open and read silently, the light vanishing from his eyes.

"Problems?"

"Nothing that can't be handled tomorrow." He tossed the note back into the mail basket.

The look on his face belied his words. Curbing her curiosity, she made a silent note to approach the subject later.

"Help yourself to some snacks. There are a couple of bags on the counter."

She checked his selection and held up one. "These look interesting. What are they?"

He glanced at the bag. "Rice crackers wrapped in seaweed."

"Uh, I think I'll try the potato chips."

"No adventure in your soul?"

She struggled to open the bag with no success and found him smiling at her attempts.

"May I?" he asked. One rip and he had it open.

Refusing to show she was impressed, she took the bag, removed a chip and munched on it while engrossing herself in the photos on the wall. She was intrigued by the quality of the portraits of animals and some townspeople she recognized. Even Tizzie looked like a movie star, decked in her finest calico dress. Photos of deer, wolves, and blue jays, which must have taken hours of patience, adorned the walls between the doors marked *STUDIO* and *DARKROOM.*

"You have quite an eye," she said.

Nick offered her a low stool and sat down on a matching one. "I know," he said, looking directly at Marissa.

He had a way of unnerving her with the slightest tilt of his head. She put down the chips, ignored the stool, and pretended interest in a camera set on a tripod. She walked behind it and looked through the lens. "What's this button for?"

He stood and approached her. "It's used to—" Suddenly the room filled with a series of rapid bright flashes.

"Take your finger off the button!"

"What did I do?"

Moving behind her, he said, "You squeezed the button for the motor drive. You just shot ten images of my Adam's apple."

"You're kidding. Why would anyone want to do that?"

"I can't imagine. But I might press the button to take images of something more appropriate, like a wolf running through the woods. The motor drive lets you take several shots in rapid succession."

"Sure, but you could blind someone with all that light."

"You practically did. I say you owe me a favor."

She sat down on the stool he'd offered her earlier and swiveled to face him. "Such as?"

He munched on a chip and then said, "An answer to another question. Have you ever been married?"

"Yes, twice. Once to my high school sweetheart. We were too young. My second marriage ended five years ago. No kids. How about you?"

"I was married once, for seven years, to a wonderful woman. Then she discovered she prefers women to men."

"You had no idea before?"

He answered quickly. "None. After the divorce, I dove into my music. That's how I met Bubba. We were in a band together in L.A."

"Any children?"

"Unfortunately, none. I'd always wanted a kid I could teach how to play guitar. Or maybe how to handle a camera." A bit of the twinkle left his eyes and he changed the subject. "I have a couple more questions."

She prepared herself for some about her last marriage.

"What got you so angry at Candi's memorial service and what's the story about the body you supposedly pulled from the ocean?"

The shock at his knowledge must have registered on her face because Nick followed with an apology.

"It's okay," Marissa said. "I need to talk about this." She stood and crossed to the window.

If she cooperated, she thought, maybe he'd share more information about himself and J.J.

Although she'd planned a short version, she was soon a pot bubbling with information, relating all that had happened since her arrival at the Cove on Christmas Eve, including J.J. and Daphne's kiss.

Nick sat forward throughout her story, his eyes eager.

"So I don't know what happened to my aunt and I don't know who the corpse is. To top it off, some guy was asking about me at the coroner's office and my uncle wants me out of town so badly that, this afternoon, he pretty much kicked me out." She stopped. "Guess I over-answered your questions."

"I'm glad. And don't worry about the guy asking about you at the coroner's office. It was me."

"You?" she said with a start.

"You looked so apprehensive at the service. You didn't finish the eulogy. Your eyes were angry when you said, 'Aunt Candi didn't dr—'" You didn't finished the word. I was curious. That's why I called the coroner."

She walked back to him and sat down. "Why go to the coroner? As far as you knew, the body had already been cremated."

"I knew the records would still be intact."

"And what did you find out?"

"Not a damned thing. But now some of the pieces are falling into place." He took the note from the mail basket and handed it to her. It was clean except for four ink-filled *e*'s. It said,

> *Nick:*
> *Curiosity killed the cat and it will kill you too. Stop your snooping or your beneficiaries will find out I'm right.*

There was no signature.

"Oh, no. Gregory got one like this, too. Someone slipped it into his pocket when he wasn't looking."

"Are you serious? Who would want him and me out of town? And look at these *e*'s. This was written on an old typewriter. I don't know anyone besides Tizzie who still uses a typewriter."

"I know. Gregory's the only one I know who kept an old one like that. Still, I can't imagine Tizzie writing threats. She'd have no reason to. And she certainly wouldn't spell 'beneficiaries' correctly."

"I agree. Whoever wrote the notes is afraid we're going to find out something we shouldn't. I need to call the coroner again. It sounds like the writer thinks I know who that corpse is."

"Maybe you should steer clear for a while. My guess is someone's been watching you."

He slipped his feet from the rungs of the stool. "Maybe so, but if the corpse is someone I know, I'm not doing the family any good by staying away. And I'm sure you're curious."

"You bet I am. I also want to find out how my aunt fits into this." She stood. "I tracked down the phone number of this Gunther guy she's supposedly run off with. I'd planned to call him tonight." She looked at the wall clock. "After midnight. It's morning in Germany." She drew the number from her purse. "May I use your phone?"

Nick nodded toward the one on the counter and she made a call to Munich.

After several rings, an older-sounding woman answered in German.

"*Sprechen sie English?*" Marissa asked.

"*Nein, nein.* Not so much."

"My name is Marissa DeSantos. May I please speak to Gunther Friedlich?"

"*Nein, nein.* Dr. Friedlich is not here."

"Doctor?"

Nick cocked his head and pointed to the button for the speakerphone. Marissa pressed it.

"Is Candi there?" she asked the woman.

"*Nein,*" her reply came over the speaker. "*Fraulein* Candi never comes. Two men before ask same question. More than one week now we wait."

"Do you know the names of the two men who called?"

"*Ja.* Husband Walter calls many times. Makes me crazy. Other man I know not."

"Let me give you my number," Marissa said. She looked to Nick and he indicated the number on the phone. She recited it to the woman. "Please call me if you or Dr. Friedlich receive any information about Candi."

"*Nein, Nein.* Too many things here I must do. How I can do my work?"

"I'm sure you're busy, but it's important I find Candi."

"I cannot help. You maybe call friends of *Fraulein.* Now I must go. *Auf Wiedersehn.*"

At the disconnect, Marissa looked up and caught Nick staring at her with a warm smile. She hoped the blush she felt didn't show.

"Tough luck," he said, offering her a chip.

She shook her head in refusal. "At least I have a contact in Munich. I wonder what kind of a doctor this Gunther guy is. Maybe Candi's sick."

"I doubt it. There are plenty of doctors right here in California. If he met Candi at an importers' conference, he probably has a doctorate in foreign commerce or some such thing. Did the woman answer your call with a company name?"

"She answered in German. I couldn't understand what she said. She could have answered with a company name. She might be a receptionist or coworker." She thumbed through her address book. "I'd like to call my police contact in Ocean Bluffs. He said I could call him at any time."

"Knock yourself out."

She punched the first three numbers for Hendrick and stopped. "Who do you think might be calling Germany for Candi besides my uncle?" Nick shrugged. "Maybe it was a business call."

She punched Hendrick's number into the phone and he answered immediately.

"I tried to get you earlier and you were out," he said. "Seems Candi only made it to the Munich airport. Then she booked a flight to Hong Kong."

"Hong Kong?"

Nick looked up.

A wave of relief washed over Marissa. Candi was alive. "How long has she been there?" she asked.

"At least a couple of days. We just got the report. Does your aunt know anyone there? Walter couldn't provide any information."

"My uncle's been told she's in Hong Kong?" His talk with the police must have been an interesting one, she thought. "I have no idea if she has contacts there. Is that where she is now?"

"Can't say for sure."

"Did my uncle mention anything about a death certificate?"

"He wouldn't believe she was alive. Said he had written confirmation of her death. Said he couldn't find it. Did he ever show it to you?"

"When I asked him, he told me the same thing."

"See if you can help him find it. Then call me. It would save me and Missing Persons some time."

Marissa ended the call. Uncle Walter would never let her search his room. Her intuition told her a search would provide nothing.

"Candi's in Hong Kong?" Nick asked.

"Looks like it. She flew in a couple of days ago. How do you track someone down in a place like Hong Kong?"

"This doesn't sound good."

"I've heard stories about women being abducted there."

"I think you're reaching too far."

She sat down again and twisted the stool to face him. "This is so frustrating."

"I can imagine it is. What can I do to help?"

"You're doing it. It's good to talk to you about it." She changed the subject. "But that's not why we're here. Tell me about J.J."

"Okay, as I said before, I have no proof except Paco's word. He says he'd been helping J.J. out when he caught him slipping the jewelry off the corpses' fingers before he buried them."

"Unbelievable. Sounds like he'll stop at nothing to make some cash. Could Paco prove it?"

"Not a chance. None of the grieving families wanted the bodies exhumed. So there was no proof. J.J.'s a sweet talker. They preferred to believe him."

"Did J.J. know Paco saw him in the act?"

"Paco caught him red-handed slipping a garnet ring off Arthur Billingsworth's finger. Paco was disgusted. Told J.J. to call someone else when he needed help."

"Do you think my uncle knows about this?"

"Can't see how he wouldn't. The rumors flew all over town. But Walter and J.J. have been friends for years. He'd believe J.J. before he'd believe Paco."

"And J.J. continues to let my uncle think he's innocent?"

Nick nodded. "J.J. isn't the kind and understanding man you see in the funeral home."

An understatement if she ever heard one. "Is there more? For instance, I'm curious as to how he got that limp? Was he in Viet Nam?"

Nick chuckled. "Nothing that courageous. An angry husband took a pot shot at him for fooling around with his wife."

"Why am I not surprised?"

Remembering she still had to find a place to spend the night, she said, "I'd better be going. My uncle was furious when he asked me to leave. He wants me out of there and I haven't even packed."

She headed for the door but Nick stayed seated. "May I ask why he wants you gone?"

Marissa turned back. She thought of Walter catching her in the bedroom with Gregory and of his disapproval of her seeing Nick. "He has a couple of personal bones to pick with me."

"Uh, I wouldn't be too hasty to accept those bones."

"What do you mean?"

"Piecing together what you've told me, I say Walter has made a bargain with J.J. to tell the town Candi drowned. This in exchange for keeping his mouth shut about J.J.'s affair with Daphne."

"Of course! Why didn't I think of that?"

"You're not as bright as I," he said with a wink. "If J.J.'s lie about the corpse isn't good enough to fool the townspeople, he knows Walter will spill his affair with Daphne. J.J., Daphne and Walter know you and your boyfriend are the only other ones who know the truth about the corpse. Your boyfriend's left town. If I were Walter, I'd want you out of town, too. He or J.J. or Daphne or anyone else involved could have written the threats."

"Uncle Walter? I can't believe he would. And how would he gain access to Tizzie's typewriter?"

"How would anyone?"

"Hmm, you're right. But I don't care what my uncle wants. I'm not leaving town until I find out what's going on." She headed for the door again and he caught up with her.

"Whoever wrote this note," he said, "wants me to stay out of your business. Would you be up for doing some sleuthing together?"

"Sure. If you really want to get involved. Aren't you concerned the threat might be serious?"

"Not if it's really from Tizzie," he said switching off the lights. "And if it's from someone else, I've done nothing for them to be upset about."

Nick walked Marrisa out and locked the door behind them. "Where are you staying tonight?"

She stood with him outside the door. "I thought I'd get a room at the Do Drop Inn."

"That's too much trouble. I'm watching Bubba's place here in the Pajama Factory while he's gone. It's too late for him to return tonight. I can stay in his place and you can stay in mine. Bubba thinks the world of your aunt. He'd be glad to help us out."

Marissa's eyes burned with fatigue and the thought of not having to drive out to the inn was a relief. "If you and Bubba don't mind, that would be a lot more convenient."

He led her outside. "Let's go get you packed."

19

FALSE ACCUSATION

The windows in the Victorian were dark when Marissa and Nick drove up the driveway to Walter's place. Marissa worried about what might happen if she showed up and her uncle were awake. But she knew Walter rarely stayed up past ten o'clock and the dark windows confirmed he was probably in bed and most likely asleep.

Nick parked next to Marissa's Miata. "If that's your car in the driveway," he said, "you might want to take a look at what's on the windshield."

Marissa headed for something white tucked under the wiper.

"I'll get it," Nick said, leaving his car. He lifted the wiper and removed an envelope. "It looks like the one I got."

"Let's go inside where there's light."

As she and Nick climbed the steps to the front door, Marissa noticed the holly wreathe on the door was gone. Inside, the house was still. She switched on the lights and noticed the Christmas tree was also gone. The removal of holiday decorations Walter had put up especially for her emphasized her visit was over.

She quietly led Nick to the back of the house. "My uncle's hearing isn't the greatest, but let's go into the kitchen where he's less likely to be awakened. Have a seat," she said, offering him a chair at the kitchen table. She joined him and he handed her the envelope.

She studied her full name, neatly typed—except for the letter *e,* which was filled with ink.

She tore open the envelope and read aloud:

> *Marissa:*
>
> *Curiosity killed the cat and it will kill you too. Go back to San Francisco immediately or you'll find out how right I am.*

She dropped the note on the table. "Who do we tell about these threats? Certainly not the deputy sheriff."

Nick laughed out loud.

"Shhh." She was more concerned Walter would know "that long-hair Nick" was in the house than she was of disturbing her uncle's sleep.

"Wait while I pack. I'll only be a minute."

"I'll be right here." He laid his note beside hers. "Maybe I can make some sense of these."

Marissa climbed the stairs and tiptoed past Walter's closed door. No snoring. He was either deep asleep or awake and trying to hear.

Once in her room, she threw clothes into a suitcase and carried it down the hall, pondering why Candi might have gone alone to Hong Kong. Could it have been for business? If so, why tell Walter she was leaving him?

Then she thought of a new angle. What if her uncle had kicked out Candi like he kicked her out? Could he have found out about

Gunther and sent them both on their way? Maybe Candi and Gunther are both in Hong Kong.

She tiptoed downstairs, trying unsuccessfully not to bump her suitcase on the steps.

"Who's there?" came Walter's voice from upstairs.

Marissa tugged Nick's sleeve and he grabbed her suitcase. "It's me, Uncle Walter. I was just leaving." She led Nick to the back door and closed it softly behind them.

Marissa waited for Nick to flick on the lights and then followed him into his studio apartment. Compact, paneled and neatly arranged, it contained a small desk and a captain's bed covered with a blue bedspread. Over an easy chair draped the tie Nick had worn to the memorial service. A tiny kitchen adjoined the living room/bedroom.

Although she could think of several ways to more efficiently organize the space, she curbed her professional suggestions. Actually, she liked the cozy arrangement.

She studied the walls, where an array of animal and nature photographs hung. Crossing a throw rug with a U.S. Marine Corps insignia, she examined a striking photo of a huge St. Bernard with bright eyes and an expression that said, "Please, take me home."

"Great shot," she said. "Your dog?"

Nick was surveying the contents of the refrigerator. "That's Brutus. I had to have him put down."

"I'm sorry."

Nick chose two Cokes, opened both and poured one into a glass and handed it to her. "It was a long time ago. I still think about that dog."

"I still think of my Mugsy, too."

"Yeah?" He offered her the chair and took a seat on the bed. "How long has he been gone?"

"He ran away when my folks were killed in an accident. I was only a kid."

Nick put down his Coke and sat forward. "You lost both your parents at the same time?"

She nodded and took a sip of her drink. "It was a tough adjustment. My brother Tony was old enough to become my guardian and Uncle Walter footed all the bills. I owe them both a lot."

"Must have been a sad childhood for you."

"It was, in the beginning. Then Tony taught me how to survive in the city. He was too proud to keep taking all the money my uncle offered."

"So how did you get along?"

Marissa stopped. "You don't want to know." Once again, she'd already told him more than she'd planned.

"Come on. That was years ago." His smile urged her on.

"Well . . . Tony accepted money for essentials. For luxuries, like roller skates and candy, he taught me how to pick locks."

"You're kidding. Can you still do it?"

She winked.

Nick chuckled. "You're a woman of surprising talents. Ever get caught?"

"Only once. Uncle Walter vouched for me and the cops let me go. Walter tanned my hide and I never stole anything again."

"You ended up a pretty sharp cookie for having been raised an orphan. What kept you going?"

"My uncle. He'd stop by every few days and we'd talk— even if we didn't have anything to talk about. He was my anchor."

"I can see why his asking you to leave now really hurts."

Marissa was impressed with Nick's concern but she'd bared her soul enough. She walked to the window and touched the shade. It snapped to the top of the window frame, revealing a moon that cast slivers of silver light on the waves lapping the shore.

"What a fantastic view!"

Nick dimmed the lights. "Looks better with the lights low," he said. He joined her at the window. She watched the waves with him for a moment, feeling his closeness behind her. Her mind wandered.

"Sure beats the view of the L.A. freeway," he said.

"Uh, what?" she asked, embarrassed she was thinking of what his arms around her would feel like.

"I said the view was better than the L.A. freeway."

"Oh, yes. Ever regret coming here?"

"Not on your life." He turned up the lights and hoisted her suitcase onto the bed. "I'll let you get situated. There's some clean towels in the bathroom. I'll give you a buzz tomorrow morning." He scribbled a note at the desk and handed it to her. "Here's Bubba's number if you get the urge to call me between now and tomorrow morning." He pressed it into her hand.

His fingers were warm and firm and lingered a second longer than necessary.

"Thanks, Nick. You've been a great help."

His eyes met hers. "It's my pleasure. And about never being sorry for leaving L.A? I'm even more sure of it now." He winked at her and left, closing the door behind him.

Marissa stared at the door until the sound of his footsteps were gone. Something about him made him different.

Marissa opened the window and let the sound of the crashing waves fill the room. Tired as she was, she studied the titles of the books on the shelves: *War and Peace, Call of the Wild,* two recent issues of *National Geographic,* notebooks filled with classical and jazz sheet music, three books on just-in-time manufacturing and several books of photo essays and techniques of photography. A framed poster on the wall, signed with more than fifty signatures, showed a cartoon fat man with a gold crown and the words, "To the best V.P. in the world."

She was slipping into her nightgown and was about to check out the contents of his medicine cabinet—doesn't everybody?— when the phone rang.

Maybe Nick had a girlfriend . . . or it could be Nick calling from Bubba's place. She grabbed the receiver.

"Hello?"

No one replied.

"Hello?"

"Marissa?"

"Gregory?"

"I knew it," Gregory said. "I've been trying to find you all night. Walter told me you left in a huff. I called your apartment. I called the Do Drop Inn. I was worried something happened to you. Then on a hunch I called you at Nick's. I knew in my gut you'd be there."

"Gregory, I can explain."

"No need to explain at this hour. I can pretty much figure out what's going on."

Marissa glanced at the travel alarm on the nightstand. "What's so important that you'd be tracking me down at four o'clock in the morning?"

"Good question. Originally I wanted to talk to you about the note someone put into my pocket. But it's taken me so long to track you down, I thought you might have been in an accident."

"I'm sorry," she said. Without thinking, she added, "We got some notes like yours." The word "we" slipped out before she realized what she'd said.

"We?"

She took a breath. "Nick and I each received similar messages tonight."

"That's really great. A *menage a trois*."

"We're not a threesome. Nick doesn't even—"

"Who would do this? Who in Spindrift Cove, beside you and your uncle, even knows my name? Does Nick know my name?"

"Nick didn't do it. News travels fast around here. It would be easy for anyone to find out your name. I'm in bed and I'm exhausted. Let's sleep on this and talk about it in the morning."

"Ha! Sure! I know what you'll be sleeping on. I hope it's soft as butter."

"Gregory—"

"Forget about New Year's. I'll find someone else to take to the party."

She winced when he slammed the phone in her ear.

20

DAMNING EVIDENCE

Marissa tossed most of the night, thinking about Gregory. For two years, she thought she was in love with him. She'd banked her future on him. And Walter considered him a perfect match, as did everyone else. But how did she really feel about him?

She reviewed the previous evening with Nick. Nothing romantic had really happened, yet she was looking more forward to seeing him than in patching things up with Gregory. How could she throw away a two-year relationship in exchange for a man she hardly knew?

It seemed she'd hardly dozed off when she woke to a bright shaft of light bursting through the window. She slipped out of bed and padded to the bathroom. She'd planned to call Gregory first thing and then decided to wait. She still wasn't sure what she was feeling.

She was about to jump into the shower when she heard Nick at the door. "Open up. I have something to show you."

A look in the bathroom mirror revealed shocks of hair standing upright. Smudged mascara and puffy eyes from lack of sleep made her look like a raccoon.

"I'm not dressed."

"Dress in the bathroom. This can't wait."

"Could you please come back later?"

"No way." His words rang with urgency. "Tell me you're decent."

Marissa grabbed her robe and opened the door. Without looking at him, she said, "At least give me a chance to shower." She hurried to the bathroom and shut the door.

Disrobing, she saw the *Spindrift Sun* slowly appear under the door.

"Read this first," he said.

The bold headline caught her eye: *Typerider stolen!*

She gasped. "What's this?"

"Read the article. Apparently someone sneaked into Tizzie's apartment while she was at work yesterday. Whoever it was brought back the typewriter. Will you come out so we can talk about this?"

Marissa splashed cold water on her face, flattened her hair and threw her robe back on. "Who could have stolen it?" she asked, emerging from the room.

Compared to her, Nick looked like a model in a magazine. His eyes showed no sign of a short night. He offered her the only easy chair, crossed the room and studied her. She looked away.

"Have you been crying?" he asked.

"No. I didn't get much sleep last night."

"Was it because of the threats?"

"Yes. I mean, no. My boyfriend Gregory couldn't reach me at my uncle's place last night so he took a chance I might be here. When I answered the phone, he thought the worst."

Nick stepped towards her. "What happened?"

"He's such a pig-headed . . ."

"Ass?"

"No, that's too strong. He wouldn't even let me explain. I could just . . . just . . ."

"Have you tried calling him this morning?"

"I was going to. I don't know what I'd say."

"You could try telling him the whole story." He offered her the phone but she stood her ground.

"He broke our date for New Year's Eve."

"Is that all you're angry about?"

"Yes . . . No. It's all over. He's taking someone else."

Nick pushed the phone toward her again. "If you really care about him, you'd better tell him that you slept alone last night."

She considered his words and then took the phone. Why was she doing this? And why was Nick so eager to save her relationship with Gregory? She pressed the numbers and relief flooded through her when his answering machine kicked in.

"You know what?" she said, hanging up. "I didn't really want to go to that party. He . . . he wears a pedometer."

Nick raised a questioning brow.

"Yes, he measures how far he walks. Can you believe that?"

"That's a pretty serious accusation." Nick ventured a grin.

His comment made her smile, which became a chuckle and he joined in the ensuing laughter.

"You have some important thinking to do," he said. "Call him now or call him later. I can't promise I can fix your problem, but it's a beautiful day and I can get your mind off Gregory for a while."

She headed toward the bathroom.

"Good. Go take your shower. Then, if you need to brood, you can use my left shoulder to cry on."

"And your right shoulder?"

"No way. That's the one I use to push the old Chevy."

She entered the bathroom and was about to undress. Instead, she poked her head out the door. "What about Tizzie's typewriter? Who could have stolen it?"

"Seems to me whoever it was took it just to write those notes."

"The only one I can think of who knows all three of us is my Uncle Walter. He may be acting a bit senile but he wouldn't do something like that. He's angry at me but he loves me and he's crazy about Gregory."

He wasn't so keen on Nick, she thought, but she kept that fact to herself.

"How 'bout getting dressed?" Nick said. "We have some sleuthing to do."

After a quick shower, Marissa threw on jeans and a T-shirt and applied a touch of makeup. She emerged from the bathroom to find Nick paying bills at the desk.

"You look very pretty," he said, rising and pushing the bills aside.

Gregory never told her that.

"My car keys are at Bubba's," he said, "I'll grab them and we'll be on our way."

She followed him along the atrium balcony, their footsteps sounding like army boots on the wooden planks.

Once inside Bubba's apartment, Marissa found the layout similar to Nick's place except for the three-foot photo of Pamela Anderson over the desk and two stacks of *Playboy* magazines on the floor. A red-and-green striped bedspread, bright yellow carpets and a blue easy chair made the room a three-ring circus. On the nightstand sat a stack of well-worn sheet music under a stuffed trout that hung on the wall.

Nick grabbed his keys from the top of the music stack. "We're off, m'lady."

Marissa did an about-face and as they left the apartment, Bubba's phone rang.

"Let it ring," Nick said.

On the second ring, Nick turned back. "I'd better get that. Someone in town might need help. I'm still standing in for Bubba as handyman."

Marissa followed him back into the room as Bubba's answering machine kicked in and a woman's voice came over the line.

"Bubba, it's Mom. I'm becoming concerned. Why haven't you answered my last three calls? Did you decide to go away for Christmas? You didn't miss church, did you? Dad and I are worried. Please—"

Nick vaulted the bed and grabbed the phone. "Mrs. Maselli? This is Nick. I'm taking care of Bubba's apartment while he's gone. Wasn't he at your place for Christmas?"

The answering machine broadcast her reply. "Nick? Why no. He never said he'd be visiting. Last I spoke with him, he said he was going on a fishing trip with J.J."

Marissa backed out of the room to give Nick privacy. He waved her in and motioned her toward the armchair.

"When was that?" he asked Bubba's mother.

"Let me see. It was December twenty-second. I was disappointed because he said he was playing in the band during the holidays and couldn't make it down for Christmas. We got no call on Christmas Day and he hasn't answered any of the messages I've left on his answering machine. I pray to God he's all right."

Nick sat down on the bed. Concerned, Marissa sat beside him.

"Last I heard, he was going to surprise you at your place," Nick said. "I tried to call him there but all I got was your machine."

"We spent Christmas at the cottage like we usually do. We thought Bubba might surprise us there." The woman's voice cracked. "Do you have any idea where he is?"

"Don't worry, Mrs. Maselli. I'll find him. Did you call J.J?"

"Yes, and my husband called him two or three times. We've left several messages on his machine. I pray the Lord is watching over Bubba."

Nick rubbed his forehead. "Give me your number. I'll see what I can find out. I'll call you back as soon as I have something."

"Oh, thank you, Nick." She gave him the number. "The good Lord will reward you. My husband and I will be right here waiting for your call."

Nick hung up and ran his hands through his hair.

Marissa asked, "What do you think happened to Bubba?"

Nick stared into space. "I don't know, unless he went fishing with J.J. and on his way to his parents' place, he stopped to see the guys he used to hang out with in L.A. But I can't imagine that he would have stayed with them through Christmas. I wonder if he's okay."

"Do you think we should call the police?"

"Not yet. I want to talk with J.J. first."

Nick walked down Main Street and crossed to the funeral home, leaving Marissa at the Pajama Factory. He figured she was probably right to stay behind. If J.J. had been avoiding her, chances are he wouldn't open up to Nick if she were along.

He thought back to the last time he'd seen Bubba. What exactly had he said about his fishing trip?

Soon he was in the lot behind the funeral home, where J.J.'s car and the hearse were parked. Nick looked up at the second-floor apartment and climbed the outdoor stairs.

"J.J.!" He pounded on the door. When no one answered, he rubbed the window with his sleeve and looked in. The door burst open and J.J. stood before him in bare feet, a pair of jeans and no shirt.

"Hey, man. You're gonna wake the dead."

"Pretty funny," Nick said. "I'm looking for Bubba. Have you seen him?"

J.J. massaged the back of his neck. "Not for a few days. I gave him time off to go to L.A. Sure could have used his help at Candi's service."

"Yeah. I bet. Bubba told me you two were going fishing a couple days before Christmas."

"We were planning to. Then Bubba changed his mind." He licked his lips. "Said he was going to L.A. a day early. You might want to call his mother."

"I already talked to her. She says she's been trying to get in touch with you."

"I haven't been around much lately, with Christmas and all."

"She didn't leave you any messages?"

"Not that I know of. Unless she called while I was in the shower. I haven't checked my machine today."

"Where do you think he is?"

J.J. shifted his weight to his good hip. "Is Bubba in some kind of trouble?"

"I sure hope not."

He rested his hand on Nick's shoulder. "Sorry, I can't help."

Nick pulled away. "Thanks." Leaving, he muttered, "For nothing."

Marissa waited for Nick outside the photo studio, mulling over the past events.

Candi was missing, Gregory had dumped her and now Bubba had vanished. How much simpler life would have been if she'd spent the holidays in San Francisco. But solving Candi's disappearance from a distance would have been more difficult. Uncle Walter might have kept it from her for even longer. She walked toward J.J.'s place.

Nick emerged from the driveway of the funeral home, strode down Main Street at a good clip and then broke into a run. His stride was even, like a marathon runner's.

Gregory could never run like that.

Nick slowed as he approached Marissa and caught his breath.

"What did you find out?" Marissa asked.

"J.J. claims he hasn't seen Bubba since before Christmas Eve. Says Bubba blew off the fishing trip. Told him he was going to L.A. a day early."

"Do you believe him?"

"Not on your life. When Bubba makes a commitment, he keeps it. And J.J. pretended Bubba's mom never called him."

He lies about Bubba? she thought. He ignores calls from Bubba's mother? The pieces were falling into place. She chose her words carefully. "Was Bubba doing the same work for J.J. that Paco used to do?"

She could tell from Nick's expression that he knew what she was thinking. "You think Bubba might have seen J.J. lifting more jewelry?"

"I hope not."

"Is Bubba about six foot two? Weigh about two-hundred-fifty pounds?" God, she hoped not.

"Well, yes. I thought you said you never met him."

"Do you know what kind of gun J.J. carries in the holster he wears?"

"As a matter of fact, I do. It's a Smith & Wesson of some kind. He once roped me into driving him to target practice in Ocean Bluffs and convinced me to try shooting it."

"Did he show you how to load the bullets?"

"No, he loaded them from the box."

"Any chance you remember what the box said?"

"Where are you going with this? If my memory serves me, the bullets were .38 caliber."

Marissa closed her eyes, picturing the Unidentified Persons report she'd left at Walter's place. "I think we better go to the police."

21

CAR TROUBLE

Marissa slid into the passenger side of Nick's Chevy and looked back at him standing by a rear wheel.

"Damn," he said. "I must've driven over a nail."

She got out and joined him in an inspection of a totally flat tire. "Let's take my car."

They crossed Main Street and walked up Ferndale Road to Walter's place, where Marissa's Miata sat at the edge of the circular driveway. She was curious about this man who seemed to take setbacks in his stride. "Would you like to drive?" she asked, testing his male ego.

"I'll play passenger," he said, holding the door for her.

He seemed to know just how to keep her interested.

He got in and Marissa turned the key. The car edged forward and a sudden blast jerked her head back, slamming it against the headrest. The entire hood shot off in a burst of flames. She froze.

"Get out of the car!" Nick shouted.

Marissa jumped at his words. My God, she thought, we're going to be killed!

She fumbled at the door handle but couldn't get it to work. The heat from the fire hit her face.

Where is that latch?

Finally finding it, she swung open the door and fell out. Nick grabbed her and pulled her from the car. Huge flames rose from the front, the black smoke stinging her eyes.

"You okay?" Nick asked.

"I think so," she said between gut-wrenching coughs. "Are you?"

He nodded, holding his hand over his mouth and nose.

"Follow me," she said. She stumbled up the steps of the house. "Uncle Walter! Where are you?" She ran through the house, calling her uncle's name.

"Nick, check for fire extinguishers. They may be in the coat closet in the foyer. I'll look in the kitchen."

She flung open the lower cabinet doors and threw aside ant traps and dishwashing powder. A rusted extinguisher leaned against the wall. She grabbed it and prayed it worked.

"Got one!" Nick shouted from the foyer.

Extinguisher in hand, Marissa scurried after him as he ran down the front steps, where several neighbors were already dousing the fire. Several more emerged through the trees. The flames had mushroomed and a huge cloud of black smoke rose from the car.

Dodging two children who were watching from the steps, Marissa shouted, "Stay back!" Her fingers seemed to move in slow motion on the extinguisher's latch. "How do these things work?"

Nick started his extinguisher with a whoosh and Marissa copied with hers. The sound of the contents hit the car with a vehemence that forced her back. She steadied her weapon and moved closer.

"Help the man in the overcoat," Nick shouted. "The one who's fighting the flames in front."

Marissa blinked her burning eyes and joined the man in the overcoat. Nick disappeared in the smoke, shouting commands to others.

Soon the man's extinguisher gave out. "I've got the front covered," she said. She moved to the other side of the car.

"Keep it up," Nick yelled. She could only judge his location through the billowing smoke. Her heart pounding, she quelled the flames until they finally died. Black smoke continued to spiral toward the sky.

Marissa dropped the extinguisher, but the crackle of the fire continued. She felt the growing heat on her back. She turned around.

Huge flames jumped from pile to pile of dry brush her uncle had failed to clear from the lawn.

Good Lord! she thought. They were heading toward two dead pine trees near the Victorian.

She picked up the extinguisher and advanced, but the searing heat and stinging smoke forced her to retreat. A man with a garden hose shouted to her to step back as a dry bush burst into flames at her side.

Blinking furiously, she tried to clear her vision. The flames continued, defying those who dared to douse them. She aimed and pulled the trigger but only a trickle of foam emerged.

"Here!" she heard from behind. She turned to see Margaret Potter running toward her in a pillbox hat and business suit. Margaret thrust an extinguisher at her. "I don't know how these things work."

Marissa grabbed it and in seconds a huge stream of foam smothered the flames nearby. She looked up to see Nick and the man in the overcoat finishing off the last embers that had been approaching the trees.

Once the final spark had been doused, Marissa collapsed on the bottom step of the house, her shoes and jeans sopped and her arms and T-shirt gritty with soot.

She watched the man in the once-beautiful overcoat wipe his hands on his sides and join Nick, who looked like an exhausted chimney sweep. They crossed the lawn to the car and inspected its remains: a burned out front end and a back end intact.

"My poor car!"

"Your *car?*" the man said. "You could have been killed!"

Marissa stepped forward. "What in the world happened?"

"I'd say someone rigged your car," Nick said, wiping his brow with his black sleeve and leaving a dark streak across his forehead.

"It had to be J.J.," Marissa said. "No one else would do such a thing." A lump rose in her throat at the sight of the smoldering heap that had once been her car.

Nick wrapped an arm around her. "I'm so sorry."

She allowed herself a moment of grief. Then with a wipe of her eyes on her sleeve, she thanked the man in the overcoat.

He removed his coat, which looked like it'd been run over, and he folded it over his arm as if it were brand new. "That's what neighbors are for," he said. He headed up the driveway with the departing crowd.

"If there's any way I can help," a young woman said, "please stop by. Nick knows where I live." She turned and followed the others up the driveway.

"Unbelievable," Marissa said, wondering where her uncle might be. "I didn't get a chance to thank everyone."

A smile emerged on Nick's face. "These people are the reason I moved here from L.A." he said, watching the neighbors leave. Then he led her to the front of the car and stooped to inspect what was left of the front tire.

"What do you think?" she asked over his shoulder.

He felt the ground in front of the wheel. "It's strange the blow-up didn't happen as soon as you started the car. The explosion came after we started moving."

Marissa bent to inspect the debris under the wheel. "Could something have been planted in front of the tire?"

"I'm no expert," Nick said, "but that's how it looks."

She stood and stretched her back. "So who do we report this to? The deputy sheriff?"

Nick chuckled. "Not the one in Spindrift Cove."

A blaring siren sounded in the distance and grew louder. "I forgot to call the fire department," Marissa said. "How did they know?"

Margaret Potter emerged from the other side of the car. "I called them." Only a smudge of soot marred her crisp white blouse.

"Margaret, I don't know what I would have done without your extinguisher," Marissa said. "And thanks for calling for help."

"Any time," she said, adjusting her hat and shouting to the crowd to wait for her.

J.J.'s phone rang and woke him from his nap.

"What the hell did you do to my niece's car?" Walter shouted.

J.J. pulled the receiver from his ear.

"And where is she?" Walter asked, his voice cracking.

"Calm down, old man. What are you talking about?"

"You know damn well what I'm talking about. I was at the hardware store when I heard the explosion. When I got home, I found my niece's car blown up and my lawn demolished."

"My God! You think because I asked you to get her out of town that I'd do a thing like that?"

"Well, if you didn't, then who did?"

"Hey, we've been friends a long time. You gotta believe it wasn't me. Maybe Marissa's boyfriend got jealous and wanted to put a scare into her. I've been seeing her in town with Nick lately."

"He wouldn't pull a stunt like that—even if he was mad."

"Then it must have been an accident. Maybe those kids you hired to clean up the brush dropped a lit cigarette on the grass before they left."

"Seems far-fetched but I'd believe that before I'd believe Gregory did it."

"I'll listen around town and see what I can find out."

"Yeah, J.J. You do that." He slammed down the receiver.

Marissa stood sooty in Nick's shower and let the hot water pound on her skin. She lathered up and pondered the future she'd once planned so perfectly. Not only had she lost her car and her boyfriend but she had no way to get home. And who knew how long it would take the insurance company to process her claim during the holidays? Without a car, how would she search for Candi, not to mention keeping her business appointments at the Clutter Clinic?

Deep in thought, she scrubbed her arms almost raw and then let the water pummel her body. Would the insurance money be enough to buy a decent vehicle? She'd put every cent she had into converting her guestroom into an office.

She rinsed off, toweled down and had finished dressing in fresh jeans and a T-shirt when a soft knock came on the door.

"Can I come in?"

She fluffed her damp hair. "It's open."

Nick entered looking shower fresh and smelling of Zest soap. "I called Tizzie," he said.

"I hope you didn't accuse her of anything. We don't have solid proof about those threats."

"No, I asked her if we could borrow her truck. Your car isn't drivable and I don't want to waste time now fixing my flat. Tizzie insisted on bringing her truck over." He took her hand. "You don't have to come with me to the police station, if you'd rather not."

"No, I'd like to come along."

"Any idea about who might have written those threats?" he asked.

"I say it was J.J. We should check your car before we leave. He could have planted a bomb in front of your wheels, too."

"You've got a point," Nick said.

Marissa crossed to the window. Below, on the street, sat Nick's blue Chevy, a car-length in front of a black sedan. She watched a green truck coming south on Main Street. It slowed down by Nick's car.

"That looks like Tizzie."

The truck stopped when it's nose was even with the front of the Chevy. "Oh, God," she said. "Tizzie's going to try to fit into the space behind your car. If there's a bomb in front of your wheels, all she has to do is bump the Chevy and it'll go off!" She tugged the window open.

"Tizzie!" she shouted. "Stop!"

Nick bounded out the door and down the stairs.

Marissa ran out and down the steps in time to see Nick arrive at the front of Tizzie's truck.

"Stop!" Nick shouted, waving at the truck.

Unheeding, Tizzie slowly backed into the spot, bumping the front bumper of the sedan behind her.

"Hit the brakes!" Marissa shouted over the music blaring from the truck's radio.

Tizzie signaled she couldn't hear through the closed window. She edged forward, toward Nick's Chevy.

"She can't hear us," Marissa shouted. "If there's a bomb, it's going to go off."

"Hit the damn brakes!" Nick yelled. He tried the door on the passenger side. It was locked.

Tizzie rolled down the window.

"The brakes!" Marissa yelled.

The car jolted to a stop and Nick dashed to the driver's side and opened the door. "Set the emergency brake. Now!"

Tizzie obeyed. Nick grabbed her arm and tugged her from the car. "You could have set off an explosion."

She stumbled from the driver's seat. "What in tarnation are you talking about? You said on the phone the explosion happened to Marissa's car."

"Yes," Nick said. "And it could happen again. Stay right here."

Marissa inspected the right front wheel of Nick's Chevy. "Here it is!"

"Another bomb?" Tizzie asked.

Nick squatted beside Marissa. "Yup. Don't touch it. I'll call the police." Nick went back into the Pajama Factory.

Marissa led Tizzie onto the sidewalk and explained their suspicion that Nick's car might have been rigged, too.

"My Lord" Tizzie said. "If it weren't for you two, I could've bumped Nick's car and ended up one dead old lady!" She hugged Marissa so hard she gasped for air.

"I'm glad we stopped you in time."

Tizzie released Marissa. "Why did you think Nick's car would be targeted, too?"

"Three of us received threats—Oh, God, Gregory!" She pushed past Tizzie. "Stay here. Don't let anyone touch Nick's car. Not the deputy sheriff. Not anyone!" She sprinted into the Pajama Factory, taking the steps to Nick's apartment two at a time. Barging through the open door, she shouted, "Let me talk to the police."

Nick signaled for her to wait but Marissa yanked the phone from him. "What the—"

"Did you tell them about both bombs and about the threats?" she asked.

"Yes, I did."

Marissa put the phone to her ear. "Is this Hendrick at the Ocean Bluffs station?"

"No, you've got McNulty in the General Works Unit. Who's this?"

"It's Marissa DeSantos. Gregory Townsend also received a threat. So I suspect a bomb in front of his wheels, too."

"Suspect?"

Damn, he didn't believe her.

"No, I'm sure. Gregory doesn't know anything about it. He lives in San Francisco at 1300 Green Street, #342. We need the San Francisco police over there pronto. And are you coming down to look at our cars?"

"We're sending someone out. Give me Gregory's—"

"And this is important. Don't send J.J."

She hung up and punched in Gregory's home phone. She tapped the desk with her free hand. "Come on, Gregory. Answer!"

Gregory's answering machine came on. The message seemed endless. "Come on!"

"Gregory, don't go near your car. It may explode." She hung up and dialed Information. "Give me the number of the Green Street West apartments."

She punched it in.

Another answering machine.

Nick brought her a chair, which she dropped into, feeling the sweat form on her brow as she waited for the recorded message to finish.

"This is Marissa DeSantos, Gregory Townsend's girlfriend. There may be a bomb planted under a wheel of Gregory's car. He has no clue. It's a black Camry, probably parked in the garage beneath his apartment. I can't get in touch with him. Please keep everyone away."

She told Nick, "I'll call his cell." She tried Gregory's number and it rang several times.

"Hello?"

"Gregory?"

"No. This is Derek, Gregory's coworker. He left his cell phone here last night. Who's this?"

"Derek, This is Marissa. Do you know where Gregory is?"

"He called about half an hour ago from a coffee shop. Said he was about to hoof it home to get his car. We have an appointment in Ocean Bluffs."

"Are you going together?"

"Yeah. He's driving. What's this about?"

"What time's he picking you up?"

"He said in forty-three minutes. Is something wrong?"

That sounded like Gregory. She checked her watch. "Listen. Gregory's car may be rigged to blow up. I can't reach him."

"You're shittin' me."

She covered the phone and told Nick, "That McNulty guy didn't believe me. I don't trust him to get the San Francisco police there in time. We've got to get to Gregory before he gets to his car.

Can you move Tizzie's truck out of that space without bumping your Chevy?"

Nick headed for the door. "I'm on my way."

She spoke again to Derek. "This is no joke. We're leaving Spindrift Cove for Gregory's place. Keep calling him at home."

"There's no way I can get in touch with him. I've got his phone." This time he sounded panicky.

"Look. He lives on Green Street. 1300. How long will it take you to get there?"

"Forever," he said. "I'd have to take a bus."

"Get yourself a ride. I'm leaving now." She put down the phone and ran out the door.

Outside, she found Nick explaining to Tizzie. "You'll be the first I'll give the details about the bombs when we get back."

Tizzie drew her brows together, nodding her understanding of his rapid speech. "You better get going. The keys are in the ignition. Sure I can't come with you?"

"Not this time, Tiz, but thanks. Marissa, wait till I pull out."

Marissa marveled at the calm he displayed and his deftness as he maneuvered the truck out of the parking space. When Nick motioned for her to jump in, he shouted out the window to Tizzie. "When the police come, tell them about both bombs. Show them Marissa's car. And tell them about the threats written on your stolen typewriter."

Marissa yelled, "And keep J.J. away!"

She hung on as she and Nick squealed onto Highway 1. "Don't hold back on the gas pedal," she said. "We don't have a minute to spare."

22

UNNERVING TASK

Marissa hung on for her life as Nick raced through yellow lights. She swayed with him as he maneuvered the old truck around winding curves as if he were driving a racecar.

"What's the best way to get to Gregory's place?" he asked.

"Hit 280. It takes him forty-seven minutes, on a good day, to get from here to his door. That's about the same time he'll be getting into his car."

"forty-seven?" Nick snickered.

"He's compulsive about accuracy."

"You don't say."

Nick changed lanes twice to pass a Buick and a Dodge. Marissa kept bracing herself until they finally reached the outskirts of San Francisco. Then the traffic crawled to a stop at a light. Nick beat his fingers on the wheel.

"Go!" Marissa shouted when the light turned green.

Nick took off in a burst of speed and then slammed on the brakes at the bumper of a Cadillac that unexpectedly stopped in front of them.

Marissa held her breath at the screech of tires. Nick swerved to pass on the right.

"Over there," she yelled. "A hole in traffic. You can get through."

"I see a bigger one." Nick squeezed the truck between a bus and a Volkswagon. He stepped on the gas.

When they reached the city, the traffic slowed.

"Ten minutes to go." Her heart beat so fast she thought it would burst.

They crawled down Larkin and Pine Streets. Nick's knuckles were white on the wheel, his eyes intent. When the next light turned red, he brought the truck to a stop. The engine died.

"No, not now!" Marissa looked ahead.

Nick tried the key and the engine sputtered and died again. He pressed the accelerator and tried once more but the engine failed to respond.

"Damn!" He pounded the wheel. "Tizzie asked me yesterday to check her carburetor."

The light changed but they sat motionless. A horn blasted behind them, followed by those of the others caught in the delay.

"I flooded it," Nick said, waving the traffic on. "We'll wait a few seconds."

Marissa chewed a knuckle. Her watch showed two minutes until Gregory would arrive at his garage.

The car behind pulled around them and the light turned red again. Nick tried again and this time the truck started. Marissa could only watch as he kept his foot on the accelerator and the gears in neutral while the speeding cross traffic blocked their path. When the light changed, he shifted into first and they took off.

"Whew! We're getting close. Take a right at the next light." Marissa clung to the dashboard when they squealed around the corner on two wheels. "Right here on Green Street. Don't pass it!"

"You'll have to give me a few feet's notice," he said, almost missing the street.

"There's the apartment house. Oh, God, there's Gregory! He'll never see us from here."

She watched him step out the front door of the apartment building and head toward the sloping driveway into the underground garage.

Nick blasted the horn. Gregory jumped and scowled at the truck.

"He doesn't recognize us," Marissa shouted.

Gregory walked down the driveway and disappeared into the garage.

"Gregory!" Marissa screamed out the window.

The truck squealed into the driveway. Nick leaned on the horn. Gregory sidestepped to avoid them. Marissa jumped out of the slowing vehicle. "Gregory! Don't go near your car!"

He looked at her. "Marissa?"

Nick bolted from the truck. "Which car is yours?"

Gregory glared at them. "Is this some kind of a joke?"

"My car was bombed," Marissa said. "And they tried to blow up Nick's. Where's yours?"

He straightened. "I can check it out myself."

A feeble attempt to save his dignity, she thought.

Nick followed close behind him. "Hey, I'm not here to cause problems. We're trying to save your ass."

Gregory's stride became more determined.

He doesn't know the first thing about cars, Marissa thought.

When Gregory reached his Camry, he handed Nick the keys. "Do what you have to do."

Nick inspected the front and behind all four tires.

Marissa watched the two men: Nick taking action and Gregory standing with his hands in his pockets, like a helpless child. She approached him and he stepped aside, avoiding her eyes.

Nick looked beneath the hood, unlocked the door and checked under the dashboard. Then he checked the trunk.

"Nothing?" Marissa asked.

"Everything's cool," Nick said to Gregory. "Sorry to bother you."

Gregory sneered and extended his hand for the keys.

Marissa felt sorry for him.

Nick dropped the keys into Gregory's hand and Gregory slid into the front seat.

On the drive south to Ocean Bluffs, Marissa rolled down the window to feel the warmth of the sun.

Nick seemed more relaxed, too. "Your boyfriend's sure carrying a grudge," he said.

"Gregory? He's got a right. He still thinks you and I slept together." She regretted the hurt she knew she'd caused him.

"Didn't you explain? Don't you two talk?"

For Gregory, explanations would do no good. She'd answered Nick's phone in the wee hours of the morning. He'd never understand why.

She sighed. "Maybe someday."

They reached Ocean Bluffs and Nick pulled into the closest parking place to the police station. Marissa looked up at the eight-story Hall of Justice and thought, so this is where J.J. reports when he's on official business.

Her thoughts turned to Nick and she imagined the burden he carried—to have to face the fact that the corpse might be his best friend.

"Would you like me to go in with you?"

Nick stared straight ahead. "I think I'll go this one alone." He patted her arm and slid from the seat.

"I'll wait for you here."

The confident smile she had grown accustomed to faded into a frown of intent.

"Nick."

He looked over his shoulder.

"I hope it's not Bubba."

He closed his eyes for a second. "Yeah, me too."

Nick climbed the steps to the tall concrete building that housed the sheriff's office. After passing through the glass doors, he followed instructions on a sign and dropped his keys into a plastic bin. He proceeded through the metal detector and retrieved his belongings on the other side.

Nondescript tan walls, tan marble floors and tanned men in suits verified he'd arrived in the land of California bureaucracy. After checking at the information desk, he headed to the third floor Sheriff's Office, Detective Bureau.

He followed three teenage boys and a stocky woman in a suit into the elevator. The boys teased each other and Nick remembered happier days. He thought of Bubba and fought a wave of nausea that lingered in his gut.

The elevator doors opened on the third floor and he crossed to a set of double glass doors leading him to a petite receptionist with a thick red braid. In the waiting area, an Afro-American man bent forward in his chair, his head cradled in his hands.

This could be him in a few minutes, Nick thought.

Next to the man sat a teenage girl with matted strands of long blond hair and eyes rimmed with heavy mascara. She cracked a huge wad of gum and tossed Nick a grin.

Nick looked away and approached the receptionist. "I need to speak to someone about the John Doe found in Spindrift Cove on December 24th."

Nick rejected her offer of a seat and paced the floor, wanting to get this blasted ordeal over.

The receptionist placed a short call and told him, "Detective Hendrick will be with you shortly."

The possible outcomes reeled in Nick's head.

Maybe the corpse doesn't look anything like Bubba.

Nick looked up when a tall, athletic-looking man strode into the reception area and introduced himself as Detective Hendrick. Thick curly blond hair topped a square face and a solid body a few inches taller than Nick's.

Nick returned his firm handshake. "Are you the officer I reported the car bombs to?" He looked different from the way Nick had pictured him on the phone.

"You would have spoken to someone in our General Works Unit," Hendrick said. "Sounds like you had quite a day."

"You might say that."

"I understand you might know something about a John Doe we're investigating." He eyed Nick quickly but Nick suspected he'd tallied a wealth of information.

"Yes, my friend's missing. I heard about the body found in Spindrift Cove. I'm concerned it might be him."

Hendrick's face softened. "Come with me."

Nick followed him through the doorway, wondering what he'd be thinking when he walked through the same doorway on the way out.

They proceeded through a high-ceilinged room large enough to house a dozen small cubicles with shoulder-high walls. He caught snatches of phone conversations as they traveled the hallways and arrived at a cubicle on the far end of the room. A stocky man sat inside studying a computer monitor, surrounded by stacks of paper that cluttered the bookshelves and the top of his desk. Newspaper clippings covered every inch of the wall behind him. Hendrick introduced the man as his partner, Detective Rudy Sanchez."

The man had a face like a bulldog and when he rose, he had the stance to match. Although short, Sanchez looked as if he could hold up his end of a dogfight with no problem. His eyes did a quick study of Nick when he offered him his hand with a grunt that was meant to be a greeting. Accepting his hand was like grasping a warm shoulder of beef.

Hendrick said, "Nick reported some car bombs a while ago."

"The ones in Spindrift Cove?" Sanchez asked. "McNulty in General Works just told me about them."

Nick nodded. "Do they have any clues?"

"Too early to tell."

Hendrick said, "Nick thinks he might also know who our John Doe is."

Life came to Sanchez's face. "Good news for us. Maybe not so good for you."

"Will I have to view the body?"

"It's not like on TV," Hendrick said. "We don't do that here."

Relief swept over Nick. "How do I ID him?"

"Pictures and descriptions are usually enough. Of course dentals and prints help, too, when we have them."

Nick had no idea who Bubba's dentist was or if he'd ever been fingerprinted. "What did the prints show?" he asked.

Hendrick shook his head. "There were none. They were blow-torched off."

Nick shuddered at the thought.

Hendrick excused himself and moved to the next cubicle. He came back with a folder. "Let's go somewhere more comfortable where we can talk."

Nick followed him and Sanchez to a place that looked much like a living room. The whole damn room, Nick thought, including the couch, two chairs and carpet, were a tranquil blue. Not at all like government supply. But until he found out what happened to Bubba, no room or color would soothe his nerves.

Hendrick motioned him to the couch while he and Sanchez settled into the two chairs.

"Want some coffee?" Hendrick asked.

"No, thanks." No coffee, Nick thought, no small talk. Let's keep this ordeal as short as possible.

"This may be difficult," Hendrick said. "We'll make it as easy as we can."

At least he had a sense of compassion. Nick wasn't so sure about the bulldog.

"What's your friend's name?" Hendrick asked.

"Bubba Maselli."

"Is Bubba his real name?"

"It's the only one I know. That's what everybody calls him."

"Would you spell his last name?"

Nick complied and Hendrick wrote it down.

"Do you happen to have a photo of Bubba?"

"Not with me." He should have searched his apartment. "I may be able to find one."

"Where does he live?"

Nick provided his address.

"When's the last time you saw Bubba?"

"The day before Christmas Eve."

"So you saw him on the twenty-third?"

"Yes."

"What was he wearing?"

Nick thought back. "Hell, I don't have a clue. A baseball cap is all I remember. And probably a T-shirt and jeans."

Was that disappointment on Hendrick's face?

"Do you know if anyone's filed a missing persons report?" he asked Nick.

"I don't think so. I thought I'd do that today."

"We can take care of it after we're through here—if we need to."

God, he hoped they needed to.

Hendrick asked, "Any idea what happened to your friend?"

Nick described Bubba's plans to go fishing with J.J.

"You talking about Deputy Sheriff Haggersby from Spindrift Cove, the town mayor?" Sanchez piped in.

"Uh huh. J.J. says Bubba never showed. Says he left a day early for L.A. Look, officer, I'm really concerned. I heard the body in the cove was shot with a .38 caliber bullet. I know that's what J.J.'s pistol takes."

Sanchez flinched and two lines squeezed between his bushy brows. "How do you know the body was shot with a .38?"

They'll never believe J.J. did it, Nick thought. He's one of their own. This is how they question a suspect. "My friend Marissa DeSantos talked to the coroner. He told her about the bullet."

"Is this the same Marissa who found the body and the one who owns the car that blew up?" Sanchez asked.

Nick nodded and the two men exchanged glances.

"She's had a lot happen to her these past few days."

Sanchez spoke up. "Do you shoot?"

Nick sat up in alarm. "Me? No. I only shoot photographs."

"How do you know what kind of bullets J.J. shoots?"

Nick relaxed. "Oh, that. He took me to target practice with him one day."

Sanchez snickered. "How'd you do?"

"Pretty lousy. I hate guns. They kill the wildlife I shoot with my Nikon."

After what seemed an eternity, Sanchez asked, "How do you know Marissa?"

"I did some work for her uncle. He needed his flue fixed and Bubba, he's the town handyman, was out of town . . . or so I thought. So I helped her Uncle Walter out. Marissa was visiting him when I arrived."

"What's Walter's last name?" Hendrick asked.

"Schmidkin."

Hendrick asked, "This is the same Walter whose wife is missing?"

"Yes."

This all sounds so unbelievable, Nick thought.

He stretched his neck to relieve the tension. All he wanted to know was whether the corpse was Bubba.

As if Hendrick read his mind, he said, "I know these seem like a lot of questions. We need to understand the circumstances here before we proceed."

"I understand."

"Tell me what Bubba was into. What were his habits?"

Shifting his position on the couch, Nick replied, "If you mean, 'did he have any routines?' I'd say no. He did odd jobs around town, filled in whenever anyone was sick. He helped Pastor John at the church and worked for J.J. at the funeral home. He didn't put in regular hours anywhere."

"Is that how Bubba met J.J.? Through employment?"

"I guess. I don't really know. He knew him before I moved to town."

"How long ago was that?"

"When I came to the Cove? About four years ago."

"Any scars or birthmarks?"

"You mean on Bubba? None that I've seen."

Hendrick seemed to digest the information. The bulldog only stared ahead.

"Did Marissa show you the composite sketch of the corpse?" Hendrick asked.

Nick sat up. "I didn't know she had one."

Damn, he thought. Marissa was so sure it was Bubba she didn't want to upset him by showing him the picture.

"Give me a description of Bubba," Hendrick said, sitting back. "Start with his hair, eyes, build, any distinguishing features."

This line of questioning was more like he expected. Nick described Bubba the best he could.

Hendrick handed him a sheet of paper from the folder he brought with him. "Is this the man you're describing?"

Nick hesitated, feeling beads of sweat on his brow. He studied the sullen face in the sketch on a page titled "Unidentified Person Report."

He exhaled. "This isn't him. Bubba has long hair . . . and a beard. I've never seen him any other way."

"How about height, weight, eye color."

Nick read the statistics. "Those are about right, but this can't be Bubba."

"Read the part at the bottom, where it says 'circumstances.'"

Nick read the text. "He was found in a tux? Bubba didn't even own a tux. And he didn't wear a Princeton ring. He went to school in L.A. Hadn't graduated from college. This isn't him."

Sanchez stood. "Let's go back to my cube. I want to show you something."

Relieved the questioning was done, he followed Sanchez to his cubicle. No, the picture didn't look like Bubba, he thought. But the fact that the height, weight and eye color were right gnawed at his gut. And the body had washed ashore the same time Bubba had disappeared.

Sanchez pushed aside a mound of papers and plopped into a chair. His stubby fingers flew across his keyboard until the monitor displayed the sketch of the man whose face was on the Unidentified Person report. "Tell me how Bubba's hair looks."

Nick peered warily over his shoulder. As he described the hair and the beard, Sanchez hit a few keys. Hair and a beard appeared on the drawing.

Nick leaned toward the screen. "His beard is fuller around the cheeks."

Sanchez added more hair and asked about Bubba's eyes. After a few more changes, the man in the sketch came to life and Nick's stomach did a slow somersault. He shoved Sanchez's hand from the keyboard. "You can stop there."

His head reeled. "That's Bubba," he mumbled, slumping into a chair. He wished the room would stop spinning. "Can I have some water?"

Hendrick left the cubicle. Nick held his head in his hands. "Oh, my God. Bubba's dead."

23

SOLEMN PROMISE

Marissa broke the silence on the way home with occasional words of comfort, soon realizing they fell on deaf ears.

Finally, Nick asked, "Why in the world was Bubba clean-shaven and bald? It makes no sense."

Eager to get him talking, Marissa said, "I can't imagine. Did Hendrick have any ideas?"

"He said Bubba might have shaved off his beard and hair, but I don't think so."

"Maybe the killer did it. It's gruesome, but it'd be a good way to keep anyone from identifying the body. The drawing on the report wouldn't look anything like him. The police would have a tougher time finding the killer if they didn't know who the victim was."

"Makes sense. It's probably why Bubba had on a Princeton class ring."

"I'm curious. Did you tell them J.J.'s gun shoots .38 caliber bullets?"

"I mentioned it. They acted unconcerned. The whole set of circumstances I described to them sounded so unbelievable, I was sure they'd say the fact that J.J.'s gun shoots the same caliber as the bullet in Bubba's chest was only a coincidence."

"Do you think they'd cover for J.J. because he's a deputy sheriff? Isn't he also the mayor?"

He looked at her. "It would take a hell of a lot of proof for them to accuse one of their own, not to mention a town dignitary."

Marissa sensed Nick's anger and tried to get his mind off Bubba. "I wonder how things went with Tizzie telling the police about the bomb in front of your car."

"The cops told me they took the report," Nick said. "They said it was too early to know anything about who did it."

"This is so frustrating." They rode in silence and then she added, "At least we know the police showed up. I'll call them later and give them any information Tizzie might not have provided. Knowing her, though, she was probably quite thorough."

"She's a pretty smart cookie when it comes to reporting the details."

"Yes, she is. And you know what I was thinking? We were lucky you had a flat tire. If we'd started the Chevy, it could have blown up."

"Yeah, real lucky," he said with a hint of sarcasm.

She could tell his mind was still on Bubba. She ventured, "Do you feel confident that J.J. killed Bubba?"

Nick's knuckles became white on the wheel. Through gritted teeth he said, "His gun shoots the same kind of bullets that Bubba got shot with."

"But weren't the two of them friends? Bubba worked for J.J. and they spent time fishing together."

"J.J. has the loyalty and morals of a jack rabbit."

She twisted toward him in the seat. "But could he have become angry enough with Bubba to kill him?"

Nick loosened his grip on the wheel. "I've been wondering about that all the way from the police station. To tell you the truth, I haven't a clue."

Marissa gave up trying to fill the silence the rest of the way back to Spindrift Cove. When they finally arrived at the Pajama Factory, Nick cleared his throat and said, "I have something to ask you."

Marissa was ready to help him in any way she could.

"You'd be doing me a favor," he said, "if you'd stay in Bubba's apartment until you have to go back to San Francisco—or until I find someone to rent his place."

Was it her needs he had in mind? Marissa wondered. Or maybe he couldn't face staying in Bubba's apartment so soon after the news.

"Thanks," she said. "I'll be happy to."

She expected him to get out of the truck. Instead, he added, "Something else. Spindrift Cove's going to go crazy when they hear about Bubba. There's not a soul in town who wouldn't empty the last dollar in his bank account for him." He paused and swallowed. "And if everyone finds out the corpse you found is Bubba's, Walter will have all hell to pay for lying about Candi."

Marissa fingered the armrest. "How do you think the town will learn about Bubba?"

"I have to tell Tizzie," he said. "I promised her a scoop."

How could he make Tizzie's scoop take precedence over Uncle Walter's tar and feathering? Marissa thought. "The scoop you promised her was about the bombs under the car tires."

"The town will find out one way or another. Wouldn't you rather they get the facts straight? The only way they will is if I personally give them to Tizzie for the paper."

Poor Uncle Walter, Marissa thought.

"After I call the police," she said, "and see what they've found out about the car bombs, you can give Tizzie the news. Then she'll have the scoop you promised. We'll hold off telling her about Bubba."

"That's ridiculous. I can't—" He rubbed his eyes. "I know Walter is your uncle, but why are you so intent on protecting him when he shows no signs of wanting your help?"

"He . . . he . . ." She really didn't want to get into this. She heaved a small sigh. "I told you about him. He's been like a father to me."

"I can see why you—"

"I love him." She swallowed the lump in her throat. "Uncle Walter saved me financially. And Candi's been mentoring me in my business since before she and Uncle Walter were married. I owe them both a lot." She held back tears.

Nick took her hand and brushed her cheek.

She said, "Give me some time to find my uncle so he can tell the town on his own about Candi."

Nick looked past the Perk and Turf and out to the ocean. Turning back to her, he kissed her hand. "Hendrick said I could be the one to tell Bubba's folks. I can't put that off. Once they know, you'll have to tell Walter. Maybe then we can both tell Tizzie. Walter can have his say in the news at the same time as Bubba's death is announced."

The warmth of his kiss lingered on her hand. Marissa leaned over and pecked him on the cheek. "Thanks."

"Make sure Walter moves fast," he said. "The news about Bubba is going to leak out even if I keep my mouth shut." He slid out of the truck.

She watched him walk into the Pajama Factory, his head hunched into his shoulders.

Marissa dropped a few coins into the phone in the booth outside the Pajama Factory and placed a call to Hendrick. When he came on the line, she asked if he'd heard any further news about Candi.

"I just checked with Missing Persons," he said. "Nothing more, but I heard the General Works Unit is making progress on the incendiaries."

"Is J.J. a suspect?"

"We have some leads."

A perfect dodge from her question.

"You can leave me a message at Nick Devereaux's place," she said.

"You mean the guy who just IDed Bubba Maselli?"

"Yes. Nick's a friend."

She hung up and leaned back in the phone booth, feeling she was making little progress. After dropping another coin into the phone, she called Nick. When he picked up, no voice came over the line.

"Nick? Are you all right?"

"I'm fine," he said with finality—an indication that he wasn't.

"How did the Masellis take the news?"

After a long pause, he said, "I haven't called them yet."

Bubba's death had hit him even harder than she'd thought.

"You calling from the booth downstairs?" he asked.

"Yes. I'm giving you some alone time, but I need to tell you that I called Hendrick. He says they're making progress on the bombs. He still doesn't know who set them and he wouldn't tell me if J.J. is a suspect."

"Guess there's no scoop for Tizzie. Let me know as soon as you talk to Walter. We can't waste any time."

Marissa walked to her uncle's hardware store and looked past the *CLOSED* sign and into the dark window. A light at the back of the store lit the aisles enough to keep anyone from trespassing. No Walter.

On the way up to the Victorian, she practiced how to confront him. "The corpse is Bubba," she'd say, "Candi is alive and in Hong Kong."

But is she? she wondered. Candi may be in Hong Kong, but the police have no proof she's alive.

She went up the driveway and past the charred shell that was once her car. A pang of loss crept through her. With the holidays in full swing, the claims examiner couldn't promise to show his face until after New Year's Day.

She was about to open the front door of the house when she stopped, guessing Walter's reaction if she walked in unannounced after he'd kicked her out.

No need to make matters worse.

She rang the bell and got no response. She couldn't keep Nick waiting. She tried the door and went in.

"Uncle Walter?" Her voice bounced off the high ceilings. "Are you here?"

After checking both downstairs and up, she scouted the backyard with no success. Then she noticed Candi's car was gone.

He must have taken it, she thought. Of all times for him to take off.

24

BROKEN PROMISE

J.J. threw his jacket over the arm of the couch before responding to the blinking red light on his answering machine.

Could be more work, he thought. He'd hoped to have time to down a few beers in Half Moon Bay.

He pressed the button under the light and smiled at the sound of Daphne's voice: "Tonight. Do Drop Inn parking lot. 7:30. It's important."

How concise her messages were. She must crave his body. He laughed out loud at the absurdity. She'd kept him at bay longer than any woman he'd ever known.

His clock radio told him he could make it to the inn with a few minutes to spare. He grabbed his jacket and retrieved a small box he'd tucked under a pile of Jockey shorts in his dresser. Lifting the lid, he admired a ruby ring surrounded by six small diamonds. No sign of the initials he'd filed off. The ring would look nice on Daphne's finger, much nicer than it did on old Mrs. Vanderholt's. He'd ask Daphne to return it to him at the end of the evening, giving her husband no cause to become suspicious.

He slipped the box into his shirt pocket and left for the inn.

Nick placed a call to Bubba's parents, half hoping they were out.

Mrs. Maselli answered. "Oh, Nick, I'm so glad to hear from you. Have you heard from Bubba?"

Nick took a sip of coffee that had grown cold. "I'm afraid I have bad news."

"Oh, no!" Her muffled voice repeated Nick's words to her husband. "He's not hurt, is he? Oh, the Lord Jesus be with us."

Nick gulped the last of the coffee and breathed deeply. "I'm sorry to tell you, Bubba is dead."

"No! This can't be!"

Nick took a deep breath. "His body was found on Christmas Eve here on the beach."

An ear-piercing wail came through the receiver followed by a loud clunk. "My baby's dead!" The volume of her wail dwindled as she retreated from the phone.

Mr. Maselli came on the line. "Nick? Is it true? Am I hearing right?"

"I'm afraid so. I'm so sorry."

Through a muffled sob, the man said, "Tell us what happened."

In the distance, Mrs. Maselli spouted cantations to Jesus, the Lord and the Holy Ghost.

"It's not a pleasant story," Nick said. "Bubba's body washed up on the beach on Christmas Eve. He had no ID so no one knew who he was."

"You mean he drowned? That can't be. Bubba was captain of the swim team in high school. And he knew the ocean. I taught him myself about currents and undertow."

Mrs. Maselli shouted, "Drowned? Impossible! Heavenly Father, save us."

"How do they think it happened?" Mr. Maselli asked.

No need to alarm him any further, Nick thought. "The police are looking into it. I have a number for Officer Hendrick. He can give you the details."

"Let me write it down."

Nick gave it to him and Mr. Maselli thanked him. "We'll call Officer Hendrick right away."

"If you need me in the next day or two, I'll either be home or at the Perk and Turf. I'll give you the number there."

"No need. It's where we always call . . ." He choked back a sob. "Where we used to call Bubba."

Nick lay down on the bed, squeezing back tears and trying to face the fact he would never see Bubba again.

Darkness had filled the room when Nick finally rose from the bed. The ache in his gut persisted.

When the phone rang, he guessed it was Tizzie. She'd want her scoop on the bombs. She'd also been asking him to check her carburetor. He couldn't talk to her now without telling her about Bubba. He was about to let his machine take the call when the caller hung up.

Nick's stomach growled from missing both lunch and dinner. The thought of food only made him feel worse.

He poured a glass of Pinot Noir and surveyed the contents of his refrigerator. A bowl of green grapes and a half carton of sour milk. He'd be hungry by morning if he didn't make a stop at the 7-Eleven. Besides, the air might do him good.

On his way out of the Pajama Factory, he knocked on Bubba's door, hoping to catch up with Marissa. No answer.

She's probably looking for Walter, he thought.

The bell over the door at the 7-Eleven jingled too pleasantly to suit Nick's mood. He selected a box of corn flakes, a quart of milk and some bread and baloney for lunch. He was paying at the counter when the bell sounded again and he closed his eyes until the throb subsided in his temples. When he looked up, Tizzie was navigating her shopping cart over the threshold.

Of all the bad luck, he thought. How could he keep the news about Bubba from her as he'd promised Marissa?

"Nick," she said. "I was so sorry to hear about Bubba."

He flinched. "You . . . what?" His stomach twisted. Marissa would have his head.

Sadness ringed Tizzie's puffy eyes. "Mr. Maselli called at the Perk and Turf, looking for you."

Must be the one who tried to call him before he left the apartment, Nick thought.

Tizzie stood the shopping cart next to Nick. "He told me the news. I can't believe Bubba's gone."

God, he thought. How many people has she told?

"It doesn't seem possible," he said, hoping Tizzie didn't also know the corpse in the cove was Bubba and not Candi.

"He was such a kind man," she said. "A friend to everybody."

Nick's thoughts whirled.

"I just finished a special edition of the *Spindrift Sun*. To soften the blow, I've been calling everyone who knew him. They're taking this real hard." She took his arm. "You don't look so hot. You going to be all right?"

His thoughts remained on his promise to Marissa. "I'm sorry Tizzie. This has been hard for me."

"You poor soul. It's so sad losing a friend like that."

Pocketing his change, Nick asked, "Have you told Walter yet?"

"Tried. I forgot he's gone to San Francisco. End-of-year hardware sale. Haven't called J.J. yet either."

Damn, Nick thought. The story will be all over town before Walter has a chance to confess.

He took his bagged groceries from the counter. "Nice seeing you, Tizzie. I think I'd better find Marissa."

Tizzie followed him to the door. "Good thing she didn't know Bubba. She's got enough on her mind what with finding her aunt dead on the beach. You two can console each other."

He bid her goodbye again, relieved that Mr. Maselli hadn't told her the corpse was Bubba.

Tizzie rushed after him. "I forgot to tell you why Mr. Maselli was looking for you. He says he and his wife want to come up and get Bubba's stuff. He'd like you to give him a call."

J.J. entered the lot at the Do Drop Inn and parked in the back, beside a clump of oleander bushes. Soon Daphne's familiar Ford rounded the corner of the inn and parked near the bushes. He watched as she left her car and slid into the seat next to him, his heart beating like a puppy's tail.

He whiffed the heady scent of Tabu as his gaze traveled to the low-cut black dress that clung to her skin.

She and Chet must be off to a holiday party, he thought.

He pulled her to him. Kissing her lips, he pretended she'd dressed just for him.

She backed off. "I can't stay. Chet'll be back to the house soon. I came to tell you the body from the cove was IDed today and the news isn't good."

A chill rushed down J.J.'s spine. He had expected he'd eventually hear the news, but not this way. "Who . . . who is it?"

"I don't know how to tell you this. Do you remember when you told me Bubba was going to visit his parents for Christmas?"

"Oh, no! It's not Bubba."

Daphne bit her lower lip. "I'm so sorry. He never arrived in L.A."

"Oh, God. Do they know who did it?"

"I don't know anything more than what I've told you."

"Who IDed him?"

"That fellow Nick."

"Devereaux?"

"Yes. And he's going to tell all of Spindrift Cove that the body in the ocean wasn't Candi. What are we going to do?"

J.J. thought for a moment. *Nick is tight-lipped, but he has no reason to keep his mouth shut about the body. The truth will spread like wildfire.*

"Don't you worry your head. Let me take care of Nick."

"We need to talk about this soon," she said. She reached for the door handle. "I'll be in touch."

"Wait." J.J. pulled the box from his pocket and revealed the sparkling ruby. "I know you can't take this home, but I want you to see it," he said, slipping the ring onto her finger.

Daphne's eyes widened. She held up her hand. "It's absolutely stunning. Where did you get it?"

J.J. reached for the ring. "I'll keep it for you until next time."

She pulled her hand away. "Not on your life." She kissed him and he fought the urge to ravage her. "This is too lovely to leave behind," she said.

Not what he'd expected. Giving a married woman a gift she can take home isn't smart, he thought, especially if her husband's a cop. And what if she wears it and Mrs. Vanderholt's kids recognize it?

"You're sure you can hide it from Chet?" he asked.

"You betcha." She winked at him. "You're something else."

She slid from the car and he opened his window. "You won't wear it till I see you again."

She leaned into his open window. "It's our little secret." Leaving, she said, "I'll call you."

Still uneasy, J.J. watched her slide into her car and drive away.

Marissa jogged in the dark down Ferndale Road looking for Walter. How could she have let this hoax get so out of hand? At times she felt like packing up and going back to San Francisco—if she had a car. And if she had the heart to leave her uncle to face the townspeople alone. If only her brother Tony were here. He'd know how to help her out of this predicament.

First Gregory dumped her. Then Uncle Walter fell from the pedestal she'd once put him on. Maybe she'd expected too much from both men. But Gregory could have at least given her a chance to explain why she'd spent the night in Nick's apartment. Besides all this, Walter's behavior was bordering on bizarre.

The Pajama Factory was a welcome sight as she slowed her approach to Main Street. How good a steaming bath would feel at her new home in Bubba's place. Maybe there'd be a message from Gregory in reply to the three messages she'd left him. He'd forced her to realize that even though Uncle Walter thought Gregory was perfect for her, she and he weren't meant to be. Having a man who was good for her career wasn't enough. And she couldn't deny that Nick made her skin tingle more than Gregory ever had—if that counted for anything.

What bugged her now was the lack of closure. As a clutter organizer, she was used to having everything in its place. Maybe they could at least remain friends.

She stopped to drop a quarter into a can on a stack of *Spindrift Sun* newspapers. The headline spread across the single page: *Bubba's gone.*

What? Nick had promised to keep Bubba's death a secret until she told Uncle Walter. How could he do this to her?

She read Tizzie's misspelled article:

> *The dead body of Bubba Maselli, one of Spindrift Cove's most beloved citisens, was identified today by Nick Deveroh. A 38-kalibur bullet was lodged in his chest.*

"I can't believe he told Tizzie behind my back!"

> *Bubba was last seen on December 23. Mayor J.J. Haggersby said Bubba never showed up for a planned fishing trip on the 24th. The mayor claims Bubba told him he was_cansilling the trip to make a surpriz visit to his parents in Los Angelees. Bubba's parents say he never arrived. Police are still investigading the shooting.*

Nick told Tizzie everything! Marissa thought. He gave her no chance to find Walter. She continued reading:

> *Plans for a memorial service have not yet been made.*
> *The anyual Spindrift Cove New Year's Eve party has*
> *been cansilled to pay respects to Bubba.*

No mention was made that Bubba's body had washed ashore on Christmas Eve. At least Nick had granted her that much of a favor. If Tizzie or the townspeople found out it was Bubba and not Candi, Uncle Walter would be served on a platter with Tizzie's turkey giblets.

Filled with the heat of betrayal, she crushed the newsprint into a ball. "Vengeance on the men in my life. Beginning with Nick Devereaux!"

She stormed up the stairs, cursing Gregory for not understanding, Walter for becoming an unapproachable stranger and Nick for betraying her.

She pounded on Nick's apartment door. "Nick, damn it, come out here."

The door slowly opened.

"How could you?" she shouted so loud her voice rang in the rafters. She smoothed the crushed paper. "You promised you'd give me time."

Her eyes met with a forlorn Nick. Barefoot, with his hair standing on end, his eyes puffed and red, he supported himself with a hand on the doorknob.

The sorrow on his face hit her full force. "Oh, God, Nick. It's Bubba. I'm so sorry."

He stood wordless.

"I . . . I've been so selfish. I forgot. I . . . I'll go now."

Nick closed the door.

25

EXPOSED DECEPTION

Marissa descended the steps of the Pajama Factory wishing she could turn back the clock. Would she ever learn to control her temper?

To calm her nerves, she inhaled the scent of the ocean, the look on Nick's mournful face haunting her.

She headed toward the Perk and Turf—the only place she hadn't looked for Walter.

An air of sadness hung over the coffee shop. The Christmas lights were gone, the usual fire in the fireplace was now only dead coals and the old juke box stood silent.

The sole customer was a large balding man, who sat at a corner table with his gaze fixed out the window. His hands wrapped around a cup of coffee. A plate with a half-eaten steak had been pushed away.

Tizzie emerged from the kitchen, her gait slower than normal. She looked as if she'd been crying. "Have a seat, Marissa."

"Can you join me?" Marissa asked, taking a table by the dead fire.

Tizzie dropped into the chair across from her. "I feel like I've lost a son."

"Bubba must have been someone special," Marissa said, feeling the corpse she'd saved from the ocean had now become a real person. From what she'd been told, she would have liked Bubba. She wished she could tell Tizzie the whole story.

"Did Nick tell you the news?" Marissa asked.

"No, Mr. Maselli did."

Nick didn't tell her? Marissa swallowed hard. How would she ever explain her behavior to Nick?

Tizzie added, "Bubba's father called here looking for Nick. Seemed in a hurry. Told me Bubba had drowned and hung up."

"Are the Masellis going to be all right?"

"I only spoke to Bubba's father. I could tell he was trying not to break down over the phone. Seems he'd only just heard the news."

What hell Nick had gone through, Marissa thought. She tried to focus on Tizzie. "I'm glad you got your typewriter back."

A glint of a smile crossed Tizzie's face. "I am, too. It was only gone overnight." The smile disappeared. "Whoever took it still's got the cover." She wiped her hand over the table. "It's a big old clunker but it's got sentimental value. My father bought that Smith Corona when I was still in high school." Leaning back, she added, "Said someday I'd be a writer. Little did he know I'd own my own newspaper."

Marissa supposed a one-pager could be called a newspaper. "Any idea who the thief was?" She was sure it was J.J. Still, she wanted to test the waters.

"I have my suspicions, but I'm not one to point a finger until I have all the facts."

"Sign of a good reporter."

"I took some fingerprints before I used the typewriter again."

"Fingerprints? How did you do that?"

"I borrowed Margaret Potter's Fingerprint Lab."

"Margaret has a fingerprint lab?"

"Not a real one. When I told her I got my typewriter back she told me she had a way to tell who stole it. Showed up with a toy called Fingerprint Lab she'd bought for her grandson Richie for thirty bucks. Said he'd lost interest in it and left it at her house. She was pretty disappointed at the time. But it was a good thing he left it behind."

"Did it work?"

"So far, so good. Considering it's a toy, we got pretty clear prints off almost every typewriter key."

"So now what'll you do?"

Tizzie leaned forward. "Next time anyone comes in, I'll check the prints on their water glass and compare them to the ones we took off the keys. I've already checked out one regular customer."

"And who might that be?"

She lowered her voice. "Marcus Frobush is safe." She nodded toward the man Marissa had noticed when she came in. "Checked his prints and no similarity at all."

Marissa wondered how accurate this toy could be. She wished J.J. would walk in. She would have loved to serve him a nice clean glass of water. "Guess that's a start," she said. She pulled her chair closer to Tizzie's. "Any idea what your typewriter was used for?"

"Can't say that I do."

"I think I might know."

"Don't hold back on me, girl," Tizzie said loud enough to make Marcus look her way.

Marissa whispered, "Those threats Nick and I received both had ink-filled *e*'s like the *e* on your typewriter."

"Well, I'll be a cross-eyed chicken. You think the person who wrote those notes used my typewriter?"

"Looks like it." She watched for Tizzie's reaction but got none. "Give me a few days. Like you, I need some more facts."

"Good. We'll touch base again later."

Marissa rose to leave. "You haven't seen my uncle, have you?"

"He's at a hardware sale in San Francisco."

Unbelievable, Marissa thought. By the time he came back, the townspeople would be breaking down his door. "No wonder I haven't been able to find him."

"Sometimes he spends the night up there. He has a couple of cronies he tips a few beers with. I wouldn't worry about him."

Pastor John jumped at the ring of the rectory doorbell. Someday, he thought, he'd figure out how to deaden the sound of that dratted thing.

He closed the pages of *Gory War Tales of the Twentieth Century* and tumbled out of the two-person hammock that took up a good portion of the living room. The doorbell rang again. "I'm coming."

He slipped into his shoes and opened the door. In the glow of the porch light stood a slender woman in her mid- forties and a taller, cleanly shaven man about the same age.

"Pastor?" the woman said, smoothing her black suit. "We're Karen and Frank Maselli, Bubba's parents."

"Come in," John said, resigning himself to the fact that his book would have to wait. "I was so sorry to hear about Bubba.

Your son was a favorite here in town." He ushered them into the living room. "Please have a seat."

The woman looked first at the hammock that still swung in the corner. She chose the couch and her husband sat beside her. The pastor wedged his enormous girth between the arms of a straight-back chair.

"We're sorry to drop in on you unannounced," Mr. Maselli said.

His wife dabbed at her eyes with a tissue. "The Lord didn't want things to be like this. The Bible says, 'He who toils for the church and community shall survive.'"

John had never heard that passage. He'd have to look it up.

"We came to town to pick up Bubba's things," Mr. Maselli said.

His wife added, "And we want to ask you a favor." She fidgeted with her pocketbook and then set it on the floor.

"Of course," the pastor said. "Would you like some coffee or maybe some tea?"

"No, thank you," the woman said. "'Caffeine doth rot the soul,' the Bible says."

John hadn't heard that one either.

Mr. Maselli said, "We know Bubba had many friends in Spindrift Cove so we'd like to ask if you'd perform a memorial service for him before we go back to L.A."

Another memorial service request, John thought. Wait until the church board in San Francisco hears the good news. Pastor John has been accepted into the community.

"Most certainly. When would you like to have it?"

The woman's eyes misted. "Sometime soon. The police told us it's been a week since that nice woman friend of Nick's pulled his body from the ocean."

John gulped. "You mean Marissa?"

"I believe that's her name, bless her soul."

Oh, my God in heaven! "Excuse me, while I get us some wine." He scurried to the kitchen.

"Wine is the blood of Jesus," Mrs. Maselli called after him. "Pray that it gives us strength."

Pastor John leaned on the kitchen table with both hands. The body in the cove belonged to Bubba? If that's true, then what happened to Candi and who did he perform the memorial service for? Whose ashes were in the urn on the altar?

He filled three wine glasses from an open bottle of Chardonnay. After downing one, he refilled it and set it on the tray.

"Yes, of course I'll perform the service," he said, carrying the tray to the living room and offering them wine. "If you don't mind my asking, who informed you that Bubba's body was in the cove?"

"The police," Mr. Maselli said.

"And we talked to the coroner," his wife added.

"And who told you it was Bubba's? Oh, I just asked you that."

Mrs. Maselli smiled. "It's pretty upsetting for all of us."

"We should hold the service as soon as possible," John said. His hand shook as he offered each of them a glass of wine. "Let me check the chapel calendar." He walked to the computer on his desk and tapped quickly on the keys. "We could have it on Thursday, if you'd like."

The woman quickly replied, "Oh, thank you."

"Have you spoken to J.J. Haggersby about the arrangements?" the pastor asked.

"I left him a message on his answering machine," she said. "We haven't heard back."

"We're new at this," her husband said. "We'd hoped you would take care of these things."

The pastor put on his kindliest smile. "Some I can and some are decisions you'll have to make. Maybe we can visit J.J. together in the morning."

The man stood. "Here's my card. Our room number at the Do Drop Inn is on the back. If you need to reach us before tomorrow, please call us there."

Mrs. Maselli gathered her purse and stood beside him.

"I'll call you tomorrow morning," Pastor John said, showing them out. "You two get a good night's rest."

When they were away down the path, he closed the door and leaned against it. "Walter Schmidkin has duped me."

26

CURIOUS UNRAVELING

Pastor John bowed his head as he sat in the first row of the Chapel of Roses. A single altar candle shed light on his hands held in prayer. Every time he thought of himself at the memorial service, extolling the virtues of Candi, his jaw locked and he gritted his teeth.

What if she's alive? he thought. He couldn't chance making a fool of himself in Spindrift Cove after failing as a pastor in San Francisco. How could he have trusted J.J.? Or Walter? The church board will say he should have checked out the facts.

"Please God, don't let them find out."

He wiped his face with a handkerchief. Bargains with God had never worked before. Then again, he'd already boiled the water for Pastor John stew.

A draft swept through the chapel and he squinted at a figure in the open doorway.

"Pastor John?"

"Tizzie, is that you?" He could barely make her out in the darkness.

She hustled toward him. "I'm sorry to bother you when you're praying, Pastor, but I have important news." As she approached, he saw her brows were drawn together and the corners of her mouth drooped.

Curious, the pastor made room for her in the pew. She slid in beside him, the candlelight throwing a macabre glow on her lined face.

"What's on your mind?" he asked.

"I called the police for details about Bubba today." She took a breath. "Usually they're tight-lipped when I ask for news, but they told me the corpse Walter's daughter found in the cove was Bubba, not Candi!"

Oh, God, she knows it all, he thought.

"I just found out, too," he said. "I assure you I didn't know until today."

"Oh, Pastor, I never suspected that you did. But that's not everything. I know who wrote the threats on Nick and Marissa's lives. It was the person who stole my typewriter. I have proof."

"Threats?" Maybe the church board in San Francisco was right about him not knowing what's going on in his congregation.

"Someone stole my typewriter and wrote Marissa and Nick threatening notes. They wrote one to Marissa's boyfriend in San Francisco, too." She explained about the ink-filled *e*'s. "When I got my typewriter back, I took fingerprints off the keys and I've been comparing them to those on my customers' water glasses."

"And?"

"You won't believe this: Walter wrote them!"

"Come now, Tizzie. Walter doesn't have a mean bone in his body. And how did you get the prints off the typewriter?"

"I used a kit Margaret bought for her grandson."

"A toy? You can't accuse someone of a crime with evidence that came from a toy."

"Yes, I can, Pastor. They're clear as day."

"But think for a minute. Why would Walter threaten his own niece?"

"Beats me. All I know is that I was closing up shop when Walter came back from San Francisco and stopped in for some chocolate pie. When he left, I compared the prints on his water glass to those I took off the typewriter and I'm sure Walter is the man who wrote those threats."

"That's hard to believe." He doubted that Tizzie had any training in reading fingerprints. "Did you show J.J.?"

She shook her head. "Can't tell him. He's Walter's best friend. He'd laugh me out of town."

So now, Pastor John thought, he'd have to play deputy sheriff, too?

"And if Walter would threaten his niece," Tizzie said, "he'd probably kill his wife."

The pastor leaned back in the pew. "Now, let's not jump to conclusions. We don't know anything for sure."

"But if that wasn't Candi in the ocean, then where is she and whose ashes are in the urn on Walter's mantel?"

John thought back to the memorial service. J.J. should have given him the urn to place on the altar. Instead, J.J. had put it there himself. And it was J.J. who gave the ashes to Walter. That was the pastor's job. Both times J.J. had gone out of his way to keep him from picking up the urn.

Heat flooded John's cheeks. I'll be damned! He thought. "Did you happen to look into the urn?"

"My goodness, no. I'd never do such a thing."

John sighed. "I didn't either."

"Do you think it was empty?"

"I can't imagine it was full. Where would the ashes come from?"

Tizzie rose from the pew. "J.J. and Walter are in cahoots. They pulled a fast one on all of us." She drew her cardigan closed and took her bag from the pew. "I wouldn't be surprised if they planned her murder together. And I'm going to tell everyone I see."

Pastor John sat forward. "Now, hold on, Tizzie. I think we better sleep on this." He stood. "Excuse me a moment while I close up the chapel."

He blew out the altar candle. "Those are some pretty strong accusations, Tizzie." He joined her. Cradling her elbow, he guided her down the aisle and out the chapel door.

What does a pastor do in a situation like this? he wondered.

A brisk breeze cooled the night and the pastor whiffed the aroma of eucalyptus. "I'll walk you home."

"Is that you, Pastor John?" a woman's voice called from down the path.

"Margaret?" Tizzie said. "What are you doing out at this hour?"

Margaret Potter scurried up the path, clutching her purse to the front of her tailored suit. A dark beret sat on her head. "I found out something I have to tell the pastor immediately. You might as well know, too, Tizzie."

John steeled himself for one of Margaret's orations.

"I just got off the phone with my sister. And she told me her husband Bill saw Walter and his niece go into Candi's office in Ocean Bluffs. You know she had an office there."

"Can we get to the point?" John asked.

"Hmph. Anyway, Bill's office is next door to Candi's and he says the walls are thin as paper."

"What are you trying to say?" Tizzie asked.

"Is it okay if I say the *s* word?" Margaret asked the pastor.

John stifled a chuckle. "If it's necessary for the story."

"Walter said Bubba was screwing Candi." She wiped her brow. "Lordy, it's hot tonight."

A laugh escaped from John and he quickly composed himself.

"Walter was mad," Margaret said. "And when someone's mad, they say things they wouldn't usually say."

Tizzie stepped in closer. "So what did Bill hear?"

Margaret said, "I'm trying to tell you that Bill heard Walter say he was going to kill Bubba."

"What?" Pastor John said.

"I told you so," Tizzie piped in.

"Now let's not be too hasty in our conclusions, ladies."

"We can't let that man get away with this," Tizzie said. "Killing Bubba and writing threats. And then making us think the body in the ocean was Candi. He probably killed Candi, too."

Pastor John's mind reeled. Could these women be right?

"And I was there when he bought the rat poison," Margaret added.

Tizzie's brows raised. "That's how he did it?" she asked. "I say he's a murderer and we need to do something about it."

Margaret said. "Let's go to his place and confront him."

"Good idea", Tizzie said. "And we'll bring the whole town with us."

"Not so fast, ladies. If there was a murder—"

"Two murders," Margaret said.

"However many, we should let the police take care of this."

"We can't call the sheriff," Tizzie said. "He's the one who bamboozled us. And by the time the police in Ocean Bluffs gather their evidence, Walter could take off and we'd never see him again."

Margaret shook her finger at John. "Walter's not only a murderer. He conned all of us at the memorial service. We've been made to look like fools."

Margaret was right about that, John thought. And if the church board found out, the deed would go on his record. He could be transferred to an even smaller community. "What do you ladies have in mind?"

"Tell you what," Tizzie said. "I've got a list of people I phoned about Bubba's death. I can call them back and we can all go over to Walter's place and make him explain."

"You're calling everybody?" John asked.

"Everyone except J.J."

"What about Marissa and Nick?" Margaret asked.

"I'll skip them, too. Are you both with me?"

If John agreed, he could make sure the confrontation didn't get out of hand. And, damn it, he was mad that Walter and J.J. had duped him.

"I'm with you, ladies."

The sun had barely risen when J.J. raced up the hill to Walter's place. He cursed his bum hip and clutched the *Spindrift Sun* so tightly the one-pager wilted in his hand. "Open up!" he shouted, pounding on Walter's door.

It opened a crack and J.J. shoved it hard, nearly knocking Walter over. "Did you see this?" He held up the page so Walter could see the *Bubba is dead* headline.

"Yes, and it's a rotten shame. Bubba was a good boy."

"The Masellis found out from the police that the body in the cove was Bubba's."

"Bubba's? That can't be," Walter said. The color drained from his face. "How . . . how did he die?"

Sweat dripped from J.J.'s brow. "I don't have the details. Daphne told me. And she said Nick knows. If word gets to Tizzie, she'll put the pieces together and the next *Spindrift Sun* will blast an even bigger headline."

Walter rubbed the back of his neck. "We can tell everybody our story is true about Candi being dead. We'll tell them she died overseas and was buried there. You can tell them the memorial service was for my sake and for her friends."

J.J. stopped pacing and thought a moment. "You know, old man, you're right. Tizzie was the only one at the service who said Marissa found Candi's body in the cove. We can say Tizzie got her facts screwed up like she screws up her spelling. Brilliant idea!"

"Wait a minute. I don't think we should pin the blame on Tizzie. That wouldn't be fair. I was the one who told her the corpse was Candi."

"Deny it."

"I can't do that to Tizzie."

"God, Walter. You've got no choice. Do you have a better idea?" Walter's glazed eyes told J.J. he still hadn't recovered from the news.

"Let me think about it," Walter said.

Loud shouts came from Walter's driveway and J.J. pulled back the window curtain. "You better think fast, old man. You have company and it looks like a lynch mob."

27

OPEN CONFRONTATION

Pastor John marched up the circular staircase to Walter's Victorian like a general leading an army. As long as Tizzie and Margaret stuck close by, he'd have no trouble taking command, he thought. He turned and grinned at the congregation from Candi's memorial service. Lulu May carried her baby in one arm and a sign that proclaimed YOU CAN'T FOOL US. Another sign showed a skull and crossbones with MURDERER! painted in bright red.

John's confidence rose at the sight of even more townspeople ascending Walter's driveway. He pounded on the door.

"That's J.J. peeking through the curtain," Margaret said.

Tizzie yelled, "Knock the door down, Pastor."

John squared his shoulders, feeling the power of his congregation. "Come on out, Walter!" He beat on the door with both fists.

"Take your medicine like a man," Margaret yelled.

The door opened a crack and Walter emerged, his hand raised to quiet the crowd. Margaret pushed past both him and the pastor. "Follow me," she shouted and the crowd filed into Walter's parlor.

I could have done that, the pastor thought, muscling his way through the noisy gathering. He looked across the room. Wouldn't you know J.J. would be here, too?

J.J. raised his hand to stop the noise, but the crowd had its own agenda. Finally, he stuck two fingers in his mouth and let out a shrill whistle.

Everyone came to attention except for Lulu May's baby, who responded with a howl.

Wishing the whistle could have been his, the pastor used an ottoman to help him step onto a chair. "Walter, you duped us," he said, hoping the crowd would back him.

The people booed Walter, bolstering John's confidence even more.

"You had us all mourning for your poor wife and she isn't even dead." His voice had gained volume, echoing against the high ceiling.

"She is, too, dead," Margaret shouted. "He killed her." The crowd cheered her. "I saw him buy the rat poison."

Walter attempted to reply over the loud jeers and J.J. let out another whistle.

"Candi is dead," Walter said, standing back from everyone. "But she wasn't washed ashore last week." He momentarily closed his eyes and whispered, "Your sympathy was appreciated."

"She sure is dead," Tizzie shouted. "Tell us how you killed her!"

The veins in Walter's temples bulged and his face turned crimson. John thought the man was about to have a heart attack.

"Take him to jail, J.J.," Margaret hollered.

The pastor wiped the sweat from his brow. The women were going to take over.

Walter was about to speak when the phone in the hall rang and the pastor detected a sigh of relief as Walter went to answer it.

"Let it ring," John said, teetering on the chair as he tried to navigate to the ottoman and then the floor.

Walter ignored him. John thought he might not have heard him. He followed Walter on his heels.

"Don't let him get away," Margaret shouted.

Walter picked up the receiver and John grabbed it and slammed it down. "Get back in there and tell us where your wife is."

Thank God Walter obeyed, John thought. He couldn't afford to lose ground.

Walter resumed his place in the room. "Candi was on a business trip to Germany. That's where she was killed."

"A likely story," Margaret said.

"Prove it!" Lulu May shouted.

Marissa jumped at the loud clang of a receiver slamming in her ear. So! Her uncle was back from his hardware sale. And he was still God-awful mad at her to hang up on her like that. It was time he came to his senses. She threw on a jacket and headed for the Victorian.

About to approach the driveway, she heard loud shouting coming from her uncle's place. A mob of townspeople filled the driveway and was trying to squeeze through the open door of the house.

Oh, God. Looks like all hell's broken loose.

She quickened her step and caught up with the crowd. Pushing her way through, she fought her way up the stairs and through the door where she could make out her uncle surrounded by an irate crowd. As he fielded angry questions, she caught his attention.

Walter rushed to her. "Marissa! Thank God, you're all right. I've been looking for you ever since your car blew up. Where have you been?"

Had he forgotten he'd kicked her out? She ignored his question, grabbed a dining room chair and stood on it. "Quiet! All of you!"

Much to her surprise, the townspeople settled down.

"What is it you want from my uncle?"

"We want to know what happened to Candi," the pastor said. "You, J.J. and Walter have made fools of all of us."

Marissa asked her uncle, "What do you have to say?"

"What?" he asked.

"Tell them where Candi is!"

"I have the death notice and I have her ashes to prove she's dead. Show them, Marissa. Get the urn from the mantel."

No way would she get roped into his ploy. Those were not Candi's ashes. "I think you'd better get the urn." She stepped down from the chair.

Before Walter could make a move, Tizzie made her way to the mantel, grabbed the urn and removed the lid. Margaret looked in and gasped. Then Tizzie looked in. "She's dead." She tilted it so everyone could see.

Or so it seems, Marissa thought, still wondering where those ashes came from.

The pastor looked in and moved beside J.J., who looked quite pale.

Tizzie said, "We want to know if Walter killed her with rat poison."

Now where did that idea come from? Marissa wondered.

Walter stood tall. "I have the death notice from Germany upstairs. If you'll calm down, I'll show you."

The people whispered to each other as Walter climbed the stairs. Marissa considered what kind of lie he'd tell this time.

Minutes later, Walter returned with a note, which he handed to Marissa. "Read this to them."

How could he do this to her?

She was about to hand it back when her curiosity won out. She unfolded it, noticing Pastor John biting his lip.

The chatter stopped as she read the note to herself. It was penned in poor English and certainly wasn't a death notice. Still, it could temporarily satisfy the crowd. "It's a personal note regarding Candi. It's written in English on a German doctor's stationery."

The pastor stepped forward. "What good is that? I want to see legal proof that the service I performed for these kind people was legitimate."

"We know it was legit," Tizzie said. "Here are the ashes. We want to know how she died and why you lied to us."

"Yeah," Marcus Frobush shouted and the crowd agreed.

Walter spoke up. "I don't have the details yet. You'll have to be patient. When they arrive from Germany, I'll let you know. Tizzie, you can put them in the paper."

The mob erupted again and the pastor held up his hand. "Listen! We've accomplished what we came for. We know now that Candi is dead and we did not mourn in vain." He put a hand on Walter's shoulder. "We all share your grief." To the crowd, he said, "Now let's give Walter a chance to grieve—and a few days to get further word. We can't ask him for information he hasn't received yet."

All except Margaret mumbled their agreement. "I'll believe it when I see it. Walter's a killer. He not only killed his wife, he also killed Bubba."

The crowd gasped.

Where did she get that idea? Marissa wondered. "Do you have proof?"

"My brother-in-law heard him threaten to kill Bubba."

Questions arose from the townspeople and Marissa exchanged puzzled glances with her uncle. "Do you know anything about this?" she asked loud enough for him to hear.

"I don't know what in tarnation Margaret's talking about."

Margaret added, "My brother-in-law, Bill Richards, has an office next to Candi's. He heard you say you'd kill Bubba. And next thing I found out he was dead."

Marissa thought back to the day she and her uncle had visited Candi's office. The man in the hall had introduced himself as Bill Richards. He must have heard her uncle through the wall when Walter threatened to kill Bubba for, as Walter put it, "screwing his wife."

Walter turned pale. "I never—"

"And on what day did Walter threaten to kill Bubba?" Marissa asked.

Margaret looked to the ceiling as if she'd find an answer. "It was . . . it was the day after Christmas."

"And on what day did I pull Bubba's corpse from the cove?" Marissa asked J.J.

J.J.'s eyes narrowed at Marissa. "Christmas Eve," he mumbled.

"Speak up. So the crowd can hear you."

"Christmas Eve," he shouted.

"Two days before my uncle's supposed threat to kill Bubba. In fact, a pretty strange threat if he'd already killed him. Why would he implicate himself? I think we've cleared my uncle of that charge." She opened the front door.

The crowd exchanged comments and Marissa hoped she wouldn't be challenged. "Now, all you nice people can go home," she said. She held her breath at the response to her flimsy explanation.

The crowd tittered. Tizzie nodded to Pastor John, who headed for the door. J.J. followed with the rest of the crowd and Marissa let out her breath.

Margaret was last to leave. "I don't believe those are your wife's ashes," she said to Walter. "I'm coming back if you don't bring us the real death notice."

Marissa looked out the window at the dispersing crowd. When the last protestor left the driveway, she held up the piece of paper that Walter had tried to pass off as a death notice. "What is this supposed to be?"

"I don't understand," he said cupping his ear as if to help him hear.

"What is this?"

"Oh, that. I got it from Candi's boyfriend Gunther," Walter said. "It says she's dead."

Marissa shook her head. "No, it doesn't. And it's not from Gunther. It's an angry note from Gunther's receptionist. It's written in broken English on the doctor's stationery, asking you to quit calling. It's signed 'Helga.' Have you been making phone calls to Gunther?"

Walter looked at the floor. "I might have made a few. I didn't get to talk to him, but I spoke to Helga. She always answers the phone in German, with what sounds like the name of an office, like a doctor's office. She knows some English. She told me she works for him."

"From the looks of this note, I'd say you made more than a few calls. How did you get his number?"

"I found it in Candi's things." He took the note from her. "It says right here, 'to you, Candi is dead.' That's enough for me."

Marissa couldn't believe his weak attempt to justify his reasoning. "As of a couple of days ago," she said, "Candi was in Hong Kong. Officer Hendrick from the Ocean Bluffs police has been tracking her."

Walter's brows drew so close together they formed one bushy line. Marissa had played her last card and Walter looked as if he'd played his last one, too. She waited for an explanation. When none came, she said, "We'll talk about this when you've come to your senses." She stomped out and down the stairs.

28

REVEALED SECRET

Marissa climbed the steps to Bubba's apartment, muttering under her breath. "What a stubborn, jackass uncle. How can he think I or anyone else would believe his stories?"

She let herself in and slammed the door behind her. Her open suitcase lay on the floor in disarray, reminding her of her recent move from Nick's to Bubba's place.

She stopped in her tracks. She hadn't left her suitcase that messy. And a pair of Bubba's shorts were hanging out of the dresser drawer. The coffee cup she'd left in the sink was now on the counter. Someone had been in the apartment.

Would Nick have come in? Certainly he wouldn't have gone through her things. She was about to call him but decided against it. She'd already interrupted his grief.

As she lay on the bed, contemplating her next move, a knock came on the door.

"Who is it?" she shouted.

Another knock.

She flung open the door and looked outside.

Nick sat on the balcony railing. "Keep scowling like that and I'll have second thoughts about coming in."

She smoothed her hair. "I'm sorry about yesterday. I wasn't—"

"You've already apologized." He moved toward her. "What's got you so mad?"

She stepped back to let him in. "I'm the one who caused problems for *you*. It's my turn to do the consoling." He walked in and she asked, "How are you handling all this?"

"All right, I guess, considering." He crossed the room to look out the window. "I miss Bubba a lot. I'm going to miss jamming with him on weekends. He was the best friend I ever had."

The ticking of the travel alarm on Bubba's desk filled the silence as Nick continued looking out the window. When he finally faced her to sit on the bed, he said, "I just came back from coffee at the inn with his folks. I'm still coming to terms with the fact that Bubba's not coming back."

Nick made space for her to sit beside him. "The police were here today," he said, "searching for clues."

"About Bubba? No wonder the apartment looked different. What did they find?"

"Not a whole lot. They took a few of his things. Didn't seem too impressed with what they found." He looked at her. "I'm finished bringing you down with my problems. Tell me what's bothering you."

"Nothing as serious as you and Bubba," she said, sitting down. "It's my uncle. The town's all against him. They showed up at his place *en masse* and angry as hell. They demanded to know about Candi."

"Good God. What'd he say?"

"He waffled. He could have saved his hide if he'd come clean and apologized. Instead, he holed himself up with his lies. We finally got everyone to leave, but I'll bet they're out shopping for tar and feathers."

Nick put an arm around her. "I wish I could help. He seems to have a mind of his own. There's not a whole lot we can do."

Rising, he said, "Mr. and Mrs. Maselli have asked me to pack up Bubba's things. I have some empty boxes at my place. What if you and I do something productive?" He opened the door to the closet and a surfboard fell out, narrowly missing his foot. "I guess we can start here."

The early afternoon sun streamed through Bubba's apartment window when Marissa folded the last of Bubba's shirts and added them to a pile in a cardboard carton.

"Think the Masellis will want this?" Nick asked, about to take the stuffed trout off the wall.

"I'd leave it. It's pretty ugly and the stuffing's coming out." She tucked some socks into the corners of the carton. "I've been thinking about J.J. Suppose he did kill Bubba. If I were him and I had access to a crematorium, I would have disposed of the body by burning it, not by dropping it in the ocean."

"It would have been an easier way," Nick said. He lifted a pile of jeans from a dresser drawer. "But Bubba never mentioned a crematorium. There's none in town. I wonder if J.J. has access to one."

"Also, when you think about it, the fact that Bubba might have seen him pilfer a ring isn't a reason to kill someone. Bubba would have had to catch him doing something more serious."

"You're right. The only link the police have is that J.J. owns a gun that shoots the same caliber bullets as the one in Bubba's chest. Nick stared at the wall, a pair of Bubba's jeans in his hands.

"The report said Bubba's clothes were at least a size too small," Marissa said.

"I'm curious whose clothes they were."

Nick carried the box of shirts to the door. "Do you have a copy of the report?"

"I have it in my bag." She retrieved it and handed it to him.

He unfolded it and read the text. "It says here that the neck size of the shirt he wore was 16-1/2. All the shirts we've packed are size 17-1/2." Looking up, he added, "Hendrick also told me they couldn't even get prints because Bubba's fingertips were burned off with a propane torch."

"The killer sure didn't want anyone to find out who Bubba was." She watched Nick sort through the contents of the file drawer in Bubba's desk. He smiled at a photo of Bubba and him and slid it into his pocket.

Marissa allowed him his moment of nostalgia and busied herself carrying Bubba's skis from the closet. She set them next to the boots by the door.

"That's about it," Nick said, checking the closet.

"All the furniture stays?"

"Yes. I furnished this place with garage sale stuff. It's good enough for a rental." He sat down on the bed, an empty hanger in his hand. "I can't believe I'll never see him again." He hesitated and added, "You know, much as I dislike J.J., in all the years I've known him, I've never seen him mad. I wonder if he could get angry enough to kill someone."

"If he did kill Bubba, and it was because Bubba caught him taking jewelry off a corpse, then why didn't he put a bullet into Paco, too, for the same reason?"

"Good question."

"Do you think J.J. might have threatened Paco so he'd keep his mouth shut? Maybe Paco got some notes like we did."

Nick rubbed his neck. "You may be onto something." His eyes took on a sparkle Marissa hadn't seen since before he'd learned about Bubba.

"I can catch him at his peewee football practice today," he said.

"What about your flat tire?"

"Ever watch a super mechanic at work?"

"You?"

"Come keep me company."

Nick fixed the flat while Marissa looked on. When he was finished, he wiped his hands and asked, "You won't mind if I visit Paco alone? He isn't one to spill his guts in front of strangers."

"Go," she said. And he took off.

The afternoon dragged and Marissa kept catching herself reaching for the phone, wondering if Gregory really meant what he said during his last call. Two years together was too long to toss aside as if nothing happened. The cooling-off period after the phone call had come to a close. If she explained, maybe they could at least be friends.

She called him at work and a machine picked up.

He probably left with everyone else to celebrate New Year's Eve, she thought. Would he go to the company party alone to show her he didn't need her? Or would he stew at home? The fight they had was crazy and about something that never happened.

She tried his home number. The phone rang twice.

"Hello?" A woman's voice.

Marissa slammed down the receiver. Gregory didn't waste any time.

Nick drove the perimeter of the park and came to a stop by a flock of cheering five- and six-year-olds in football uniforms. Another group of outfitted kids nearby looked as if they'd been told there's no Christmas.

Paco stood tall above the crowd that was jumping with game-winning glee. He looked toward the street. "Hey, Nick! Come meet the best peewee football players in Spindrift Cove."

Nick scooped up an errant football and joined them. He threw a short pass to a towheaded boy with mud on his face. The boy caught the ball and Nick approached him. "Great catch. Did you play a good game?"

The boy eagerly described the last scoring play while Nick and Paco listened with rapt attention.

"Go load your gear into the van," Paco shouted to the boys. "It's pizza time!"

The boys cheered and raced to the van. Nick followed behind with Paco.

"What a surprise to see you," Paco said. "What brings you out here?"

"Actually, Bubba does."

Paco stopped walking. "God, I'm sorry. I read about him in the paper. He was your best friend."

"Thanks. That's why I need to find out how he died. I know you don't like to talk about you and J.J., but it's important to me. I think Bubba might have caught J.J. doing something he shouldn't have."

Paco put his hands in his pockets and looked down at the grass. "You think J.J. killed Bubba?"

"I can't say that for sure. I'm hoping you can shed some light on a possible motive."

"Whatever you need." His dark eyes filled with fire. "I'd do anything to get back at that bastard."

"Does J.J. know you were the one who told Martha Billingsworth about the ring he stole from her husband's body?"

Paco's eyes narrowed. "Does he ever." He lowered his voice. "I know this won't go beyond you. J.J. put a gun to my head and threatened to kill me and come after my girl if I confirmed Martha Billingsworth's accusation."

"And that's why the case was dropped?"

"She had no proof and she didn't want her husband's grave disturbed."

"Mr. Rodriguez," a boy shouted from the van. "Hurry up. We're hungry."

Paco waved and he and Nick continued walking toward the van.

Nick asked, "Is it possible that Bubba might have seen J.J. steal a lot more than one ring?"

"I don't know!" came his immediate reply.

Nick stepped back at his fervor.

Paco smiled and winked. "And I don't know anything at all about the others he kept in a locked cabinet in the preparation room of the funeral home." He turned and walked away.

"Thanks, man," Nick yelled after him. "I owe you a big one."

29

SURPRISING DISCOVERY

Marissa answered the persistent pounding on Bubba's door and Nick burst in, out of breath.

"You were so right," he panted. "J.J.'s into something more serious than the theft of a single ring." He took her by the shoulders and sat her on the bed. "Paco wouldn't give me the details. J.J. scared the hell out of him—so bad that Paco won't report him to the police. But I found out enough to start some snooping. Are you up for it?"

"You bet I am. What do we need to do?"

"We need to make a move. It seems J.J.'s got a stash of stolen jewelry at the funeral home. Enough for him to kill anyone who finds it."

"That J.J.'s a real nice guy." Marissa fished in her purse. "Here's the key ring you gave me with Bubba's apartment key. Maybe one of the other ones is to the funeral home."

Nick flipped through the keys. "No luck. These are for the apartment and a storage shed."

Marissa paused. "Then I'm all for breaking and entering."

Nick smiled. "You seem pretty confident we can get in. How long since you picked a lock?"

"It's been a while, but I can do it."

"What other little tidbits about your past do you have up your sleeve?"

"Maybe a few more." She winked at him. "You only get one at a time."

Her adrenaline was already pumping at the prospect of exposing J.J. The break-in would keep her mind off the woman who answered Gregory's phone. That voice sounded like Candace from the Accounting Department. Marissa had previous inklings that Gregory had the hots for her. Candace the status seeker, in her French perfume and Liz Claiborne suits.

Nick nudged her. "Are you with me?"

"Let's go tonight. J.J.'s sure to be celebrating New Year's Eve at some big bash. He'll probably be drowning his sorrows because Daphne will be out with her husband."

"If you think you're up to it, I'm with you. We'll need to stake out his apartment to make sure he's gone. Maybe from the bushes in the back. I'll bring a flashlight. We may be out in the cold for a while. Better wear your 'woolies.'"

"No need," Marissa said. "We can watch from the side window in Uncle Walter's hardware store. From there, we can see whoever comes up J.J.'s driveway. We'll be more comfortable in the store and I know a secret entrance."

"Clever woman," Nick said. "It's exciting hanging out with a cat burglar."

Marissa and Nick nodded to a teenage boy walking his dog on an otherwise deserted Main Street. A clouded moon provided the only light.

"This must be how the cops feel," she whispered, "before they nab someone." Nervous energy filled her and, by the time they arrived at the hardware store, she was almost skipping. She motioned Nick down the driveway between Walter's store and the funeral home.

A bright light shone in the apartment window above. "Looks like J.J.'s home," Nick said.

Marissa crept farther down the driveway, eyeing the side of the hardware store. "If you'll shine the flashlight along the bottom row of shingles, I think I can find Uncle Walter's secret door."

Nick flicked on the light, shielded it with his hand and scanned the shingles with the beam.

"Right there," she said. "You can hardly see it. It used to be a dog door for a Dalmation."

"I didn't know Walter had a dog. Does he leave him here all night?"

"No, Rosco's been gone since last year. My uncle replaced the dog door with a small door with a lock. Now he uses it for loading supplies from the driveway into the storeroom."

She rotated the dial on the lock, stopping at the numbers for the month, day and year of Walter's birthday. The lock clicked and she opened the door. "The opening is small but I can fit through. I'll let you in at the front of the store."

Nick shone the flashlight into the opening and Marissa crawled into the dusty storeroom. She curbed a sneeze and brushed the dust from her clothes. Unable to see in the dark, she felt for the wall switch and turned on the light. After making her way down an aisle, she doused the light from the control by the front door. The bells over the door seemed to jingle extra loud when she let Nick in.

Nick made his way to the side display window that faced the funeral home. "This'll be a good vantage point. We can see the lights in J.J.'s apartment."

Marissa joined him at the window. Nick stood behind her and leaned forward, holding her so she wouldn't fall into the display. His warm breath on the back of her neck made her feel warm all over. "We can see anyone coming up the driveway, too," he said.

"We might be here a while," she said. "Let's see if we can find some chairs in the back."

Nick shone the beam on the wooden floor and down the aisle. Marissa followed him to the storeroom. Nick entered and beamed the light on the walls.

"Here's a couple of folding chairs," he said. "Take the flashlight and I'll carry the chairs to the window."

He handed her the flashlight and tossed her a dark cloth that had been draped on them. Then he loaded both chairs in one arm and headed for the window.

Marissa was about to deposit the cloth on a shelf, when she felt its stiffness. She shone the light on it and gasped when the beam revealed a typewriter cover with Smith Corona printed on it. "Nick, come back and look at this."

Nick came back and inspected the cover. "Does Walter have a typewriter?" he asked.

"Not as far as I know. But Tizzie told me her stolen one was a Smith Corona and its cover was never returned. This one's not even dusty."

Nick put down the chairs. "Walter wrote those threats?"

"I can't believe this. That would mean he probably set the bombs, too."

Her words were drowned by the bells that jingled over the door and her uncle's voice demanding, "Who's here?"

Marissa froze.

"I know you're back there," Walter said. "I could see the beam from your flashlight from the street."

The lights clicked on and flooded the store, revealing Walter at the light switch.

"It's me, Uncle Walter. Nick and I thought we saw a light inside and when you didn't answer the door, I came in through the storeroom to make sure you were all right."

Walter walked toward them.

"Marissa." He nodded. "And Nick."

Marissa prepared herself for whatever he had to say. But unable to keep their discovery from him, she shoved the typewriter cover at him. "Where did you get this?"

Walter took it and inspected it. "Don't know what you mean," he said, handing it back. "Where'd you find it?"

"It's Tizzie's. She told me it was taken when her typewriter was stolen. Nick and Gregory and I received threats that were written on her machine while it was missing. We found the cover in your storeroom."

Walter looked at them. "You've got to get out of town." His words were urgent. "Someone is after you."

"Who?" Marissa asked.

He shifted from one foot to the other. "I can't tell you anything without risking your safety."

"What can you tell me about the bombs that were put in front of our cars?"

"What cigars?"

"Not cigars. Bombs were placed in front of Nick's and my cars."

"Bombs? Is that how your car got burned up?"

"Did you put them there?"

Walters eyes filled with fire. "I'd never try to kill you."

"How about the threats?"

He looked at his feet and mumbled. "Okay, so I wrote the notes. The only way I could keep you two and Gregory safe was to get you out of town. But I know nothing about bombs. You've got to believe me. You have to leave town."

Nick stepped forward. "If our lives are in danger, we need to know who's after us and why."

Walter took them each by an arm and steered them to the door. "The less you two know, the easier it'll be for you." He faced Nick. "You've got to convince Marissa to leave Spindrift Cove."

Marissa had seen that look on Walter's face before. "I think we've reached a stalemate. I'm not leaving town until I find out what's going on."

"Think about what's happening, Walter," Nick said. "You'll be way ahead of the game if you'll tell everyone Candi is alive. If you don't now, they're sure to find out on their own." He slid his hand into Marissa's. "Come on. Let's go."

As they were leaving, Walter shouted, "Marissa! I'm asking you to leave because I love you!"

30

EVIDENCE SEARCH

Marissa sat shivering beside Nick in the oleander bushes outside J.J.'s apartment. Their stakeout place was not so good nor as comfortable as the one they had in the store, but it would work. No jingle came from the bell over the hardware store door, so Marissa knew Walter hadn't gone home. The pleading look in his eyes haunted her. He'd told her he loved her many times before but never with such fervor. He was actually shaking.

So her uncle wrote the threats to protect them. This she could believe. As for the bombs, she didn't know what to think.

The light shining through the side display window went out and she heard the bell jingle when Walter left.

"Do you think he'll eventually come clean?" Nick asked.

Marissa warmed her hands in her pockets. "Oh, how I wish he would do something soon. He could end up in jail if he doesn't come up with a believable explanation."

Nick pulled her below the tops of the bushes. "Here comes a car."

A dark sedan drove past and parked behind J.J.'s apartment, next to his black hearse. A wiry man and a stocky woman emerged.

"Only you would get us invited to a party in a funeral home," the woman said.

Marissa nudged Nick.

The man led the woman up the steps to J.J.'s apartment. "It'll be something to tell the kids about tomorrow."

J.J. came onto the landing above and Marissa crouched down even farther. "Where the hell you been?" J.J. asked. "Come on in."

Once the couple was inside, Marissa stood to ease the cramps in her legs. "He's going to be up there partying all night. Now what do we do?"

A light sedan drove into the driveway and she and Nick ducked again. The car drove past, parked beside the first one and a woman staggered out, full of New Year's cheer. A short man, singing "Michael, Row the Boat Ashore," stumbled from the car and helped the woman up the apartment steps with three others from the car chiming in behind.

"We may be in luck," Nick said. "If they're all as noisy as these people, no one will notice we're here."

Several more cars crept down the driveway and then a lone man appeared, his shoes crunching on the gravel.

Marissa whispered, "That's Uncle Walter."

"He must have been on his way to the party when he stopped at the store."

She held her breath as Walter passed them. When he was out of earshot, Marissa asked, "Do you think everyone's arrived?"

"Let's wait," Nick said. "It's almost midnight. Everyone should be inside by then."

A cold wind blew down the driveway and Marissa leaned into Nick for warmth. Huddled in the bushes, they waited until the first paper horn tooted and shouts of "Happy New Year" came through an open window.

"I'm ready," Marissa said. She ventured into the driveway, but the loud crunch of her shoes on the gravel warned her to move onto the grass.

Nick led the way on the grass next to the wall until they reached the front of the funeral home. He tried the door. No luck. He pulled a small screwdriver from his pocket and began working on the lock.

"Where'd you get that?" Marissa asked.

"I 'borrowed' it from your uncle's store. Thought we might need it."

He tried opening the lock several times without success. Marissa took the screwdriver from him. "Let me do it," she said. She pulled a hairpin from her pocket.

Nick chuckled. "Thank your brother for his burglary lessons. While you're fiddling with the lock, I'll check the other side for an open door."

Marissa ensured the coast was clear and proceeded to work on the lock. She'd almost conquered it when she heard a vehicle slow to a stop in front of the funeral home. She quickly hid her hairpin and the screwdriver.

"Great place for a party," a roly-poly man in a party hat said to her, joining her at the door.

"Uh, yes, pretty great. You might want to go around to the back. There's a staircase that'll take you there."

A pudgy woman in a long black coat and reeking of perfume clung to his arm. "Have you rung the bell?" she asked. "J.J. always answers the bell."

"Yes," Marissa said, hoping J.J. was in no rush to answer the door.

"What's a looker like you doing alone on New Year's Eve?" the man asked.

"Cliff, that's enough," the woman said. She turned to Marissa, "You probably refused more than one date for tonight, haven't you, honey?"

Nick joined them, putting his arm around Marissa's waist. "What do you think's keeping J.J.?"

The man offered Nick his hand. "Cliff Masters. I run Shady Oaks Cemetery in Ocean Bluffs and this is my wife, newly elected city councilwoman Francine." He puffed out his chest. "I hear J.J. throws one hell of a party."

"Herman Scruggs, hardware," Nick said, introducing himself. "And my new wife Bessie. Bessie's a ballerina."

Marissa kept the straightest face she could.

"How nice," the woman said. "My sister's neighbor sells tickets for the San Francisco Ballet. Maybe you know her."

The man leaned on the bell and Marissa thought quickly. "Maybe this place has another entrance. Herman, will you take a look?"

"Only if you come with me, sweetie," Nick said. He dragged her off just as J.J. opened the front door.

They rounded the corner of the building and Marissa burst out laughing. "Ballerina?"

"I hate showoffs," Nick said. "Francine is on the City Council," he added, mimicking the man.

"Shh."

"Cliff and Francie," J.J. said to the guests at the door. "I wondered where you were. Come on in." His words were slurred.

"Got a credit card with you?" Nick whispered.

"Does Santa have a beard?" She handed him a stack of several and he selected one.

Marissa and Nick watched as Francine and Cliff passed through the front door. When the man had cleared the doorframe, Nick whispered, "Quick. Follow me."

Marissa dashed with him to the closing door.

Nick inserted the card between the lock and the doorframe as it was about to shut.

"Something tells me you've done this before," Marissa said.

He pinched her side and she subdued a laugh. "I've had a bit of a lurid past myself."

They waited outside until they heard J.J.'s and his guests' footsteps shuffling up the inside stairs.

"There must be an inner staircase from the funeral home to J.J.'s apartment," Nick said. "We'll need to be extra quiet." He shoved the front door open.

Marissa stepped into the reception area and inhaled a strong scent of roses. A faint light from wall sconces lit the space on each side of a massive stone fireplace. Sounds of the party carried down through the ceiling. She was relieved any noise she and Nick might make would be masked by the celebration.

Suddenly the room went dark.

"He doused the lights from upstairs," Marissa said. "I can't see a thing." She felt her way in the dark. "I hope there aren't any corpses on display. We could easily trip over them."

Nick scanned the room with the flashlight. "According to Paco, we need to look for something called the preparation room."

Marissa's gaze followed the light around the huge carpeted reception area where the fireplace was flanked by two antique chairs that faced the front door. Then Nick shone the light down a long carpeted hall.

"Let's go this way," Nick said.

Marissa trailed him, pausing at an open door on the right. Nick walked in and scanned the room with light, resting the beam on two baskets of flowers with Italian words written on ribbons. He continued to move the light around the room. A chill shot through Marissa when it landed on the shoes of a corpse. She let out a muffled cry.

"Shhh." Nick put an arm around her waist.

A quick look and Marissa averted her eyes from the body—but not before she saw his pin-striped suit and a full view of the drawn face of a robust man who could have passed for a Mafia godfather.

"Keep going," she said, prodding Nick. "This place gives me the creeps."

She followed the light as Nick shone it along the wall to a door, which he slowly opened. The beam scanned across a room full of several empty caskets. "This must be where you choose a casket."

He closed the door and they proceeded down a hall that ended in a staircase to the second floor. "The steps to J.J.'s apartment," Nick said.

He trained the light on the wall and a third closed door. Nick tried the handle and the door opened.

Marissa's shoes made scuffing sounds when the carpeted floor gave way to cement as they entered the small room. An empty metal table, large enough to hold a body, stood next to a rack of men's clothing.

"This must be where J.J. puts the clothes on the bodies." She shivered. "How gruesome."

She walked to the back of the room and opened another door.

Nick flashed the beam inside. Marissa looked into the room as the light scanned two metal tables extending from a wall of cabinets. On the cabinet shelves stood a collection of filled bottles.

"Looks like this is where J.J. does the embalming," Nick said.

He walked in but Marissa held back. "Tell me there's no business today."

"No bodies," he said. "Come on in. This is the preparation room we're looking for." He led her to one of the tables.

She touched a small block of wood in a set of several that were spaced evenly along both edges of the table. "What do you think these are for?"

Nick studied them. "Maybe they elevate the body."

She moved closer and reeled backward at a resounding clang and a sharp pain that shot through her temple.

Nick's light flooded her face. "Are you okay? Judas Priest, you're bleeding."

She winced when he dabbed at the blood above her eye with his handkerchief. "What hit me?"

Nick directed the flashlight above the table, where a huge metal and fabric sling dangled from the ceiling. "He must use this thing to hoist the bodies off the tables."

Marissa shuddered and held his handkerchief to her throbbing head. "Let's do what we need to do and get out of here." She headed toward the cabinets and was about to check the doors when heavy footsteps thundered down the stairs to the hallway.

"He heard us." She clutched Nick's arm, her heart racing.

The footsteps approached them and stopped on the carpeted floor outside the dressing room. A light switch clicked and Marissa dug her fingers into Nick's arm.

We're caught, she thought. And there's nowhere to run.

They waited.

The steps receded and then faded.

"He's heading for the reception area," Marissa said. She heard the front door open and, after a pause, it clicked shut. Then came the sound of a latch being set.

The footsteps grew louder as he approached the room again. Nick's arm crept around Marissa but she couldn't stop shaking.

The footsteps stopped outside the door. She clung to Nick, hardly breathing.

Then the steps went up the staircase and the light switch clicked again. She heaved a sigh and waited for her shaking to stop.

"We better be quick," Nick said. "One more noise and he's going to come find us."

He let go of her and opened the doors to several cabinets but found only bottles of chemicals. Marissa winced with the creak of each hinge.

"No cabinet like Paco described," Nick said

"Don't bother with the rest of the cabinets." Marissa tried the door on the one at the end of the room. "It's got to be in this one."

Nick aimed the light on it. "Why's that?"

"It's the only one with a lock. It must contain something valuable. It could have been designed to hold lab coats but I'll bet the jewelry is in here."

Nick directed the light on a small lock below the handle while Marissa worked her hairpin and screwdriver. Within seconds, she opened the door.

"You really are good, wife Bessie Scruggs."

The light exposed shelves of shallow pull-out drawers stacked on shelves from floor to ceiling. She selected one from the middle shelf and pulled it out.

"Oh, my God!"

An array of emerald and diamond rings set in rows of black velvet sparkled before her. Even in the low light, the gleam of the stones stole her breath.

Nick pulled out another drawer of a similar array of garnet rings. "He must have cataloged them by stone. These have to be worth millions."

"It would take him years to steal this much. How do you think he did it?"

"There's too much here for one mortician to pocket by himself. I'll bet J.J. isn't the only one who's been pilfering jewelry."

"Other funeral directors?"

"Sure. Maybe even our friend Cliff, who we met at the door. They probably sell off this stuff a little at a time. All they need are contacts who can buy and resell it in other cities. Spindrift Cove is a perfect sleepy town to hide the stash."

Marissa's mind whirled. "Did you bring your point-and-shoot?"

Nick slipped a tiny camera from his pocket and shot photos of several of the drawers. "This should be enough evidence for Hendrick."

Marissa shoved the drawers back into the cabinet.

"Unbelievable," Nick said, slipping the camera back into his pocket.

"Wait a minute." Marissa slid open another drawer. "I'll bet he has a case for class rings, too. Let's check a few more."

She viewed drawers of amethysts, sapphires and several of diamonds.

"I think I found it," she said, pulling out a drawer of college rings. "Alabama, Harvard, Yale. He even has them alphabetized." She felt Nick lean over her shoulder. Her finger traced a row to an empty indentation between the rings for Oberlin and Rutgers.

"Princeton," they said in unison.

Marissa couldn't believe her eyes. "This is where the ring he put on Bubba would have been,"

Nick lingered a moment. Marissa could almost see the visions of Bubba reeling through his mind. "Are you okay?" she asked.

He took a breath, snapped another photo and slid the drawer back into the cabinet. "Let's get out of here."

Marissa followed him out of the room and into the dressing room.

"I could kill the bastard," he said. He stopped at the rack of clothes. "I'll bet he got Bubba's tuxedo jacket from this rack. It was probably meant for some other body. Here, hold the light."

Marissa shone the flashlight on the clothes and Nick pawed through the rack. He stopped at a pair of light blue trousers. "These are the same color as the jacket described in Bubba's report. Throw a light on the label."

He folded back the waistband and she aimed the beam on an Oscar de la Renta label.

"Oh my God," she said, reeling back. "Matching pants to the jacket Bubba had on."

"Are you sure?"

"Positive. An Oscar de la Renta label in the jacket was in the report. Except why would J.J. only use the jacket?"

Nick snapped a photo. "It's the biggest one here. He may have been able to squeeze Bubba into the jacket but not into these small pants."

Back outside, Marissa breathed deeply, welcoming the change from the stuffy air in the funeral home. "I can't wait to see Hendrick's face when we show him the photos we took. Can you develop them in your darkroom?"

"If you want to bring in 1999 in a darkroom. I was thinking we could spend the rest of New Year's Eve on the beach. I know a good one a short ride south of Spindrift Cove."

Marissa thought of snuggling with him at the ocean. An evening with Nick on the beach would be much more fun than schmoozing at the stuffy ComTech party she and Gregory had planned to attend.

"That's an even better idea," she said. "We could take the undeveloped roll to Hendrick."

"You're right, Sherlock." He pushed her bangs from her forehead. "How's that lump?"

Marissa touched the dried blood over her eye. "The patient will survive."

"And will sport quite a shiner in the morning."

"Not many can say they've been whacked in the skull by a corpse sling."

Nick kissed the top of her head. "I'll load some firewood into the trunk of the old car and we'll be off to a bonfire on the beach."

"That sounds perfect," she said.

31

UNANTICIPATED FIND

Marissa carried the beach blanket and flashlight and Nick lugged his guitar and firewood to a spot on the beach near the ocean. Both went back to the car a couple of times for empty buckets, paper, kindling and the picnic basket they'd packed from leftovers in his refrigerator.

Marissa gazed at the stars twinkling in the black sky. She scanned the sea beyond the crashing waves, remembering the corpse that had drifted in the week before. So much had happened since then. How alone she'd been that night on the beach and how lonely she would have felt tonight if Nick hadn't asked her to join him here. She'd hardly had time to think of Gregory.

Marissa helped Nick spread the blanket on the sand. The moonlight playing on his face reminded her of the way the flames from the fire in Walter's fireplace had thrown shadows on his face the first day she met him. She was glad she'd ventured to take him up on an evening of jazz at the Do Drop Inn.

She helped him dig a hole in the sand and stack the kindling.

"Would you toss me the matches?" Nick asked. "They're in the box with the wood."

She found them and dropped them into his hand. Feeling free, she twirled around in the sand, almost losing her balance.

Nick chuckled. "The San Francisco Ballet will disown you, Bessie Scruggs, if you screw yourself into the beach."

She laughed, dancing toward the ocean. "You're the one who would have to explain to the paramedics."

A series of flashes caught her unaware as she danced back toward him. She stopped. "I've been blinded. You used your camera motor thing!"

"Perfect action for a motor drive. Blink a few times and your eyes will clear. Wait till the paramedics see these shots."

Nick's joke fueled her giddiness and she laughed until she had him laughing and she had to hold her sides. His comment wasn't that funny but it released the tension from their escapade.

Nick gained enough composure to kneel and strike a few matches without success. He said, "That couple at J.J.'s is probably still looking out the back door, wondering why Bessie the ballerina didn't show up for the party."

Marissa bent to shield the match in his hands from the wind as he tried to light it. "And if they asked J.J., he's probably wondering who in the world he'd invited from the San Francisco Ballet."

Soon a spark ignited and spread from the match to the paper and the kindling, causing Marissa to gasp and withdraw from the huge blaze. Memories of her flame-engulfed Miata overcame her.

Nick leapt up and pulled her away from the fire. "We're both going to be a little crazy around fire for a while."

He gave her a gentle squeeze and knelt down on the blanket. She joined him, pleased at the way he comforted her. Composing herself, she scanned the waves. "How did you find this amazing place?"

"J.J. told me about it a while back," he said, opening the cooler. "I ran into him one night at the Perk and Turf and he gave me directions. Said it was his favorite spot. I never expected to be spending New Year's Eve on 'his beach.'" He made two baloney sandwiches and handed her one. "Some New Year's, isn't it? If I'm not taking you to a mortuary, I'm handing you lunch meat in the sand."

Better than the Comtech party, she thought. She would have worn her new black dress. Her hair would be piled on top of her head and her feet would hurt so much from her new heels. She moved closer to Nick.

"You seem a little quiet tonight," he said.

"I'm worried about Uncle Walter." She steadied two plastic wine glasses on the blanket as he filled them with chardonnay. "How could he lie to me about things so important? Had he been lying to Candi, too? Maybe she had good reason to leave him. I don't know if he's becoming senile or if he really could be dangerous."

There, she'd said it. She'd been thinking it for so long and hadn't the nerve to voice her feelings.

"You think your uncle has it in him to hurt someone?"

"Who can say? We know he stole Tizzie's typewriter and wrote those threats, so he might be the one who blew up my car."

"I can't imagine he'd do that. What would be his motive?"

"I wish I knew. He's done some pretty strange things lately. I don't know if I should fear him or fear *for* him."

"I don't think you need to worry about Walter. From what I've heard, he's a decent man. A man doesn't change overnight." He poked at the fire. "Walter took a lot of kidding after he married

Candi. No one thought his marriage would last. The man's got a lot of pride to protect now that she's gone."

"Did you think it would last?"

Nick took a sip of wine. "Hell, what do I know? I couldn't even tell my own wife was a lesbian. Who knows what problems they might have had?"

"I can't believe they had problems serious enough for her to leave him. Candi and I were pretty close. She seemed to adore him. Back then, I didn't realize how Uncle Walter could lie."

"You never know what might have gone on behind closed doors." Nick tossed a stick into the fire.

Marissa remained silent, considering the possibilities.

"I'm sorry," Nick said. "I know your uncle means a lot to you."

She sat entranced by the orange flames weaving into blue and green. Walter and Candi had seemed such a happy couple, she thought.

Finally Nick asked, "What do you think happened to Candi?"

Marissa had pondered over this so many times. "I don't know. First my uncle said she was sick. Then he told me she left to join some guy in Germany. Now he says she's been killed. Hendrick says she was last seen in Hong Kong. He doesn't know for sure whether she's alive or dead." She jammed her cold hands into her pockets. "Not knowing is the worst part."

Nick slipped his arm around her waist. "You've helped me put together the pieces about Bubba. Let me help you find out about Candi." His gaze met hers and a warmth traveled down her spine. She leaned into his shoulder, enjoying the comfort of his body. Having someone to help her find some answers would be welcome, she thought.

"I'd like that," she said. She placed a hand on his shoulder. "I'd also like to hear something come out of that guitar you brought with you."

He pulled her to him and gently kissed her cheek. She anticipated a long kiss. Instead, he reached for the instrument case and
pulled out his guitar.

He was playing the same game she was. Her reticence was
because of her recent breakup with Gregory. What could be the
cause of his?

After strumming a few chords, Nick played "Black is the Color
of My True Love's Hair," the ocean waves seeming to keep time
with the lilting rhythm. The second time through, he sang the
words directly to her. His voice wrapped her in velvet and she
could have listened to him until the sun rose.

When the last note faded into the ocean air, he set the guitar back into its case. "Your shiny black hair was the first thing
I noticed about you." He stood and helped her to her feet. "It's
midnight somewhere in the world," he said, drawing her to him.
"Happy New Year."

She yielded to his arms. He kissed her lightly on the forehead
and then gently on the lips, followed by a slow, tender kiss, leaving
her wanting more.

"Thank you for coming into my life," he whispered. His ten-
derness became a warm, deep kiss. Nothing else seemed to matter.

She clung to him, catching her breath.

Soon he lifted her chin. "How about a walk on the beach?"

She was reluctant to let go of him when she answered, "A walk
would be nice."

Marissa helped Nick fill buckets with ocean water and they carried them back to the smoldering fire. Then she packed up the
food and laughed with him as they folded the blanket in the gentle
wind. This was a simple joy she'd never shared with Gregory.

After she helped Nick load the car, he led her to the shore for a leisurely stroll. As they passed a boat launch, Nick shared stories of him and Bubba and their days on the ocean. The wind came up and Nick hurried Marissa away from the water. "See that grove of trees to the left? There's some picnic benches inside. Let's head over."

Marissa struggled to keep from stumbling in the dark, so Nick flicked on the flashlight and shone it on their route through the trees. She led the way, following his scanning light until it landed on a picnic bench inside a small gazebo. Sliding onto the bench, she made room for him and he joined her.

"You really have a shiner from that sling," he said, inspecting her eye with the light.

"I'll bet it makes me look real tough."

"I sure wouldn't mess with you."

"You may have to if you don't get that flashlight out of my eyes."

He placed it on the picnic table, and as the beam flicked past the trees, Marissa caught a glimpse of something shiny in the bushes.

"Wait. Shine the light outside the gazebo."

Nick played the beam around the picnic area in front of them.

"There," she said. "Beyond the trees. A green car." She lowered her voice. "You think someone's watching us?"

"I doubt it. It's probably some kids necking."

But her intuition told her otherwise. "Let's get out of here. This place feels creepier than the funeral home."

"Where's your sense of adventure?"

She ignored his challenge to investigate. He aimed the flashlight toward their return route and she followed him and the beam back to his car.

Thoughts of the green car remained with Marissa as they drove away. She sat up when Nick unexpectedly pulled onto the shoulder and pointed the headlights toward the grove where they'd been sitting. Glints of the green car shone through the trees. He drove closer.

"What are you doing? You're going to get somebody really upset."

He kept creeping nearer to the car.

"Nick, stop!"

"Oh, my God." He closed his eyes and seemed to be catching his breath.

"What's the matter?"

He opened his eyes. "We've found Bubba's car."

32

RISING DOUBTS

Nick switched off the ignition, keeping the headlights pointed on the green Ford.

"We better call the police," Marissa said.

"You have a cell phone with you?"

She shook her head. "I lost it in the ocean."

"You did what?"

"A wave swiped it from me when I was pulling Bubba out."

He snickered. "You have the strangest experiences, woman. Let's get out and take a look at the car."

"Mmm, I don't think so. This is a crime scene. We don't want to destroy any footprints."

He smiled. "Damn, you're smart." He started the car and they backed out. "Let's find the nearest phone. The town of Granville's a stone's throw from here."

They drove down the dark highway. "What does your watch say?" Marissa asked.

He waved a bare arm and increased the lights on the dashboard. "You're in the country, woman. We don't live by the clock here."

Marissa bent toward her wrist, surprised to realize she'd forgotten her watch. In fact she couldn't remember the last time she'd strapped it on. Maybe she'd already adopted the country way of life.

She switched on the radio and navigated past the squawks until an announcer shouted above raucous turmoil, "It's almost 2:30 in San Francisco and the crowd is as wild as it's been since nine o'clock tonight." She switched off the program. "It's 2:30."

The sign for Granville popped up almost immediately. Nick drove until they saw a street with some activity. He stopped outside a large home with a brightly lit picture window. Rock music and laughter spilled from inside. Marissa could see a crowd of men and women with party hats dancing among streamers.

She and Nick left the car and approached the front door. Nick rang the doorbell, but the dancing continued.

"I don't think they can hear us above the music," Marissa said. She knocked on the door while Nick rang the bell again and then pounded on the door. Suddenly it opened and a shapely woman in a slinky black dress stood before them with a half-full cocktail glass.

"Hi there," she said, weaving. "You must be the Hoffmans. Come on in." She flung open the door and waved her hand with the glass, spilling some of her cocktail on the plush carpet.

"We're not the Hoffmans," Nick said, dodging the remainder of her drink. "My name is Nick and this is Marissa. We need a phone. It's an emergency."

"Hey, everybody," the woman shouted. "The Hoffmans are here." She turned to Nick. "Let me take your coats." To Marissa, she said, "Quite a shiner you got there."

Sounds of the Rolling Stones drowned out all conversation.

"We're not staying," Nick shouted. "We need a phone."

Marissa spotted a wall phone at the far side of the room and dodged a dancing couple to reach it.

"Where'd you get the black eye?" a gray-haired man in an Oakland Raiders sweatshirt asked her. "Have a fight with your boyfriend?"

Marissa rubbed her fingers across the crusted blood.

"Wanna dance?" He whirled her around to the music.

"No thanks," she said, struggling to keep her balance. "I need to make a call."

He frowned. "Okay, let me show you to the phone." He led her to an end table and cleared the streamers until he unearthed a phone.

Marissa punched zero for the operator and asked to be connected to the police in Ocean Bluffs.

"The police?" the man said. He poked at a dancing couple. "Shhh. This lady's calling the police!"

Word spread fast and everyone stopped partying. Marissa felt all eyes on her. "This call is an emergency," she said. "It has nothing to do with your party."

The crowd tittered and then became quiet. She knew they were listening as she described the green car to Officer Hendrick.

"What's the address here?" Marissa asked anyone who could help.

Someone shouted it and she provided it to Hendrick.

"Excuse me," a wiry young man said as she hung up. He crossed to her. "I couldn't help overhear. Were you reporting that green Ford parked in the trees down the road?"

"Do you know something about it?" Marissa asked. "Like how long it's been there?"

"I first saw it there a couple days before Christmas. I've been curious about it ever since."

Nick joined them. "Do you know how it got there?"

"No. I wasn't around there before that."

"Did you see anything else unusual happening around there?"

"I did," a man with streamers around his neck piped up. 'My dog Peppy had to go out late the night of the 23rd. It must have been past midnight and I see this car pull up. It was towing a small motorboat."

"What color was the boat?" Nick asked.

"It was too dark for me to see the color of the car or the boat, but I can tell you the car was a big one, like a Caddie or one of those big fancy ones."

"Did you see who was driving?"

"A man. He was a big guy. I stopped to watch him back the car and the boat to the launch. When he got out to put the boat in the water, I thought it was pretty weird that he'd be taking a cruise after midnight."

"Which way did the boat head?" Nick asked.

"Can't remember. I didn't watch for too long. I guess he headed straight out."

Marissa asked the crowd, "Did anyone here see him come back?"

The man with the streamers said, "I didn't see him again, but next morning when I took Peppy out, both the big car and the boat were gone."

"Did you see the green Ford, too?" Nick asked.

His questions were interrupted by the ring of the doorbell. The tipsy woman answered the door again.

"Ocean Bluffs Police," a familiar voice announced. A hush fell on the room. "I'm Officer Hendrick and this is Officer Sanchez. Is Marissa DeSantos here?"

Marissa directed the officers to the men who had seen the car and boat before Christmas. While Hendrick questioned Marissa and Nick, Sanchez disappeared into another room with the men.

When both officers had finished their interrogations, Hendrick asked Marissa, "Want to show us where the car is?"

She heard a scuffle behind her and turned to see the partygoers putting on their coats.

"Cool," one said. "We'll all go in my van."

"Only Marissa and Nick," Hendrick said. Several in the group groaned.

The stereo music started up again and Sanchez raised his voice to ask Nick, "Where's your car?"

Marissa and Nick took the officers outside and Nick pointed out his Chevy.

"We'll follow you," Hendrick said.

Marissa slid into the passenger seat and she and Nick drove down the road to the beach. She opened the window to feel the cool air on her cheeks.

"Do you think the big car the man described was J.J.'s?"

"J.J.'s Lincoln sure fits his meager description."

When they arrived at the spot where they'd been earlier, Nick pulled over and the police car parked behind. Marissa opened the car door to get out but Hendrick stopped her. "You folks can go home now. We'll take it from here. Thanks for your help."

She tucked her feet back into the car and Hendrick closed the door.

Leaning over Marissa, Nick asked Hendrick through the open window, "What'll you do now?"

Sanchez joined Hendrick at the car. "We'll tape off the area and wait for help."

"Would you guys take care of what's in the trunk?" Nick asked. "There are probably some Christmas presents in there for Bubba's folks."

"Sure thing," Hendrick said. "We'll see to it. You folks look like you could use some rest."

"Rest?" Marissa said. "I've been wondering if you two ever sleep. I've been calling your department at all hours and you're always there."

Sanchez replied, "We work some days but mostly nights. Not so bad for me. I'm single. But Hendrick's a newlywed."

Although it was dark, Marissa could tell Hendrick was blushing.

"Wife's a real looker," Sanchez added.

Hendrick elbowed him. "On your way, partner."

When they moved to leave, Marissa said, "But we've only told you half our story."

"I thought you told us everything about the car."

"Yes, about the car, but we made another discovery tonight."

Nick took his camera from under the seat and removed the film. He described what they found in the funeral home. "It's all in here," he said handing the cartridge to Hendrick.

On the way back to Spindrift Cove, Marissa rehashed the evening's events in her mind. Nick spoke little, his eyes intent on the dark road. "What do you think happened to Bubba?" Marissa finally asked.

"You mean considering all we found out tonight?"

Should she couch her words? She tried a direct approach. "Do you think J.J. killed Bubba?"

She could see Nick's jaw tighten. "I think there's no question about it."

Thank goodness he agreed with her, she thought. "How do you think he did it?"

Nick squinted at the unlit road. "I've been trying to piece together what might have happened. Maybe J.J. invited Bubba to go fishing in the boat and Bubba agreed if they could take two cars so he could leave from there for L.A."

"And then what?"

"I'm thinking J.J. tricked Bubba. When they rendezvoused, he didn't bring the boat. When Bubba got out of his car, J.J. shot him."

"You mean the fishing trip was a ruse to get Bubba away from Spindrift Cove?"

"Yes. And in the early hours of the morning when no one was up yet."

"So then he took Bubba's body back to the funeral home in his car? That makes sense. He shaved, dressed and wrapped him there. Eugh. That's gruesome."

"Then after midnight, he brought him back in his boat, a distance from the Cove."

"He probably figured no one would see him at that hour," Marissa said.

"Then he took Bubba out to sea, got rid of him and drove back with his boat."

Marissa squirmed in her seat. "What a sick man."

"Deranged," Nick said. "I hope the cops see him that way. Who knows what they might drum up if he's one of their own?"

Nick rose the next morning, remembering he'd promised Pastor John he'd help clean the chapel. After showering and dressing, he arrived to find himself alone, glad to have time to think of the night before.

He was fairly confident Hendrick believed their story about searching the funeral home. But Sanchez didn't seem convinced that Nick and Marissa weren't breaking and entering. This could throw a wrench in a case against J.J. Nick had explained they didn't knock down any doors or climb through any windows. They just walked in. Neither he nor Marissa had mentioned keeping the lock open with a credit card nor picking the lock on the cabinet.

Nick grabbed a dust cloth and began dusting the pews, his thoughts roaming to Marissa. She was a good detective and seemed earnest in finding out what happened to Bubba. He liked her but feared he was breaking a promise to himself about shying away from attachments to women. At least Marissa wasn't a lesbian. Still, he'd had no clue about his ex-wife, either. But that wasn't his fear this time. You never knew what kind of secrets a woman could be hiding. He'd better cool it. At least till he got to know her better.

He scraped a piece of gum from the end of the pew and deposited it in the trash. The next service here would be Bubba's. Damn! He felt so alone.

He considered waxing the pews to keep his mind occupied. Naw, he thought. Bubba wouldn't have given a rat's ass whether the pews shone. Damn J.J.

The creak of the chapel door opening announced Pastor John waddling in. "I thought I might find you here, Nick." His eyes intent, he motioned Nick to sit in a pew. "Got a minute to talk?"

Nick nodded.

"I've been meaning to ask you, how well do you know Walter Schmidkin?"

Now where could this be leading? "I only met him a couple of times," Nick said. "We've never spoken more than a few words. What's the problem?"

John squeezed in beside him. "Tizzie and Margaret have told me a few things that, at first, I ignored. Today I've had other thoughts."

Nick waited for him to continue.

"They both think Walter may have killed Bubba and Candi."

Nick sat up. "You've got to be kidding. Where did they come up with that?"

The pastor picked up a polishing cloth and ran it across the top of the pew in front of them. "Margaret says Candi applied for a passport for herself but none for Walter. And she said she saw Walter buying rat poison. She thinks Candi told him she was leaving him and the country. So he killed her with the poison."

Nick laughed. "Pretty rash assumptions. You don't believe her, do you?"

"Tizzie took Walter's fingerprints off a water glass. She says they match the prints on her typewriter."

Nick remained unconcerned. Walter had already admitted he'd sent the threats to get Marissa and Gregory to leave town and to keep Nick from snooping. But he wondered where Tizzie might have learned how to take fingerprints.

The pastor added, "Tizzie was right when she said Candi flaunted herself. That had to get Walter mad."

Nick silently agreed, letting John continue.

"And you won't believe this. Margaret's brother-in-law heard Walter threaten to kill Bubba."

"I hadn't heard that."

"According to Marissa, he said it after Bubba was already dead."

"So what's your point, John?"

"Just that, after I thought about it, I wondered if Walter only said it to make people think he didn't know Bubba was already dead. So nobody would consider him a suspect."

Hmm, Nick thought. Bubba had a real crush on Candi. He hoped his friend had been smart enough not to pursue it. If Bubba was messing with Candi and Walter caught him, could Walter have killed him? Had he gone with J.J. when J.J. supposedly went fishing with Bubba? No way. That's ridiculous.

Nick shook his head as if to shake off the thought. Walter wouldn't have the guts to kill anyone. But J.J. would. Could Walter have paid J.J. to help him kill Bubba? If Bubba was screwing Candi and Bubba knew about the jewelry thefts, both Walter and J.J. would have motives for wanting him out of the way.

Nick changed the subject. "I'm pretty sure Candi's still alive. The Ocean Bluffs police have trailed her to Hong Kong."

The pastor's eyes narrowed. "You mean I performed a memorial service for a woman who's alive? Then whose ashes are in the urn?"

"I wouldn't worry about it, John. I don't believe there's a law against it. The ashes could have come from anywhere."

"But what about Bubba? Do you think Walter could have killed him?"

"I wouldn't even consider it," Nick heard himself say. "Walter's an upstanding man."

Now what made him say that? he wondered. Marissa had gotten to him. He was protecting her uncle when Walter could have been in cahoots with J.J. Or maybe Walter was capable of committing a crime of passion. If Nick told Marissa he suspected her uncle, their working together to find out the truth about both Bubba and Candi would halt immediately. What's more, he'd lose Marissa's respect.

The pew shook when the pastor rose. "Thanks, Nick. I'm not sure I agree, but I'll think about what you said. To tell you the truth, I don't know who I can trust anymore." Wiping his brow with a handkerchief, he said, "The people I feel most sorry for are Bubba's parents. There's not much I can say to comfort them."

"I'm sure they appreciate whatever you've been saying."

"You think so? I'm not so sure. Thank the Lord for J.J. He's better at these kinds of things. I'll be taking the Maselli's to the mortuary to introduce them to him."

Marissa sat on Bubba's bed and used his phone to check her voice-mail at the Clutter Clinic.

"Marissa, Judd Marks here. You helped me out last year with the mess in my apartment. Unfortunately, the clutter's pretty much all back. Can you give me a call?"

Marissa frowned. Keeping a place clutter free required developing good habits. Some clients never learned.

After the beep, another message.

"Marissa, this is Ralph Kravitz." The sound of her landlord's voice brought her to attention. "Sorry to bother you on New Year's Day. Frank, in the apartment above yours, started filling his bathtub and left home without shutting the water off. The floor flooded and dripped through your ceiling. Most of your floor and furniture is shot."

Marissa's breath caught in her throat. Her brand new carpet! And the beautiful desk Candi gave her!

The message continued. "We're airing out the place now. You might want to look into your insurance to see what it covers."

Marissa replaced the receiver in a daze. No car. Damaged furniture. She dialed Gregory's number to ask for help and stopped short. No boyfriend either.

She called her insurance company and then her landlord and asked him to let the claims examiner in whenever he arrived. Good lord. Two insurance men in a matter of days.

Satisfied she'd done all she could, she lay down on the bed. What else could go wrong?

33

ABRUPT EXIT

Pastor John led Mr. and Mrs. Maselli up the concrete walkway to the funeral home. Passing the red geraniums and pink begonias surrounding the gray wooden building, he wished the flowers at the chapel would thrive like them. Mrs. Maselli seemed to appreciate the setting as she nodded her approval to her husband.

"The doorbell's connected to J.J.'s apartment upstairs," the pastor said, pressing the button. A chime sounded loud enough to hear across the street. "Sometimes it takes him a while to get down."

Mrs. Maselli smiled nervously.

The door opened and J.J. welcomed them, dressed in a white shirt and black tie that matched his blazer and pants. Perfect attire for his role of funeral director, the pastor thought.

"Please come in," J.J. said.

The soothing harp music coming from the speakers in the reception area made John wish he could afford church music better than Margaret's.

J.J. offered his hand. "You must be Mr. and Mrs. Maselli. I was so sorry to hear about Bubba. He was a favorite here in town."

As much as Pastor John wanted to dismiss the conversation he'd had with Tizzie and Margaret, he found himself wondering if Walter might have killed Bubba. Walter and J.J. were good enough friends for J.J. to help Walter.

John followed everyone through the spacious reception area where cream-colored walls rose to a high ceiling. His feet sank into the deep red oriental rug. The pastor was always impressed when he visited the funeral home. If only he could convey a similar rich and respectful aura in his chapel.

They passed a huge fireplace flanked by antique cherry-wood chairs with seats and backs that matched the carpet. John admired the cut of J.J.'s blazer as he led them into an office, where more harp music was piped in. Thick green wall-to-wall carpeting and potted palms lent a feeling of a lush sanctuary.

John's gaze traveled the room and rested on a cherry book-case that displayed three metal urns softly lit from behind. Spaced equally, the urns left room for a fourth on the end.

J.J. hadn't rearranged them since he sold the one for Candi, the pastor thought. If the Masellis choose cremation, at least J.J. will have some authentic ashes to put into the urn this time.

His gaze went to Mrs. Maselli, whose eyes were fixed on the urns. She quickly looked away and blinked back tears.

J.J. offered seats to the pastor and the Masellis. Mr. Maselli cradled his wife's elbow and led her to one of the chairs.

J.J. sank into a huge chair behind a massive cherry desk. "I know this is a terrible time for you," he said. "I hope to make it as easy as possible."

"Thank you," the couple said in unison.

J.J. had a comforting manner that John had practiced in front of a mirror. But his rendition never achieved the smooth quality of J.J.'s.

Mr. Maselli cleared his throat. "I understand you were among the last to see our son."

"Would you tell us about it?" his wife asked.

J.J. leaned back, his head almost touching the potted palm behind him. "I may have spoken to him last. I don't know who might have been the last to see him." He formed a steeple with his fingers. "Bubba and I had planned to go fishing two days before Christmas." Collapsing his fingers, he said, "I was surprised when he called the night before and told me he was canceling so he could drive down early and see you."

"And that was the last time you spoke to him?" Mrs. Maselli asked. "The night of the twenty-second?"

"Yes, it was."

An uncomfortable silence followed, forcing J.J. to speak again. "Pastor John tells me you'd like to discuss a memorial service."

John thought J.J. had changed the subject a bit too fast. "Doesn't Bubba usually help you in the funeral home during the week?" he asked.

"You're right. And he did a fine job."

"Bubba told us he helps . . . I mean, he helped out every week-day morning," Mrs. Maselli said. "So you would have seen him the morning of the twenty-third."

Pastor John sat back, satisfied he'd reopened the subject.

"Yes," J.J. said, crossing his arms and looking at the ceiling. "I forgot. I believe I did see him that morning. He said he didn't feel much like fishing."

"That's not at all like Bubba," Mr. Maselli said. "If Bubba makes plans, he sticks to them—especially when it comes to fishing. Nothing could come between him and a day on the water."

J.J. avoided the man's eyes. "I wish I could explain," he said, wiping his forehead with a handkerchief. "I'm as stumped as you are."

Mrs. Maselli sat up straight with an air of confidence that surprised the pastor. "We're not interrogating you, Mr. Haggersby. We're only trying to find out how he spent his last day."

John waited eagerly for the funeral director's reaction.

J.J. rose, approached Mrs. Maselli's chair and placed a hand on her shoulder. "Now, now. I know it's very upsetting that I can't provide you the information you want. I don't know anything else."

The woman edged her shoulder from his hand until it dropped away.

"Maybe we should get on with making the arrangements," her husband said.

J.J. drew a leather binder from the desk drawer. "Yes, I have several plans we can discuss."

"I don't think so," Mrs. Maselli said, rising from her chair.

Her husband looked up in surprise. J.J. stepped back.

Uncertain what to do, John rose. "Maybe we can come back another time?"

"I'm sorry if I've upset you," J.J. said. "I hope you'll come back when the initial shock wears off."

Mrs. Maselli turned up her nose and marched to the door, her husband rushing after her. The pastor waited for J.J. to move and then followed them all out.

Once John was outside with the couple and the door closed behind them, Bubba's mother said to him, "I'm sorry, Pastor. I must make amends with the Lord. There's something about that man that sets me off."

Marissa leaned Bubba's surfboard against the back of the Maselli's rented trailer.

Bubba's father hoisted the board into the trailer bed. "Is that the last of everything?" he asked.

Nick hustled down the stairs of the Pajama Factory with one more box and shoved it beside the surfboard. "If we find anything else, I'll send it to you." He slid three envelopes off the top of the carton and handed them to Mrs. Masselli. "Bubba had asked me to pick up his mail. I found these bills in his box."

After leafing through them, Mrs. Maselli opened the one marked Pacific Bell.

Her husband downed the last of a Dr. Pepper. "Thanks, you two, for referring us to that nice funeral director in Ocean Bluffs. And thanks for helping Pastor John make the memorial service just like Bubba would have wanted it. I don't know what we would have done without you. Isn't that right, Karen?"

Mrs. Maselli looked up from the phone bill. "What? Oh, yes. Thank the Lord in heaven you were here." She pasted on a smile that vanished when she continued to read the bill. "Frank, did Bubba have any friends in Munich or Hong Kong?"

34

WEDDING SURPRISE

Marissa and Nick waved goodbye as Mr. and Mrs. Maselli drove from the curb and headed south on Main Street toward L.A.

Nick stared into the distance, looking as if he'd just bid goodbye to his good friend. "That was nice of you to offer to pay for Bubba's phone bill," he said to Marissa.

Marissa slipped the bill out of the envelope. "I wish I could say I did it out of kindness." She scanned the bill. "I want to trace these calls."

"Let's see," he said, edging beside her.

She flipped to the second page. "A call to Munich on December 22nd. Also, two to Hong Kong the morning of the twenty-third. That's between the day Candi disappeared and the day Bubba was found." She inserted the bill back into the envelope. "Do you know if Bubba knew Candi well?"

"He did some work for her a few times. In the garden and in the house."

"And she apparently asked him to look after her business in Ocean Bluffs. Were they good friends?"

"I'd say so." Nick smoothed his mustache. "I always thought Bubba had a crush on Candi. She's a striking woman."

"They must have a pretty big age difference. Did he ever mention he had any feelings for her?"

"He didn't have to. Bubba's feelings were written all over his face. Paco and I used to look forward to poker games with him."

"You don't think he and Candi—"

"Now don't go putting words into my mouth."

"He did, didn't he?"

"I don't know anything for sure."

"Why didn't you tell me?"

Nick stepped back. "Nice first impression I'd have made: 'Hi. I'm Nick Devereaux. I suspect my best friend is screwing your aunt.' Besides, I had no idea Candi's disappearance had anything to do with Bubba's Christmas vacation."

Marissa waved the bill. "If anyone sees this and links these numbers to Candi, they're going to suspect Walter. If Walter thought something was going on between Candi and Bubba, he'd have a real motive for killing Bubba."

Alone in Bubba's apartment, Marissa dropped a teaspoon of instant coffee into a styrofoam cup. How good a cup of espresso would taste about now, she thought. Her mind traveled to her water-soaked San Francisco apartment and the hope that her espresso machine made it through the flood. She lifted the whistling tea kettle from the stove, grateful for Nick's generosity in lending it to her, and poured boiling water over the coffee granules.

Thank goodness Bubba's apartment is furnished, she thought. The coffee isn't great but at least she had a place to sit and to sleep.

She opened a window wide enough to hear the waves crashing on the beach. She thought of the claims examiner who had declared her Miata a total loss. Sadness had combined with relief when the truck towed it down Walter's driveway. At least the burned-out shell was no longer a reminder of her once-prized possession. She'd deal with the loss of her car another time. Now she was more concerned with Hendrick's imminent visit.

She was straightening a cushion on a chair when a knock came on the door. She ran a hand through her hair. "Coming!"

When she opened the door, she found Hendrick and Sanchez both dressed in suits and ties.

"Sorry we're late," Hendrick said. Sanchez only nodded, reinforcing Marissa's dislike of dealing with this man who kept most of his thoughts to himself.

Sanchez's eyes swept the room. "Nice studio," he said. He walked to the stuffed trout over the bed and added. "You and Nick both live here now?"

Marissa quickly answered, "No. Nick owns the building and has a place of his own. He's letting me stay here. We cleaned out all of Bubba's stuff."

"You still have your place in San Francisco, like you told Haggersby?" Sanchez asked.

"Uh huh. This is only temporary." Why did Sanchez always make her feel as if she had to explain? "Have a seat," she said, indicating the only two chairs. "You fight over which one. Both of you up for coffee? All I have is instant."

Sanchez refused but Hendrick was game. She took a Perk and Turf cup from the cupboard and spooned in some Nescafe.

"Cream and sugar?" she asked. "Bubba only stocked Cremora."

"Black is fine," Hendrick said. "I see you still have your shiner." Accepting the cup she offered, he asked, "How'd you get it?"

"Oh, it's nothing. I bumped into something."

Sanchez was silent, his gaze continually traveling the room.

Hendrick asked, "You and your boyfriend getting along?"

"You mean Nick? He's not . . . We're getting along fine."

Hendrick looked for a place to set his cup and, finding none, put it on the floor. "That thing you bumped into wasn't his fist?"

"Absolutely not! I got it in the funeral home while Nick was taking pictures. I collided with the sling J.J. uses to move the corpses."

Hendrick laughed and Sanchez showed the first sign of a smile.

"If Nick hadn't told me about your night at Haggersby's place," Hendrick said, "I wouldn't have bought that one."

"Not an evening I'd want to repeat."

Sanchez sat forward. "By the way, thanks for the snapshots." Each time she became wary of him, he would throw her off guard with a pleasantry.

"My pleasure. Are they enough to nail J.J.?"

"Unfortunately, no," Hendrick answered. "As a matter of fact, that's why we wanted to see you. We have a few more questions about the night you found Bubba's body."

"Whatever I can do to help."

Hendrick started by asking about the exact time she saw the body in the ocean. The session soon became an interrogation about J.J. Hendrick would ask and Sanchez would follow up. When they finished, she pressed them again. "Do you believe J.J. killed Bubba?"

Shifting in his chair, Hendrick said, "I wish we could talk about it. It's still under investigation."

Good lord, how much more evidence did they need? "Maybe you can explain something. If I were J.J. and I wanted to dispose of a body and I had access to a crematorium, I think I'd burn it rather than toss it into the ocean where it could surface later."

Sanchez came to life. "You would think so. Except J.J. doesn't have a crematorium at the mortuary."

"Closest one," Hendrick said, "is several miles away. They tag the bodies on arrival."

"Control over them is tight," Sanchez added. "It would be tough to sneak in a body for cremation."

Not such a good idea, Marissa thought. She collected Hendrick's empty cup. "Would you like more?" He refused and she couldn't blame him. That instant stuff was awful. "Any idea yet who set the bomb in front of my car?"

"That one we're getting closer on," Sanchez said.

They told her the same thing last time. "And?"

"Nothing concrete yet. We're working on it."

They must practice these replies from a script, she thought.

She crossed to the desk where she'd put Bubba's phone bill. "Thought you might want to see this," she said, handing it to Hendrick. "Looks like Bubba might have been making calls to my Aunt Candi. I tried calling the numbers in Hong Kong and they belong to hotels. No one there remembers her. The calls to Gunther Friedlich in Germany I already told you about."

Hendrick glanced at the bill and handed it back. "Thanks. You can keep this."

"We got copies from the phone company." Sanchez said.

An awkward silence followed, broken by Marissa. "Can you tell me what you think about my aunt?"

The two men rose as if on cue. "We think she's all right," Hendrick said. "We don't know much beyond that."

Marissa smiled. At least they thought Candi was alive.

"I'll walk you downstairs," she said. "I could use a breath of fresh air."

The men's steps on the wooden stairs shook the staircase and resounded in the atrium. When a gray-haired woman peeked out of her apartment door, Marissa thanked God the men weren't in uniform. A visit to her by the cops wasn't something she wanted to hear in the next morning's gossip.

When Marissa and the men reached the street, she was surprised to see Daphne, the deputy coroner, pull up to the curb. "Glad I caught you, hon," she said to Hendrick through the open window.

Marissa did a double take. Hon?

Daphne nodded to Marissa. "Nasty bruise you have there."

Sanchez grunted his thanks to Marissa and got into the squad car.

"I had some business here at the Cove," Daphne said to Hendrick, "and they told me at your office you were in town, too."

Daphne had business at the Cove? Marissa wondered. Maybe kissy-face business with J.J. What's going on?

"Would you pick up the champagne on the way home?" Daphne asked. She ran her fingers through her loose hair and licked her lips.

"Will do," Hendrick said. He gave her a playful wink and turned back to Marissa. "She's the new wife I told you about. Two months today."

Marissa bit her lip to keep her jaw from dropping. Daphne is Hendrick's brand new wife? And already she's having an affair with J.J? Something's not right.

Hendrick offered his hand. "I may have more questions in the next couple of days. Will you still be here?"

"You bet," she said, shaking his hand. After both cars pulled away, she proceeded down Main Street, her head still spinning.

She thought about Christmas Day when she'd caught J.J. kissing Daphne. Although his hands had been wandering, had Daphne returned his advances? When J.J. hadn't invited Marissa into his apartment, she'd assumed he was covering clues to their personal relationship. Actually, she had no evidence this was true. Nothing made sense any more.

Maybe the police were using Daphne to get information from J.J., hoping to nail him for Bubba's murder. No. If the murder occurred on the 24th and she saw Daphne and J.J. in a wild embrace on the 25th, that's not much time to plan and execute a sting. How long had their *tête-à-tête* been going on? And just where might they have met?

She headed down the bluff to the Perk and Turf. If anyone knew the dirt on J.J., Tizzie would.

The Perk and Turf was unusually busy. Marissa took a seat by the fireplace and opened a menu. Keeping time with "You Ain't Nothin' But a Hound Dog" on the jukebox, she waited until Tizzie finished serving orders to several customers.

"Marissa, I'm so glad you stopped by," Tizzie shouted over the music. She bent toward her and studied her face. "My lord, woman, what did you do to your eye? You want some ice?"

"No thanks," she shouted. "The bruise is a couple days old. I ran into a door."

Tizzie sat down across from her. "I'm sorry about the fuss we made over nothing at Walter's house. We here at the Cove can get pretty riled up when someone tries to pull the wool over our eyes."

"I can understand why you'd be upset. I'm concerned myself."

"Any news from the police on who blew up your car?"

"I wish there was. The wheels of bureaucracy turn slowly." The music had stopped and she was shouting for no reason.

"What can I get you from the kitchen?" Tizzie asked, seemingly practiced at lowering her voice with the volume of the music.

"How about a piece of your . . ." She studied the menu. "Blazin' Raisin pie?"

"Comin' up." Tizzie headed for the kitchen.

"Before you go, I'm looking for J.J. Has he been here?"

Tizzie came back. "Lordy no. He used to come in here regular. I haven't seen him for quite a while. I think maybe he's got a new girlfriend."

"When's the last time he came in?"

She tapped her pen on her order pad. "Guess it was September. In fact, it was early September. I remember 'cause school was back in session and this place was quiet without the young ones around."

"Was he alone?"

"He came in alone, but he left with some woman I never saw before or since. You got itchy bloomers for J.J.?"

"What do you think?"

"You got that boyfriend from San Francisco I saw you with and sometimes I see you with Nick. What do you want with J.J.?"

No hiding the newsworthy gossip from this woman.

"If you can answer a couple more questions and hold tight for a few days, I can give you a scoop that'll blast all your other stories out of the *Spindrift Sun*."

"Shoot them questions at me," Tizzie said, putting the order pad into her apron pocket.

"Describe the woman J.J. left with the day in early September."

"Sure. A real knockout. Long blond hair and really built. I'd say she was about forty."

"Do you remember how they met?"

"Clear as day." She leaned over the table as if to impart a secret. "Usually J.J. makes eyes at a women as soon as he sees her. But this woman moved in on him first. Seemed funny to me 'cause she was a real looker. Probably could have had any man she wanted. She sat at the table next to him and started batting her long lashes." Tizzie affected a poor imitation, making Marissa stifle a laugh. "Had on one of them short skirts," Tizzie said. "And made it a point to cross her legs so he could see halfway up her kazoo. She sure wanted his attention."

"What happened then?"

"Next I knew he was at her table. They shared a piece of Blazin' Raisin and then left together. I haven't seen him in here since."

"Any idea where he takes his meals now?"

"I heard he shows up a lot at the Do Drop Inn. You think maybe he doesn't like my pie?"

"Not a chance, Tizzie. Would you please box my dessert to go?" She left the price of the pie on the table plus a hefty tip.

J.J. walked with Walter to alley number four at the Ocean Bluffs Bowl-o-Rama and set down his bowling bag. "I'll beat your hide tonight," he shouted over the din of the alleys. He slipped into his polished bowling shoes. Beating Walter was usually a cinch.

"Not on your life," Walter shouted. He sat down beside J.J. "I'm in top form. I did me a 200 game last night."

J.J. watched Walter tie his laces with his usual double knot. The man was as predictable as a two-day old corpse. After filling out the top of the score sheet, J.J. shouted in Walter's ear. "You go first. I feel generous tonight."

"Suit yourself."

Walter approached the foul line and called back to J.J. "Fifty bucks says I win. You can start cryin' now."

"You're on, old man."

Walter held the ball at his chin, swung it back like a pro and released it. The ball rolled straight down the alley and knocked down eight pins, leaving a split.

J.J. hooted. "You old coot. There's no way you'll get those two pins."

Walter picked up the returned ball, approached the alley again and stood for several minutes before moving. J.J. watched as he delivered it down the right side of the alley, almost into the gutter. The ball knocked the right pin hard enough to send it sliding into the other pin and topple it. Walter walked back to his seat with a giant grin.

"A short-lived triumph," J.J. said.

Walter took the pen from him and wrote down his score in oversized numbers. "Speaking of short-lived triumphs, how's Daphne these days?"

"You're a jealous S.O.B.," J.J. said, rubbing chalk on his hands. "Daphne and I are just fine."

Walter leaned toward him. "What? I can't hear you."

"I said, 'Daphne and I are really hot for each other,'" he said into Walter's ear.

"I don't think so."

J.J. took aim down the alley.

"This is the first sweetie you haven't boasted how fast you got her into bed."

J.J. cussed under his breath and swung the ball.

"I think there's trouble in paradise," Walter shouted.

J.J. released the ball and watched it teeter on the edge of the alley and fall into the gutter. "Foul play," he said.

"Best you keep your mind on the ball and not on the fact you're not gettin' any."

The heat rose in J.J.'s face as he aimed the next ball in the same way with the same results.

Damn Walter, he thought.

"She's not such a hot number after all," Walter said. "Right?" He wrote a giant zero on the score sheet and underlined it.

The heat remained in J.J.'s cheeks. "She only needs a little more of J.J.'s T.L.C. She'll come around."

Walter took his turn and knocked down nine pins. "I'd worry if I was you. There's got to be a reason she's a cold fish if she likes you as much as you say she does."

"Cut it out, pal. I told you, 'she'll come around.'" He took aim.

"I think she's not as hot for you as you say."

J.J. swallowed the lump in his throat and delivered the ball, knocking down only two pins. "Damn." He clenched his fists. "Shut your mouth, Walter."

"Hey, J.J. How come your face is so red?"

J.J. sat alone at the bar in the bowling alley. Although Walter had left, J.J. was still fuming at him. Actually, he wasn't mad at Walter. He was mad at Daphne. His old friend was right about her holding out.

When the bartender took his order of scotch on the rocks, J.J. looked forward to a good belt of booze.

A whiff of perfume signaled a female presence and he looked up from his drink to see Margaret, the church organist, slipping onto the stool beside him.

"Hello, J.J." She ordered a glass of sarsaparilla.

"This is a surprise, Margaret," J.J. said. "I didn't know you bowled."

"I don't. It's the only place in Ocean Bluffs that serves sarsaparilla. I'm on my way to pick up some music I loaned to the organist at the Hendrick wedding a couple months ago."

J.J.'s ears twitched at the reference to Daphne's name.

"Can you believe it?" Margaret said, "I've been looking for that music for two months." She sipped her drink with relish. "Don't ever get old, J.J. Your mind starts playing tricks on you."

"Do you mean Daphne and Chet Hendrick?"

"Yup. Mighty nice people. They sure are made for each other. Look like a couple of love birds."

J.J. took a swig of his drink. "Married two months ago?"

"You got something wrong with your ears? You know, my hearing's not what it used to be, either. I'm having it checked next week. Do you know Doc Masterson, down the road?"

Son of a bitch. Daphne told him she'd been married for eleven years and was on the verge of divorce. What was she trying to pull?

"No, I can't say that I do," he said, tossing some bills on the bar. He picked up his bowling bag. "I gotta run. It's been nice talking with you, Margaret."

35

MURDER PLOT

A brisk wind rose as Marissa left the Perk and Turf and headed toward Nick's photo studio. She walked through the door as a young brunette in tight jeans stood at the front desk writing a check. A red satin dress was slung over her arm.

"Your boyfriend should be pleased with your photos," Nick told the woman. "Especially if he likes red."

"Thank you so much." She tilted her head with a smile and gazed at Nick a bit too long for Marissa. Then she trotted out, her stiletto heels clicking on the floor, a waft of Chanel following her.

Marissa took the woman's place at the counter. "I'm going to get you a stick to fend off the women."

Nick smiled. "Jealous?"

"Me? No." She was caught off guard by the blasted heat she felt in her cheeks and wished she could have responded with a smart remark.

Nick offered her a stool. "What did Hendrick have to say?"

"Not much," she said, sitting down. "But you'll never believe this. I found out Hendrick and Daphne are newlyweds."

"No way. And she's already two-timing him with J.J.?"

"I don't think so. My take is she and Hendrick are setting a trap. Tizzie told me Daphne came onto J.J. at the Perk and Turf in September—only a month before she and Hendrick got married. I think Daphne and Hendrick are trying to nail J.J. for something. It couldn't be Bubba's murder. J.J. and Daphne have been together since way before Bubba went missing."

"So what are you thinking?"

"Remember when you told me about the first time J.J. was caught stealing jewelry from a corpse?"

Nick nodded.

"When were the charges dropped?"

"I think it was sometime in September. Say, you may be onto something. Maybe Hendrick and Daphne were trying to nail J.J. for theft and then he up and commits murder." He reached for her hand. "Did anyone ever tell you you're a genius?"

"All the time," she said with a grin. "Care to join me in some sleuthing down the road? I hear J.J. eats at the Do Drop Inn now. I'll bet we can get some dirt from one of the waitresses."

"Would like to if I hadn't promised Tizzie I'd figure out why her truck won't start. She needs it for her book club in Ocean Bluffs tonight." He fished in his pocket and tossed Marissa his keys. "Take my car and stop by on the way back. We can catch a bite for dinner and you can tell me what you find out."

After Marissa left the photo shop, Nick thought about J.J. Could he have murdered Bubba to keep him quiet about the jewel thefts? Or maybe Walter could have made a bargain with J.J. to kill Bubba because Bubba was fooling around with Candi. They could have planned the murder together. Nick's impression of Walter was beginning to change.

Marissa arrived at the Do Drop Inn to find the lot filled with cars. She parked and joined a small group on their way into the inn. The dinner crowd had arrived and she was pleased to see the booth that she and Nick had shared was empty.

A waitress seated her there and started to pour her a cup of coffee. "Hey, nice shiner."

Marissa was tiring of comments about her eye. "No coffee for me. I'll have some tea."

"Comin' up."

When the tea arrived, Marissa asked, "Would you by chance know J.J. Haggersby from Spindrift Cove?"

The waitress slid the cream and sugar toward Marissa. "Sure. He used to come in here with Bubba and Walter. It's a shame about Bubba. Did you know him?"

"No, I didn't." She squeezed a wedge of lemon into her cup. "When was the last time J.J. came in?"

"Hmm. Not since Bubba's been gone. He was a stud. I used to look at those big black boots and picture them under my bed."

"J.J.'s boots?"

She laughed. "I'm talking about Bubba. J.J.'s ancient."

Marissa tried the scalding tea and set it aside. "You said he stopped coming in after Bubba disappeared?"

"Now that I think of it, it was way before. What are you? A cop or something? Some crook take a slug at your eye?"

Marissa kept her cool. "I'm an old friend of J.J.'s. I'm in town for a short while and can't seem to catch him at home. Someone said he hangs out here."

"I don't know much more than I told you. I'm about to go home. You might check with the guys on the evening shift."

Marissa thanked her, paid for the tea and left.

The sun was setting as Marissa waited and watched the customers come and go in the parking lot. Soon she spotted a young man in dark pants and a white shirt emerge from a car. He walked to a bench, where he took a drag on a cigarette.

She approached him and asked. "Do you work here?"

He looked up. "Yes, ma'am," he said, making her feel old.

"I wonder if you might help me. Would you know someone by the name of J.J. Haggersby?"

"No, ma'am," he said, "Maybe if you tell me what he looks like."

"Blond, Nordic type, about six foot two, over two hundred pounds. He's got a limp and likes the ladies."

"Oh yeah, I seen him."

"Does he come in regularly?"

"I only seen him out here in the parking lot." He dropped his cigarette and ground it into the blacktop with his foot. "At least once or twice a week, for the past few months, he meets a lady here. I usually duck out here about then for a smoke. They come in two cars and leave in one."

"Can you describe the woman?"

"You ain't no angry wife, are you?"

"No. I promise."

"Uh, I don't know much else."

Marissa took a twenty dollar bill from her purse and held it out to him. "Will this help you to remember?"

Pocketing the bill, he said, "Wouldn't forget a lady like her. Tall. Long blond hair. Walks like a model. Built like one, too."

"You say they get here in the early evening?"

"Yup. Hey, are you a reporter? Maybe you can get my name in the papers. I'm—"

"I'll see what I can do."

The sun was beginning to set when Marissa drove Nick's car behind an oleander bush and stopped in a spot where she could see every car that entered the Do Drop Inn parking lot. Soon J.J.'s black Lincoln drove in, crept around the side of the restaurant and disappeared.

Marissa started the car and followed. Once she rounded the building, she caught sight of him again. As soon as J.J. parked, she pulled into a row of cars where she could watch. He immediately opened his door and went around to the back of the car. She had a perfect view.

Decked out in a brown sport coat, tan pants and brown oxfords, he looked as if he were dressed for a date. He lifted the trunk lid to reveal a folded red blanket in the trunk. He felt beneath it, apparently searching for something, which he found and then shut the trunk lid.

Curious, Marissa leaned closer to the window and watched him return to his open car door, survey his surroundings and place the object on the seat. Then he removed his jacket and slipped the article into his belt.

My God, Marissa thought. He's brought his gun!

She clutched the steering wheel as he put his jacket back on and patted the bulge at his waist.

Somehow she had to stop him.

Should she call the police? She'd have to get out of the car to find a phone. She could lose him. Maybe she should wait to see his next move. But what if she's too late?

Just then a small car drove into the lot and parked beside J.J.'s Lincoln. Marissa watched Daphne leave her compact and slide into J.J.'s passenger seat. J.J. pecked her on the lips and wasted no time starting the car. Within seconds they sped out of the lot and onto the highway.

"The scum!" Marissa muttered. She took off, her knuckles clutching the wheel tightly as she followed them south.

Small drops of rain began to spatter the windshield and she flicked the wipers on low. By the first red stop light, J.J.'s car was far ahead. Marissa slowed and then ran the light, gripping the wheel even tighter as the shower became heavy rain.

What would she do if J.J. stopped? The wipers beat almost as fast as her heart.

As she approached Spindrift Cove and the Pajama Factory, she saw Nick slamming down the hood of Tizzie's truck. She quickly pulled up beside him and rolled down the window, the cold rain splashing her face. "Jump in. Fast!"

Nick tilted his head in question but when she scowled, he hopped into the moving vehicle and slid in beside her.

"What's up?"

Marissa gunned the Chevy, keeping her eyes on J.J.'s taillights.

"J.J.'s onto Daphne's plan. I think he's going to shoot her, like he shot Bubba. They're in the car ahead." She told him what she'd just seen.

"You're sure you saw a gun?"

"Positive. It's in his belt." She sped up until they were a safe distance behind.

"What in hell can we do to stop him?"

"I don't know but we better do it fast."

J.J. sped through the driving rain, one hand on the wheel and the other caressing Daphne's. "Is this the ring I gave you?"

"Yes. I love it."

Yeah, I'll bet she loves it, he thought. She's probably already shown it to her old man and then to all his cop friends.

"Aren't you afraid Chet'll find it?" he asked.

"No way. Like I told you, he could care less about my panty drawer. He's been staying out late nights again, the S.O.B."

Damn, she's full of lies, he thought. He slowed at the spot where he'd left Bubba's car.

Empty! The cops found it! Shit! They're probably onto him. He glanced into the rearview mirror. No cops. No sirens. Only one car in the distance. He gritted his teeth. "How long did you say you've been married?"

"It'll be eleven years next month."

He squeezed her hand hard, wishing both of his were around her throat. "I don't think so," he said. "I heard you and Chet had a nice little wedding only two months ago."

Complete silence. He knew he had her.

He swung off the road onto a rain-soaked gravel shoulder. The car swerved on the loose stones and for a moment he lost control.

"What do you think you're doing?" Daphne asked, grabbing for the wheel.

He flung her hand aside. "You don't even deny you're a newlywed?"

So furious he couldn't speak, he swerved off the shoulder and into an asphalt parking lot lined on the right by groves of trees. Then he gunned the car straight ahead toward the ocean.

"Stop!" Daphne shouted.

J.J. squinted at a lookout point beyond, where he knew a rocky cliff dropped hundreds of feet to the ocean.

Daphne reached for the door handle. "Let me out!"

J.J. laughed. He locked all the doors with a switch and let up on the gas. He had her now. Exactly where he wanted her.

He was wise, he thought, in scouting this place out earlier. He had every detail planned. Not like last time on his fishing trip with Bubba.

As he neared the edge of the cliff, he drew to a stop, doused the headlights and killed the engine. He knew what he had to do. Heat filled his face as he turned to her.

"He's left the main highway," Marissa said, looking through the sheets of rain.

Nick cracked his window and wiped off the condensation. "Damn, I was afraid of this."

"What?"

Nick seemed lost in thought so she asked again.

"Devil's Folly is on the other side of that parking lot," he said. "No one's ever survived a fall from those cliffs."

"Oh, God! We've got to act fast."

"To do what?" Nick asked. "The only weapon we have is a flashlight."

"How about your camera? I saw one in the back seat."

"You mean shoot him to death with a Nikon?"

"We can distract him with the motor drive thingy you showed me."

"What?"

The rain pounded the roof so loudly she had to shout. "Does your camera have a motor drive?"

Nick grabbed his camera from the back seat. "What's your plan?"

Marissa doused the headlights and slowly pulled toward the grove of trees on their right. She could barely make out J.J.'s car. She didn't dare drive any closer. She switched off the ignition. "If we get out and hide behind that clump of trees, will we be close enough to blind him with the light on your camera?"

"Not with this dinky flash . . . but . . . with this strobe and the motor drive we can. It'll keep flashing. Enough to freak him out."

She checked the back seat. "Is that a tripod back there?"

"Not a very heavy one, but it'd make a good weapon."

"Give it here," she said.

J.J. slipped the gun from his belt and pointed it at Daphne. "I'm only saying this once, so listen carefully."

Daphne looked at the gun. J.J. expected fear to flood her face, but instead, she stared straight ahead.

Damn! he thought. She knew how to get to him.

Heat surged through him. His hand shook. He jabbed her in the shoulder with the pistol. "It's time for a drink," he said. "Open the glove compartment and take out the flask."

"Are you kidding? What in hell for?"

"Now!" he shouted, waving the gun at her.

She opened the glove box and retrieved the flask.

"Good job, my dear," he said. "Now unscrew the top and take a big swing."

Daphne struggled with the cap.

"And you might as well enjoy it," J.J. said. "You'll be finishing off the bottle. When and if the cops ever find your body in the ocean, an autopsy will show you're so full of booze they'll think you were plastered and fell over the cliff." He put the gun to her temple.

Daphne flinched.

"Open the damn flask!"

Daphne tried. "I can't. The top's on too tight."

J.J. swore. He lowered the gun, pointing it haphazardly at Daphne. "Hold the frickin' thing with both hands. I'll take off the top." Biting his lip, he tried to unscrew the cap with his free hand until it finally came loose.

Daphne let go of the flask.

Pain shot through J.J. as Daphne twisted back the hand that held the pistol. The gun fired, putting a hole through the windshield as J.J. let go. Scotch splashed over Daphne. She dove for the gun.

"Oh, no you don't," J.J. shouted.

He grabbed the gun. One left jab to the chin and Daphne's eyes glazed over. Her head fell to her shoulder, her body limp.

"Out cold," J.J. whispered. He was halfway there.

Flashlight and tripod in hand, Marissa flung open her car door only to have the wind crash it shut against her. She winced and tried again, using her shoulder to stabilize the door. Stumbling out, she bucked the gale that pasted her hair to her head and into her eyes. "Hurry! J.J.'s leaving the car. He's going to the passenger side."

Nick struggled inside the car with the strobe. "Where's Daphne?"

"I can't see. It's too dark . . . Oh my God, he's lifting her from the passenger seat. She looks like she's . . . Oh God, I think she's dead. Come out here!"

She shivered with cold as Nick joined her, looking ahead while fumbling to attach the cord of the strobe light.

"Hurry!" Marissa said straining to see through the dark rain. "He's carrying her to the cliff."

Nick slammed the strobe into the connection and Marissa ran ahead, the wind howling in her ears.

She barely heard Nick as he caught up. "Call out J.J.'s name when I tell you," he said.

"Call his name? Are you crazy?"

Rain pelted J.J.'s face and the mud slowed his steps as he left the asphalt parking lot carrying Daphne. He walked toward the cliff, pain shooting through his bad hip, the cold rain pelting his hand with the gun.

Damn, Daphne was heavy.

The wet mud sucked at his smooth-soled shoes, but without traction, they gave way, leaving him to slip and slide, almost losing his balance. He puffed and gasped at Daphne's dead weight in his arms.

Only a few more yards and it would be over. No one to squeal on him. No one to testify. All they could accuse him of was having an affair with a cop's wife.

"He's almost to the edge of the cliff!" Marissa panted, racing far behind and to the left of J.J. She glanced at Nick, also behind J.J. but to his right. The wind continued to lash her hair over her eyes, sometimes blinding her. Without warning, her toe hit a rock and she catapulted forward, slamming to her knees.

"Now!" Nick shouted.

Mud-drenched, Marissa struggled to her feet. "Hey, J.J.!" she yelled.

Nick ran toward him, firing the strobe lights in quick succession. Limping, Marissa circled behind J.J. and trained the flashlight on his feet.

J.J. whipped around, Daphne still in his arms. "What the—?"

Marissa shoved the flashlight into her pocket and with one sound whack, she smashed J.J. in the knees with the tripod. Down he went, flinging Daphne to the side and the gun in the other direction.

"My ankle!" he screamed.

Nick threw his camera down and jumped him, pinning him to the ground. "Find the gun!" he shouted to Marissa.

Instead she raced to Daphne and knelt beside her. She was breathing. "She's okay!"

"The gun!" Nick shouted. "Get the gun!"

"You're going to be all right," Marissa whispered to Daphne. "I'm on it!" she yelled to Nick. She scanned the beam of the flashlight on the ground until it landed on the gun. "Got it!"

Nick kept J.J. pinned down, ignoring his groans about a damaged ankle.

"One move and I shoot," Marissa said, her voice trembling. She pointed the gun at J.J.'s head.

"Keep it on him," Nick said, releasing his hold. He bent to remove his shoelaces. "Steady until I tie his hands together."

A low moan came from Daphne's direction. "The son of a bitch."

Marissa stood her ground, her eyes never leaving J.J. "Are you all right?" she asked Daphne.

Soon she felt Daphne's presence beside her. "I've felt better," Daphne said. The wet rain from her hair splashed Marissa's face as Daphne shook her head to clear it. "But I'm okay. You two saved my life. Here let me have that," she said, reaching for the gun. "Chet's taught me how to do this."

"Can't I at least shoot the S.O.B. in the foot?" Marissa asked.

"You don't know how much I wish you could," Daphne said, taking the pistol from her. "You can let go of him," she said to Nick. "I can take it from here." She approached J.J., keeping the gun on him. "Up on your feet."

J.J. moaned again about the pain in his ankle. He struggled to rise.

"Into the car," Daphne said.

She turned to Marissa and Nick. "We should have no trouble getting this bozo back to the station."

36

STARTLING SENDOFF

Still shivering from the cold, Marissa sat in the police station with Nick while Daphne led J.J. to the booking officer.

Marissa watched as J.J. placed his Rolex and the contents of his pockets on the desk and an officer cuffed his hands. As J.J. was led away, he looked over his shoulder at Marissa and Nick and snarled.

Marissa smiled sweetly. "Have a nice vacation!"

Nick nudged her with a chuckle. She leaned toward him and whispered, "Do you think Daphne's been drinking? She reeked of alcohol."

"That smell was scotch," Nick said. "I was wondering the same thing, except she was so coherent. She knew what she was doing when we brought J.J. down."

Daphne joined them, still smelling of liquor, her jaw swollen and her wet hair hanging in strings. "I don't know how to thank you two."

"Our pleasure," Nick said, squeezing Marissa's hand.

"I must smell like the local pub," Daphne said. She explained J.J.'s plan for her and the spilling of scotch from the flask in his car. "You look as cold and bedraggled as I feel," she added. "Want some hot coffee?"

Marissa pulled Nick's jacket around her. "Thanks, but we better get home and out of our wet clothes."

"But before we go" Nick said, "can you tell us the charges against J.J.?"

Daphne ticked off the counts on her fingers. "First is grand theft. Then comes my attempted murder and now we're working on Bubba's murder. We've been trying to get the goods on J.J. and those jewels since before he and Walter concocted their crazy hoax. I had a feeling he was fencing more than a few rings."

Oh, God, Marissa thought. She hoped Walter wasn't even more involved with J.J. than she'd guessed. "So you were on to J.J. the whole time?"

"At first our plan was simple. You know my husband Chet is a cop?"

Marissa nodded. "Officer Hendrick."

"We knew J.J. would chase any skirt that would give him the time of day. I had no problem getting him interested."

Marissa wondered why he'd never made a pass at her and then figured her discovery of the body of the man he'd murdered was probably reason enough to rule her out.

Daphne continued, "When I heard about the jewel thefts, I suggested the sting to Chet. If I came on to J.J., I was pretty sure he'd respond. Then I'd have the advantage."

Nick rose a brow. "And your husband thought this was a good idea?"

"Not at first. After all, we were engaged to be married. Eventually I got him to convince Coroner Williams to loan me to the police department. All I had to do was get J.J. to give me one of those stolen rings."

"Quite a setup," Nick said.

"So Coroner Williams was also in on this little 'love affair' plot," Marissa said.

"You bet. In the beginning, we thought J.J. was only a jewel thief. But by the time he finally gave me the ring, we were pretty sure he'd killed Bubba. Now, since he's tried to bump me off, he's added another charge to his list."

What a scoop for Tizzie, Marissa thought. She could picture her typing up the headlines.

"It must have taken quite an acting job to make J.J. think you were crazy about him."

Daphne smiled. "Four years as a college Thespian and a couple parts in some local plays paid off."

"Oh yes, I remember my Uncle Walter telling me about J.J.'s insistence that he go with him to that play in Ocean Bluffs."

"They were quite a twosome in the front row," Daphne said. "I was surprised to see J.J. had brought Walter along."

"You probably know J.J. has quite an influence on my uncle. Is Walter in trouble, too?"

Daphne hesitated. "Your uncle is another story. We're not sure exactly where he fits into this picture. Chet will have some questions for him."

Marissa hoped the fake memorial service was his only involvement but couldn't help but fear there was more. She and Nick were about to leave, when Nick asked, "Daphne, do you know anything about the bomb that blew up Marissa's car?"

"Or the one that almost blew up Nick's?" Marissa asked. "Were those the work of J.J., too?"

"Sure looks promising," Daphne said.

"What do you think will happen to him?" Marissa asked.

Daphne's eyes narrowed. "If I have anything to say about it, he'll burn in hell before he's free to kick up his heels again. Spindrift Cove better start looking for another deputy sheriff . . . and a new mayor."

J.J. sat at a large metal table in an interrogation room, wishing he were any place but there. The gray walls were cold as ice and the bright light made him feel as if he were already on trial.

Howling drunks had kept him up all night and his hard cot smelled like stale beer. He rubbed the stubble on his face. "Damn, I wish I had a drink."

He came to attention at the rattle of a key. The door opened and his lawyer, big Marty McGowan, strode toward him in a suit and finely stitched topcoat. Bushy salt-and-pepper eyebrows nearly touched his deep-set brown eyes. His dark hair had grayed since J.J. had last seen him. His skin had the pallor that comes with sunless afternoons in county courtrooms.

Marty set his briefcase on the floor and placed a small tape recorder on the table. He extended his hand. "Good to see you again, J.J. I wish it were under better circumstances."

"You got to get me out of here," J.J. said. "The charges against me stink as much as the jail cells. And it's damn cold in here."

Marty's grim expression deepened. "It's not going to be so easy this time. You've got some serious counts against you."

He said the same thing last time, J.J. thought. But he wasn't worried. Marty always came through.

His lawyer moved the tape recorder toward him. "You mind? It'll help me out."

"Suit yourself."

He switched on the machine and J.J. sat back, his arms outstretched, palms down on the table. "These cops are full of crap."

Marty cocked his head. "Let's start with the grand theft charge. Tell me about that."

J.J.'s mind whirled. He had to say this perfectly right. "How much do you have to steal for it to be grand theft?"

His lawyer shook his head. "Always looking for an angle." Leaning forward, his eyes bored into J.J.'s. "If you want me to help you, you have to leave the fancy sidestepping to me. Give it to me straight."

Better think about this one, J.J. thought. "They say I took some jewelry."

"How much do they say you took?"

"Uh, several rings and necklaces."

"Several, like ten or twelve or like one or two hundred?"

"Um . . . I guess the latter."

Marty took an envelope from his briefcase and handed it to J.J. "Would these be a good sample?"

J.J. opened it, slipped out several eight-by-ten color photos of jewelry and swallowed hard. He studied one that showed seven rows of college rings. How in hell did Marty get these? he wondered. Mumbling, he looked sideways at him. "These are a good sample."

"And are there more?"

"Maybe a couple more drawers worth."

When Marty didn't respond, J.J. added, "But I didn't sell all of them."

Marty's voice rose. "You mean you were fencing them? Who did you sell them to?"

J.J. smiled. "That I really don't know. I gave them to someone who sold them for me."

"And what would this someone's name be?"

"I dunno. Calls herself Stephanie."

Marty leaned back in his chair. "Don't you have a daughter named Stephanie?"

J.J. flinched and covered it with a cough. "Yeah, you're right."

His lawyer rose from his chair and pounded a fist on the table. He loomed over J.J. "That's enough of this crap. You either spill what happened or I'm out of here. I don't have time to waste pulling facts out of you. It's your ass that's on the line. If you want me to save it, you tell me like it is and tell me now."

J.J. hadn't been scolded like this since the last time Marty helped him out.

His lawyer's pale face flushed. "Agreed?"

J.J. sighed. "Agreed."

"Did your daughter sell the jewels for you?"

J.J. looked at the table. "She had contacts in Phoenix."

Marty paced, rubbing his chin. Then he faced J.J. "Spindrift Cove doesn't have more than a few deaths a year, does it?"

J.J. knew what he was getting at. "Not many. My funeral services include Ocean Bluffs, too."

"But Ocean Bluffs can't have more than one or two hundred deaths a year. These photos show a couple hundred rings. Where and how did you get them all?"

It was no use. "Stephanie collected them from morticians in the Bay Area. She needed money. It was the first time I could be there for her as a father."

Marty sat down and closed his eyes, seeming to compose himself. Opening them, he said, "How about the attempted murder of Daphne Hendrick? Tell me about that."

J.J. thought of the witnesses: Nick Devereaux and Walter's niece. "I was only trying to scare her."

"With a loaded pistol?"

"I wasn't going to use it."

"And the murder of Bubba Maselli?"

J.J. shot up from his chair. "Now that's a trumped up charge!"

"Where were you when he was killed?"

"I was fishing that day."

"With Bubba?"

"He was supposed to come but he begged off."

"You know why?"

"Said he was going to L.A. to see his family, being Christmastime and all."

Marty made some notes on a pad of paper.

"Have you heard from Bubba since?"

J.J. shook his head. "No reason he should call."

"What do you think happened to him?"

"I don't think. I know for a fact."

"And what's that?"

J.J. looked Marty in the eyes. "Walter Schmidkin did it. He told me so. He had it in for Bubba."

Marissa picked up the phone on the first ring. "Nick?"

"No," came the familiar voice. "It's Gregory."

"Gregory?" Marissa sat down on the edge of the bed, uncertain of what was to come.

"I wondered how you were doing . . . and when you're coming back."

What? Last she'd talked to him, he'd made it quite clear he was through with her. Or at least she thought so.

"I'm fine," she said, curious to hear more.

"And your uncle?"

"He's in deep trouble. Everything's hit the fan." Then her curiosity won out. "How was the New Year's Eve party?"

"Oh, it was all right."

She worked up her nerve. "Did you go with Candace?"

"Yes, but I should have gone with you."

What was he trying to pull? "She dumped you, didn't she?"

He hesitated.

She should have known. He was calling because he was lonely.

"I wanted to see how you and Walter are doing. If your uncle needs help, I'll be glad to come down."

If Walter needs help? And what about her? What if *she* needed help? "We're doing fine. There's no need for you to come down. Is that it?"

"No, I wondered how your New Year's Eve was."

Marissa thought of her evening with Nick at the funeral home. Her getting conked in the head with the corpse sling. Nick beside the bonfire at the beach and most of all, their first kiss. "My New Year's Eve was quite cozy. I spent it in front of a big fire."

"It's good you spent the evening with your uncle. He needed someone to talk to."

Well, she'd be damned. He'd expected her to wait for him. He'd always been filled with expectations—about how she should dress, where they'd go, whom they'd see. And at the same time, he was so adept at dodging a commitment to her. "Look, Gregory. You wanted out and that's what you got. I've moved on."

She heard china rattle and water running. He was doing the dishes! He couldn't even put her first when he was begging her to come back.

"Now, Marissa, don't be hasty. We've had some good times together."

"Yes, we did. But unfortunately that's all they were. Nothing more . . . for two years. I've put them all behind me. Good luck, Gregory."

"Uh . . ."

The water stopped running.

Marissa smiled to herself. "Goodbye."

The rattle of keys in the jail cell caused J.J. to lift his head from the hard bunk.

"Call from your lawyer," the guard said.

Hot damn, J.J. thought. He followed the guard down the hall to the pay phone. "Hello, Marty? Are they letting me out?"

"What in hell are you trying to pull?" his lawyer asked. "The police searched the funeral home and found the matching pants to the tux jacket Bubba had on."

J.J. thought fast. "What in damnation does that prove? I've got families that bring in de la Renta tuxes all the time."

"And do they bring in the razor that shaved off the corpse's hair and beard?"

"What do you mean?"

"They found the razor they say you used to shave Bubba."

"You got to be putting me on. Can't a man keep a razor in his own apartment?"

"Maybe so," Marty said. "But not with the whiskers of a dead man attached. And I suppose there's also nothing wrong with keeping the goods for making car bombs in the mortuary, too. Makings that match those found under Marissa's and Nick's cars."

Good God. The cops have been tracing his every move. "Damn. I knew those kids would get me in trouble. More than once I found them in the back room taking a smoke while their parents visited the deceased. I've found everything from cigarette butts to firecrackers to car bombs back there. I asked Bubba to clean that room out a couple weeks ago." It was a flimsy excuse, he thought, but maybe Marty would buy it.

"We've gotta do better than that, pal. Best you think a lot more about this because you're in deep shit."

"Uh . . ."

"I'll give you a call tomorrow, J.J."

A day's rest had rejuvenated Marissa and she was eager to resume her quest to find Candi. She sat in the waiting room at the county sheriff's office without an appointment.

Hendrick strode toward her with a smile. "I'm glad you came."

Marissa stood. "Good news?"

"Right. Missing Persons has some information about your aunt."

"Really? What did they find?"

"Normally we don't follow an adult once she's found unless her life's in danger. As an adult, she has a right to do as she pleases. But, in this case, I asked the guys to do a little extra checking. It seems Candi went back to Germany."

Germany, then China, then Germany? What possible explanation could Candi have for this behavior? And why had she left Uncle Walter? "Is that where she is now?"

"Could be. We know for sure she was there yesterday. We won't be keeping track of her anymore. If I were you, I'd try to call her at Gunther Friedlich's place before she takes off again."

Marissa got up to leave. "Thanks for your help. I'll do that."

"Hey, not so fast. You saved my wife's life. How can I ever repay you? How about you and Nick coming to our place for dinner sometime soon?"

"How about you keeping J.J. in jail? That and dinner and we'll call it even."

The next day, J.J. ambled down the hall of the county jail just fast enough to keep the guard from prodding him. Marty's threat that he was in deep shit hadn't left him since the day before. Maybe springing him from this place wasn't going to be so easy after all.

J.J.'s slow pace became a swagger as soon as the guard un-locked the door to the visiting room. A din from several inmates and visitors bounced off the walls and high ceiling.

J.J. had expected a visit from Marty. Instead, he found Walter sitting on the other side of the metal screen, a deep scowl spread across his face.

J.J. sat down across from him. "Walter, my old buddy. What a surprise. Really no need to bail me out. These trumped up charges'll be cleared up in no time."

Walter's eyes narrowed. "Don't 'buddy' me. The police think I was with you when you and Bubba went fishing. You know I was at home that day."

J.J. leaned forward. "Hush up. So what if they think you spent the day fishing? It's no skin off your back."

"What do you mean?" Walter's voice rose. "They think you and I killed Bubba."

J.J. suppressed a smile. "You've got to be kidding. I'll have to talk to Marty about that." He sat back. "Good man, Marty. He's helped me out before, you know. We don't have anything to worry about."

"We? There's no 'we.'" Walter's lower lip trembled. "First you kill Bubba and then you try to kill my niece. You can be sure there's no 'we' anymore." He wiped his face with a handkerchief. "And after all these years." He looked about to cry.

"Hey, buddy, we've been through worse than this."

Walter wouldn't look at him.

J.J. added, "And I didn't try to kill your niece. That bomb wasn't enough to harm anybody. You weren't getting her out of town fast enough."

Walter glared with rage. "Damn you! And what about Bubba? I suppose you had nothing to do with that, either."

J.J. motioned for him to lean closer to the screen. "It's a setup," he whispered. "They're looking for a scapegoat and I'm the one who saw Bubba last."

"I can't hear you," Walter whispered, moving closer.

"I said you don't have to worry."

Walter leaned even closer. "They say he got it with a .38. Same bullets you shoot. They even have the shell casing. How you gonna fight that?"

"They got the casing?"

"Damn right they do. Found it a ways from Bubba's car."

"No way they could."

"What?" Walter whispered. "I can't hear you over all this noise."

"Come 'ere, old man. Closer to the screen."

Walter leaned in.

"They're lying to you, man. I have the casing at home, in the top drawer under my Jockey shorts."

J.J. smiled at the look on Walter's face.

"You mean you killed him?" Walter asked.

"Give me your ear, man."

Walter turned his head.

"Damn right I did," he whispered. "He was about to unload to the cops about the jewelry."

The din in the room grew louder when several more visitors entered and the guard let in three more inmates.

"You mean you took all those jewels like they said?"

J.J. loved to watch the look of astonishment hit Walter's face. He was so easy to excite.

"Did you?" Walter asked.

J.J. whispered, "Of course I did. But there's no way you can prove it or that I shot Bubba. No, man, you're gonna fry in hell for me."

Walter twisted his handkerchief, his hands shaking.

"I . . . I got to go now." He was sweating beads the size of baby pearls.

J.J. sat back and snickered. "So nice of you to come visit me," he shouted as Walter got up to leave.

Man, he looks nervous, J.J. thought.

The guard approached J.J. and motioned him toward the door as Chet Hendrick walked in. J.J. watched as Walter extracted a small box from under his shirt and handed it to Hendrick.

Holy shit, J.J. whispered. "It's a tape recorder."

37

TOWN MEETING

Marissa rushed to the nearest pay phone at the sheriff's office and fumbled through her bag for Gunther Friedlich's phone number. She punched the buttons and prepared for a bout with Gunther's receptionist.

"Please be there, Candi."

The phone rang several times and Gunther's voicemail clicked on with the voice of Gunther's receptionist.

"Drat!"

Marissa took a deep breath of the cold night air before making her way up the steps to the high school auditorium. Inhaling the quiet, she anticipated the turmoil inside. It was the first city council meeting since J.J. had landed in jail and since the locals had accused Walter of killing his wife. With Mayor Haggersby out of commission, Walter would be forced to move up from vice mayor and muster enough self-confidence to take command. Confidence?

That was a laugh, Marissa thought. Walter hadn't even gained enough courage to explain why he'd told everyone Candi was the corpse in the cove. Marissa had learned from the showdown at Walter's place that the townspeople rebelled when they were taken for fools. And those who still believed Walter might have killed Candi were not about to allow a murderer to continue living in their town. The council meeting was sure to be a raging assault on Walter.

She tugged open the huge oak door and the peace outside gave way to the sound of hundreds of chattering people filling the auditorium aisles. As she pushed through the crowd, a small group of men, still in their fishing gear, stopped laughing. "Shh. Here comes his niece."

"You betcha," she said, smiling at all of them.

She covered her ears from the screech of the microphone on stage, where Nick was working on the sound system. He looked up for a moment, waved at her and smiled.

She surveyed the room, looking for Walter, hoping he wouldn't compound his problems by arriving late. She worked her way to Tizzie, who stood below the stage, and lent her a hand lifting a coffee urn onto a table.

Tizzie smoothed the tablecloth. "Thanks again for the story you and Nick gave me about J.J. and Daphne. I sold more copies of the *Spindrift Sun* than in all its history."

"Glad to be of help." Marissa spooned some coffee into the urn. "Do you always have this many people at your meetings?"

"Lordie, no," Tizzie said, setting out cups. "We're lucky if we fill the first eight rows. Everybody's wondering what's going to happen now that J.J.'s locked up. You better sit down here by Pastor John, where your uncle can see you. He's gonna need all the support he can get."

Marissa searched again for Walter. Surely he wouldn't flee from this responsibility. She flipped down a seat near the aisle and sat next to Pastor John.

"Here comes Walter," he said.

Walter strode from the left wing, past Nick, to center stage. The noise in the room halted and then became whispers.

He must have come in the back door, Marissa thought.

She sat forward as Walter stopped and stood erect in a gray suit and blue tie with a Windsor knot. His neatly pressed pants exposed black and yellow argyle socks Marissa remembered her grandma knitting before she died.

He walked to the lectern, squared his shoulders and stretched his neck from the tight collar.

"Will the meeting come to order?" Walter's voice blasted through the auditorium.

"Turn the mike down, Nick," someone shouted. "For those of us who still have eardrums."

The crowd tittered.

Walter opened a notebook on the lectern. Marissa could tell he was tracing down the page with his finger, as he had done when he read fairy tales to her. She held her breath until he finally looked up and said, "Everyone rise for the prayer." His voice varied from soft to loud as Nick adjusted the volume.

"You're gonna need more than a prayer," a woman in the second row shouted.

"You'll need the whole Bible," a kid with spiked hair added and his friends cackled with him.

Marissa curbed her urge to deck them.

Nick stood and raised his hand for quiet. Walter waited until the laughter from the comment subsided. His gaze settled on Marissa and he smiled nervously.

She wondered how he could ever save face after what he'd done.

Pastor John extracted himself from his seat and lumbered up the steps to the podium. From there, he led the prayer followed by the pledge of allegiance. When Walter resumed the meeting, Marissa could see his eyes skimming the back of the auditorium, where the latecomers stood behind the last row of seats and spilled into the aisles.

"As you all probably know," Walter said, "J.J. will no longer be performing his duties as mayor."

"Hell, he's in jail," a man piped up.

Walter ignored him. "As vice mayor, I'm assuming his duties. We have a lot to talk about tonight. So take a seat if you can find one." He looked down at his notes. "Is there any new business?"

"Old business first," a man in the back shouted. "How 'bout talking about Candi? Where is she?"

Oh, God. The trouble's starting already, Marissa thought.

"Walter killed her," Margaret shouted, rising from the center of the room. "And he killed Bubba, too."

Marissa's gaze bounced around the room, following the jeers.

Walter mumbled into the microphone. "I did not kill—"

"Speak up!" someone yelled.

Walter pulled the mike closer. "I did not kill my wife!"

The statement blasted through the mike so loudly that Marissa's chair shook.

A burly man in a fishing cap stood and shouted, "If you didn't kill her, then where is she?"

"Why did you make fools of us at the chapel?" another man yelled.

Several more stood and shouted their concerns.

Walter stepped from the podium. "I didn't kill anyone!"

The crowd hollered at him.

Someone had to stop them. Marissa stood and headed for the stage. In one quick move, she hiked herself up and stood beside Walter.

Grabbing the mike, she yelled at the top of her lungs, "Wait a minute!"

Her heart pounded.

"Cut out this childish nonsense and let's talk about this," she said in a confident tone. But her pulse was racing.

The man in the fishing cap shouted, "Talking ain't gonna bring Bubba and Candi back from the dead."

The crowd shouted its agreement.

"You're right about Bubba," Marissa said, glad to have the advantage of the mike. "And we don't know for sure what happened to Candi. But I can provide you an explanation." Her words echoed off the walls. "Now everyone sit down and act civilized."

She looked to Walter, who smiled proudly at his niece.

"Most of you have known my uncle for many years and you've all respected him."

"Until now," Margaret Potter called. "We were feeling sorry for him at the same time he was telling us boldface lies."

Marissa hid her astonishment when Walter nudged her aside and took the mike. She looked to Nick who tilted his head and shrugged.

"When I married Candi," Walter said, "most of you told me she'd tire of me. And when she left, I couldn't face you." He loosened his tie. "So I made up the story about her being dead."

The crowd exchanged comments and Marissa expected pandemonium to resume.

"That's my only mistake," Walter shouted above them. "And I'm sorry. For trying to fool you and for . . ." He looked at Marissa. "And for pretending I'd contacted her family and ours."

The crowd became silent.

So my brother Tony doesn't even know? Marissa thought. No wonder he didn't show up.

Walter continued, "But I didn't kill Bubba."

Margaret shot up from her seat. "Not true! You told your niece you were going to kill Bubba! My brother-in-law heard you!"

Marissa stepped forward and calmly said, "We've already decided my uncle's statement was uttered after Bubba was already dead."

"That doesn't prove anything," Margaret said. "He could have already killed him."

The men jeered and the women supported them. Chaos was about to erupt again. Marissa had played her last card.

She looked to Nick for support.

Suddenly the door at the back of the auditorium flung open.

"Just hold your tongues!" a woman shouted from the doorway.

Marissa gasped. "It's Candi!"

"Candi!" Walter cried. His eyes lit like sparks in a campfire.

A wave of relief swept through Marissa at the sight of her aunt, backlit in the doorway, resplendent in a flowing ankle-length red dress, her bleached blond curls piled high on her head.

Marissa watched, speechless, suppressing an urge to run to her as all heads turned and a hush swept the room.

"She's come back from the dead," Margaret said.

Marissa ignored the snickers. Where had her aunt been? How long had she been in town? And how did she know everyone would be gathered here?

Candi strode down the center aisle with her eyes intent on the stage. Her head high and her back straight, she lifted her long skirt to climb the steps in her three-inch heels. Marissa almost expected a band to play "Pomp and Circumstance."

All eyes followed Candi.

Marissa could hardly contain herself. She caught Candi's eye and her aunt winked at her on her way toward Walter. The scent of expensive perfume followed as she reached the lectern and planted a long kiss on Walter's lips.

Marissa surveyed the faces around her, realizing she, too, must look shocked. What could her aunt possibly say to explain her disappearance?

When the kiss ended, Candi took the microphone, her arm around a grinning Walter.

"You're all probably wondering where I've been."

Several people chuckled and a few shouted remarks. Only Margaret rose to voice her opinion but Tizzie tugged her back into her seat.

"I left my wonderful husband," Candi said, "because I have terminal cancer."

Marissa gasped. She reached for her uncle, whose face was ashen. "Candi—," he whispered.

His wife pulled him close. When the murmurs from the audience subsided, she continued. "I understand lots has happened since I left. I've even heard rumors about me having an affair with Bubba, bless his dear departed soul." She took a moment and continued. "For crying out loud, use your heads! Bubba was half my age! I was his confidant."

Marissa tried to piece together what might have happened.

Margaret shot up. "Who killed him? That's what I want to know."

Candi frowned and Marissa thought her aunt was about to cry. "I wish I knew more about Bubba. I only learned about him an hour ago when I got into town and saw a copy of the newspaper. Thanks to the paper I also found out about this meeting." She took a breath and composed herself. "Bubba was like a son to me. He sought my words when his mother put her religion before his needs." She approached the edge of the stage.

Marissa had never seen a crowd look so hypnotized.

Walter seemed about to say something and then held back.

Candi continued. "Bubba was the only person I confided in because he was the only friend I had who could keep his mouth shut and not feel he was betraying family."

No one even coughed.

"I swore him to secrecy about my illness and I left him my business—after I'd moved the office to a place he could afford. Bubba drove me to the airport when everyone was asleep. He called me a few times to keep me posted. Then his calls stopped. The last I heard from him was before Christmas."

She gracefully sat down on the edge of the stage and made room for Walter beside her. He quickly joined her, while Marissa stepped back to give them time together.

Candi said, "You're the best man I've ever known, Walter. I'm sorry for any problems I've caused you. I didn't want you to go through the misery of watching me die."

Marissa held back tears. Tizzie pulled a tissue from her pocket.

"Where did you go?" Margaret asked, her tone more civil.

"That's an appropriate question, Margaret. I met a doctor in San Francisco who's researching a cure that might give me a chance to survive."

Marissa sat forward in her seat.

"His work," Candi said, "is in Germany. So I went to Munich to take some tests to see if I was a likely candidate for treatment. Only ten percent actually qualify."

Marissa exhaled, torn by the good news/bad news nature of her aunt's story.

"Did you pass the test?" Tizzie asked.

Walter looked dazed as Candi went on.

"When I arrived in Germany, I got cold feet. If I didn't qualify, I didn't think I could survive the disappointment. I know this sounds strange but I put off my decision to take the test and I went to Hong Kong. If I didn't take the test, I couldn't come back here to explain my actions and if I was going to die, I wanted to spend my last days in a place I'd only dreamed of."

Marissa believed her. Candi's import business was her fantasy come true because it allowed her to spend her time shopping. Hong Kong would be her shopping paradise.

"What changed your mind?" Tizzie asked.

"Not what but who. Bubba insisted I come back." She struggled to go on.

"My God," Walter said. "No matter who changed your mind, I'm glad you're here. How are you feeling?"

"I'll get to that," Candi said. "And I'll finish my story, but does anyone know anything more about Bubba?"

Walter spoke up. "I do."

Marissa flinched, uncertain what her uncle was about to announce.

Please don't let him be involved with Bubba's death, she thought.

"I knew it," Margaret said. "I knew Walter had something to do with it."

Tizzie shushed her. "Let the man talk."

"J.J.'s not in jail only for jewelry theft," Walter said. "He shot Bubba while they were fishing. I got his confession on tape."

The crowd tittered at Walter's statement. Marissa wondered how this could be true.

"And we should believe you?" Margaret asked. "After you duped us before?"

Daphne rose from the second row and walked to the stage. She reached up for the mike. "For those of you who don't know me, I'm Deputy Coroner Daphne Hendrick from Ocean Bluffs. I'm here to support Walter and to assure you what he's told you about the confession is true. My husband, Officer Hendrick, has confirmed that J.J. has confessed."

"Oh, my lord," Margaret said. "I'm absolutely beside myself."

Marissa sat down beside her uncle, whose expression of pride for his niece became great pride for his wife. The Uncle Walter Marissa knew had finally come through.

"I'm so glad you're back," Marissa said to Candi. "Please finish your story. How did Bubba persuade you to take the tests?"

With a wistful sigh, Candi continued. "Bubba made me believe I could pass and live a happy life back here with my Walter." She pulled her husband closer to her. "I went back to Munich. I passed the test. Next week I start Dr. Friedlich's treatment and he tells me I have a ninety percent chance of beating this thing."

"Hot damn!" Walter shouted and wrapped his arms around her. The townspeople burst into applause.

"I'm glad you're all right," Marissa said, reaching her hand to her.

Candi squeezed it. "I missed you, Marissa. So many times I picked up the phone to call. I couldn't ask you to lie to Walter for me."

Marissa tried to put herself in Candi's place. She released Candi's hand. "I ought to be fuming. You sure had me worried."

"Would you have spilled the beans?"

She thought of the anger she'd felt for her uncle when he was acting so irrationally. "I probably would, only to knock some sense into him."

Her aunt winked at Walter. "He can be a crotchety coot when he wants to."

"You'll have to speak up," Walter said, nudging Candi. "I can't hear you."

Pleased to see how happy her uncle was again, Marissa slipped her grandmother's diamond ring from her finger and placed it in Candi's hand. "This belongs to you."

Walter took the ring from Candi and slid it onto her finger. Candi's eyes filled with tears and Walter handed her a handkerchief. Marissa rose from the stage to leave and after Candi wiped her eyes, she and Walter followed.

Nick caught up with them. "Funny how things turned out," he said, taking Marissa's hand.

"And why do you look so sheepish?" she asked.

The smirk left Nick's face. "Let's say I made an error in judgment about someone." He patted Walter's back.

Walter looked up at him. "I did my share of prejudging you, too. You're a fine man, Nick. I heard how you and Marissa saved Daphne's life. You make a good team." He pulled Nick aside. "But you know Marissa has an ornery streak."

Nick looked at Marissa. "Ornery women are my favorite kind," he said leading them out of the auditorium.

Tizzie rushed past them. "Scuse me folks. I got a newspaper to get out." Marissa exchanged glances with Nick at the energy and determination of the old woman.

Daphne came from behind. "Will you be going back home to San Francisco?" she asked Marissa.

Nick answered before Marissa had a chance. "Marissa has no car. Her office is flooded. She has to stay here."

"I have to what?" Marissa asked, perturbed he wouldn't let her answer the question.

"What would I do without you?" Nick said.

"I . . . I don't know." Her life away from the Cove flooded back to her.

Nick said, "I know a great place you can rent for an office. It's already furnished and I'm sure it's much roomier than the one in San Francisco."

"And where might that be?"

"Right on Main Street, next to your uncle's hardware store."

"You mean the funeral home?"

"It would make a great office," Daphne said.

"Absolutely," Walter piped in. "And J.J.'s apartment upstairs is going to be vacant for a long time."

Nick said, "I'll bet he'd be happy to sell you his hearse. It's perfect for hauling around gear for your clients. Face it, city girl. You've become a small town woman."

He pulled Marissa from the crowd and she walked with him toward the ocean.

Her eyes rested on the reflection of the moon on the water and she inhaled the fresh night air. How much brighter the stars shone than in San Francisco.

"A small town woman," she said, contemplating her future. "With a big black hearse."

Made in the USA
San Bernardino, CA
29 January 2018